REVIEWERS CHEER FOR DARLENE GARDNER AND *THE MISCONCEPTION*!

"A wonderfully entertaining read that belongs on the keeper shelf, *The Misconception* wins the WordWeaving Award of Excellence."

—WordWeaving.com

"A delight! This story [is] quite a fun read!"

—*Romantic Times*

"A treat from start to finish . . . here's hoping Ms. Gardner will provide readers with more of her type of romance, and the sooner the better."

—*The Romance Reader*

"*The Misconception* was an absolute joy to read. Treat yourself to a great love story and a good laugh with this book!"

—*Interludes*

"I was laughing one minute and crying the next. I cannot wait to see what Darlene Gardner will write next!"

—*The Best Reviews*

THE ONE SHE WANTS

"I can think of better things for us to do than talk about horses and carriages," Peyton said in a low, husky voice.

It was a moment before Mitch could speak. "What did you have in mind?"

She turned from sultry to playful in an eye blink as she grabbed his hand and tugged. "Come on and I'll show you."

He didn't figure out her intention until they reached a wet place on the sidewalk and she stopped. Before he could move, she looped her hands around his neck and grinned up at him. A second later, the wind whipped the salty water into the sea wall with such ferocity that it shot upward into a wet arc that showered golden spray down on them.

In an instant they were drenched, but Peyton didn't seem to care that she'd very likely ruined her expensive dress. She swiped the wet hair off her forehead, threw back her head and laughed. Then she rose on tiptoe, plastering herself even closer to him. "For the record, you don't have any reason to be jealous of Gaston," she said when her mouth was very close to his, "because you're the one I want."

She meant she wanted his brother, but his brother wasn't the one who was holding her in his arms. Cary was God only knew where, and Mitch was here. How could he be expected to resist the mad pounding of his heart and the beautiful woman in his arms?

Other *Love Spell* books by Darlene Gardner:

THE MISCONCEPTION

Bait & Switch

DARLENE GARDNER

LOVE SPELL

NEW YORK CITY

To my mother, Mary Gorta Hrobak, who loves a good twin-switch story, and who's still miffed at her obstetrician for being wrong when he predicted that I was twins.

LOVE SPELL®

October 2002

Published by

Dorchester Publishing Co., Inc.
276 Fifth Avenue
New York, NY 10001

ISBN 0-505-52521-6

Printed in the United States of America.

Bait & Switch

Chapter One

Grant Mitchell covered his head with a down-filled pillow, desperately trying to silence the high-spirited strains of *La Cucaracha* resounding through his apartment.

Mitch should have known better than to let Mrs. McGillicutty talk him into buying one of the musical doorbells her grandson peddled.

A cop who worked evenings didn't need to wake up to the joyful sounds of an oldie that didn't come close to being a goody.

La Cucaracha kept playing, so he flung the useless pillow aside and checked the time on the bedside alarm clock. Two forty-five. Which meant he'd been asleep for less than an hour.

He considered ignoring the doorbell, but his conscience wouldn't allow it. Not when the next youngest tenant in his Atlanta apartment building was a good forty years older than he was and might need his help.

"I'm coming," he grumbled as he switched on a light and pulled on the pair of pajama bottoms he kept at the foot of the bed. He'd learned early on it was best not to embarrass elderly sensibilities by answering the door in plaid boxer shorts.

He yanked open the door, expecting white hair and wrinkled skin, but found himself looking at what could have been his own reflection. The man standing there had features every bit as familiar as the ones he saw every morning in the mirror.

Thick, dark hair springing back from a high forehead. Blue eyes set a couple millimeters too deep. A long nose that went a tad bit wayward somewhere in the middle. A square jaw with clefted chin. A wide mouth. All atop a six-foot frame.

"Lord, we're a good-looking pair," his visitor said.

"Cary." Mitch's lips curled upward in the same grin reflected on his identical twin brother's face. In a space of a heartbeat, they enfolded each other in a hearty bear hug, complete with appropriate male backslapping.

"I've missed you, big brother," Cary said when they drew apart, referring to the fact that Mitch was older by a whopping three minutes. Their mother often joked that, from birth, Cary had never done anything until he was good and ready.

"I've missed you, too," Mitch said truthfully. Nearly six months had gone by since he'd seen his brother, far too long in Mitch's opinion. "But what are you doing ringing my doorbell at almost three in the morning?"

The corner of Cary's mouth lifted in the crooked grin that Mitch also possessed. Only on Cary, it appeared effortless and infinitely more charming. "Visiting?" he answered, but it sounded like a question.

"Just like that? You want me to believe you're here for a visit, at this hour of the morning, when I've been asking you to come see me for months?"

"Then you won't mind if I stay a while," Cary said, dragging an oversized suitcase into the apartment and shutting the door behind him before flashing a smile that seemed forced.

Mitch stared at him, trying to figure out what was going on. The face that he saw was his, but, at the same time, not his. They'd looked so much alike as children that relatives couldn't tell them apart until they figured out they were mirror-image twins. Mitch, the right-hander, had hair that swirled to his right and a tiny mole atop his right cheek. Cary, the left-hander, had left-swirling hair and a mole on his left cheek.

In adulthood, Mitch thought the differences more pronounced. Cary's usual expression was more carefree than his own, probably because his brother wasn't preoccupied with the details of everyday life, such as keeping a job for more than six months. But now Mitch spotted tiny, unfamiliar worry lines fanning out from his brother's eyes and mouth.

"You're in trouble," Mitch said with sudden conviction. "That's why you're here."

"You know me pretty well, don't you, bro? Is that an advantage to having an identical twin or a disadvantage, do you think?" Cary didn't wait for an answer, but strolled around the small apartment. The saying "Policemen are your friends" was stitched into a needlepoint frame and hung on the wall near a quilt-covered plaid sofa. The furniture in the room, though sturdy, was as old-fashioned as the frilly moss-green curtains covering the windows. One of the lamps even had a fringed shade.

Cary whistled long and low. "With this for a bachelor pad, no wonder you don't have a girl. What do you call this decorating style? Senior-citizen chic?"

Mitch felt the corners of his mouth head south. "The old folks are always showing me how much they like having a cop in the building. I couldn't hurt Mrs. McGillicutty's feelings when she offered to help me fix it up."

Cary kicked off his Italian loafers, tugged the crease of his slacks up slightly at the knees and settled onto the plaid-covered sofa. "I hate to break this to you, bro, but you should have."

Mitch sank into a matching armchair across from the sofa, rubbed his bleary eyes, and waited. He had little doubt Cary would soon confess his problem and ask for help in solving it, because that's what he always did. He didn't usually take so long in coming to the point.

Cary put his hands behind his neck and leaned

back against the sofa, a relaxed pose that struck Mitch as more forced than natural. "I was going to check into a hotel and come see you in the morning, but I'm short on cash."

Mitch bit the inside of his lip to stop himself from asking what else was new. "Why didn't you wait until morning to leave Charleston? You know it's a six-hour drive. You must've figured you'd get here after I was asleep."

"I thought it'd be best if I left under the cover of darkness."

"Why do I have a premonition I'm not going to like what you came here to tell me?"

"Because you're not?" Cary quipped.

"Just tell me what you did this time." Mitch shut his eyes as his mind whirred with possibilities. Before his brother could answer, he voiced one of them. "You didn't sleep with your boss's wife again, did you?"

"Of course not." Cary sounded indignant. "And that's not fair. How was I supposed to know Mimi was married to the owner of the spa? She wasn't even half his age."

"Why'd you get fired, then?"

"I didn't get fired this time," Cary said. Mitch watched him absently rub the elbow of his pitching arm, which had been damaged in a car crash that changed his future. It had been a tough blow, one Mitch suspected his brother hadn't gotten over. Instead of starring in the major leagues, Cary was now coordinating Charleston's city-run sports leagues and teaching clinics. "They seem to like me, not that it means much. A trained monkey could do my job."

"I don't want to play twenty questions, Cary. Just spit it out."

"I got on the wrong side of this guy," Cary said, still rubbing his elbow. "Flash Gorman's his name."

"What is he? A superhero?"

Cary gave a short laugh. "An antihero is more like it. Flash Gorman's a criminal."

The mention of crime wiped away the last vestiges of Mitch's fatigue, and he sat up straight. "What kind of criminal?"

"I don't know exactly. A loan shark for sure and I'm pretty certain he's laundering money through his bar and God knows where else. He's probably hiring out prostitutes and doing whatever else can make him some easy money."

Mitch's eyes narrowed as a suspicion grew of how else Flash Gorman made that easy money. Knowing his brother, Flash was probably Cary's bookie.

"And you're involved with this guy how?" Mitch asked, hoping he was wrong.

"I owe him money."

"Why's that?"

Cary rubbed his forehead while a trickle of guilt dribbled through him. No matter how he broke the news, Mitch would go ballistic. Especially after the foolish promise he'd made the last time he got himself into a jam. "I made a bet that didn't pan out."

"Darnit, Cary." Mitch slapped the arm of his chair. Hard. He was too much of a Boy Scout to swear. About the worst thing Cary could remember Mitch doing was swig milk straight from the carton. "Don't you learn? The last time I gave you money, you said you'd stop gambling!"

"I tried, really I did," Cary said as the trickle of guilt widened to a stream. Hell. How did Mitch do that to him? Nobody else could manage it. "But there was this basketball game, and—"

"How much?" Mitch interrupted. His mouth had thinned, and his eyes were hard. "One thousand? Two? Five?"

Cary raised his hand, palm up, over his head. "Try twenty."

"Twenty grand!" Mitch sprang to his feet. "I don't have that kind of money!"

Cary's shoulders sagged. It would have helped if Mitch had won the lottery since the last time Cary'd hit him up for a loan. "I'm not asking for twenty grand."

"Then how much are you asking for?"

From the grim expression on his brother's face, Cary figured he'd better go for the minimum. "One grand."

"One? Just one?" Mitch paced from one end of the small living room to the other and back again. "Where're you going to get the other nineteen?"

"I'm not."

"What do you mean, you're not? This Flash guy isn't going to forget you owe him big. He'll hurt you if you don't pay."

"Honestly, bro," Cary said, "sometimes I think

you don't pay attention. Why do you think I left town under the cover of darkness?"

"You're skipping out on the debt?" Mitch's voice was incredulous.

"It's either that or get my kneecaps busted." Cary crossed one leg over the other. He thought it best not to tell his brother that Flash Gorman wanted *him* to break the kneecaps of some of the *other* poor souls who were slow in paying. Especially since he'd left town before his first assignment. He patted his left knee. "I *am* rather fond of them. Especially when I'm walking."

Mitch stopped pacing and tapped his chin with his fist. Cary relaxed slightly. He could see the wheels in his brother's brain turning as he calculated how much he could afford to lend him. Finally, Mitch let out a long sigh.

"You have to go to the Charleston authorities."

Cary's mouth dropped open. Mitch wasn't supposed to say that. He was supposed to say he'd get his checkbook. "No way. No how. That's the stupidest idea you've ever had."

"You said Flash Gorman's a criminal. Turn him in, your problems are over."

"He *is* a criminal, but I can't prove that. Besides, if I go back, I could be the one who ends up getting prosecuted."

Mitch peered at him with the all-seeing eyes of the cop he was.

Cary fought the urge to squirm. "Just because we're twins doesn't mean I have to tell you everything."

Mitch's eyes narrowed farther.

"Oh, all right," Cary said. "It's nothing, really. Just that the original debt was closer to thirty thousand dollars, and I've been whittling it down."

"How, exactly, have you been doing that?"

"I have a second job tending bar." Cary paused, figuring there was no point in telling his brother what kind of bar it was. He could take only so much disapproval in one sitting.

"You made ten grand in two months?" Mitch sounded suspicious.

"They do let me open the cash register."

"You *stole* the money?" Mitch paced back to the chair and dropped into it, extending his pajama-clad legs in front of him. He leaned his head back. "Here I am in Atlanta upholding the law, and my twin's in Charleston breaking it."

"Don't sound so self-righteous. The bar's the same one Flash uses to launder money. Don't you think there's poetic justice in paying back my debt with Flash's own money?"

"I can't believe this." Mitch sat up. "I'm a cop. What do you expect me to say?"

"I just told you it was dirty money."

"It's still stealing!"

"It doesn't count as stealing when the money's dirty."

Mitch rubbed his temples, disregarding that truth. "Here's what you're gonna do. You're gonna drive back to Charleston and replace that money."

"Like hell I am." The unfamiliar rumbling inside him, Cary realized, was his temper erupting. "For starters, I don't have the money to replace. And Flash is only giving me two weeks to come up with the rest. I can't go back to Charleston. I have a better idea, bro."

"Then let's hear it."

As quickly as Cary's temper erupted, it extinguished. If he approached this rationally, Mitch would have to agree. "I thought I'd disappear for a while, which is why I need the cash."

Mitch rested his hands on his knees and leaned forward. "Let's say I do loan you the money, and you do disappear. What if, in the meantime, this guy finds out you were stealing from him? He could have a warrant put out for your arrest."

"Do you mean I'd be a fugitive?" Ugly thoughts ran through Cary's mind. He saw himself being pursued by Tommy Lee Jones. He pictured himself coming to the edge of a dam and leaping. "Like Harrison Ford in that movie?"

"Harrison Ford was innocent. You're not."

He had a point there. "So what do you suggest?"

"I already told you. Go back and straighten this out."

Cary's stomach clenched. "And I've told you I can't come up with twenty grand in two weeks."

"You won't have to," Mitch said. "I've got a plan."

Cary grimaced. He didn't like the sound of this. He remembered hearing those exact words ten years ago when they were eighteen. He'd asked Mitch to trade places with him long enough to ace the SAT, but Mitch had a plan. It turned out he planned to help Cary *study*.

"The police in Charleston want to nab this guy, right?" Mitch asked.

"Well, yeah. I guess so. If they could pin something on him."

"Then deliver him to them." Mitch started to smile. "You spend the next two weeks gathering evidence against Flash Gordon. Before he can collect on the debt, you go to the police with what you know."

"And what if Flash finds out I was"—Cary paused, because he couldn't bring himself to say "stealing" when it was so obviously the wrong word—"*rerouting* the money. What then?"

"You deal. The authorities will probably let you off with a slap on the wrist after you deliver the bad guy."

Usually, Mitch's plans made at least a modicum of sense. This one didn't. "There's just one problem with your little plan."

"What's that?"

"I'm not doing it."

Mitch threw up his hands. "You've got no choice."

"I choose to run as far away from Flash Gorman as I can." Mitch was about to protest again, so Cary interrupted. "I'm not you, Mitch. I don't fight bad guys for a living. And I'm a lousy liar."

"*That's* a lie," Mitch shot back. "If you were a bad liar, you wouldn't have gotten so many women to believe you were in love with them."

"I *was* in love with them at the time," Cary said, experiencing a pang of hurt. His own twin didn't understand that he never deliberately set out to wound anyone.

"Okay, then. If you're such a lousy liar, why did Mom believe you when you told her I threw the baseball through the living-room window?"

"Honestly, Mitch. We were twelve. And you could have told her you didn't do it." Cary sighed, then shrugged. "Okay, I'll admit I've told a lie or two in my time. But this is different. I can't do this."

"You can't walk away from it either. This could ruin your life. I can't let you do that."

Cary put both hands on his head, because Mitch had a point. He'd really gone and done it this time. This time, his problem didn't have an easy fix. There was no teacher willing to raise his grade because he was a star athlete. No father taking the blame for wrecking the family car because Cary'd gone on a joy ride before he had a license. No mother telling the principal he'd had a doctor's appointment so he wouldn't get in trouble for skipping school.

This time, there was only himself. He stared across the room at his brother, who looked so much like him. The brainstorm hit him so hard he almost keeled over. Because there wasn't only himself. There was Mitch, too.

Mitch, who didn't work undercover but was surely better suited for it than Cary. Mitch, who had never refused him a thing in his life. Mitch, who looked exactly like him.

The only person who might be able to tell them apart was Peyton, his latest lady friend. But after what he'd done last night, chances were she never wanted to see him again.

"Hey, bro," he said, his face creasing into his most persuasive smile. "You ever hear of bait and switch?"

Chapter Two

Lieutenant Harold Snow's eyes were as cold as his surname as he ripped the badge from the breast pocket of Mitch's police uniform. Mitch's heart went with it.

"Get this turncoat out of my sight," the lieutenant bit out.

Two police guards with Popeye-sized biceps hooked Mitch under the arms and pulled him toward a jail cell. His heels dragged on the cheap linoleum floor.

"But I didn't steal the money. All I did was try to help my brother," Mitch protested as they threw him in the cell and locked it. He scrambled to his feet, grabbing on to the vertical bars. His brother leaned negligently against a nearby wall, watching. "Do something, Cary."

"Can't do anything, bro." Cary shrugged carelessly. "You should have known better than to trust me."

Alarm bells went off in Mitch's brain. Alarm bells that had sounded far too late.

One of his eyes snapped open, then the other, and the prison cell disappeared. The alarm bells didn't stop. Groaning, he reached out and hit the snooze button on the alarm clock. Still, the ringing persisted.

He tried to sit up, but rolled to the middle of the bed instead, feeling as though he were navigating the seas of insanity. As his head cleared, he realized he was stuck in the middle of Cary's water bed and somebody was ringing Cary's doorbell. Somebody who expected Cary to answer the door.

Except Cary was safely ensconced in Atlanta, thanks to Mitch's grudging agreement to switch places with him and straighten out his mess. Cary didn't seem to appreciate that Mitch was taking risks that involved his career as well as his kneecaps. One misstep, and Mitch'd land in a jail cell. Then his career would surely be over.

He needed to focus on the positive side of their agreement. As a concession, he'd gotten Cary to promise to stop gambling. Granted, he'd promised before. But this time he seemed to mean it. Besides, considering who could be on the other side of Cary's door, Mitch would much rather take the gamble of opening it than Cary. He was a cop. He could take care of himself.

Mitch executed a logroll that took him to the

edge of the water bed. Then he stuck out a bare leg and foraged for dry ground. All the while, the doorbell kept buzzing. Then the pounding started.

What was it about him that encouraged others to wake him out of a sound sleep? First Cary had come playing *La Cucaracha* in Atlanta. Now this.

He pulled on jeans over his boxers and tucked a handgun at the small of his back. Then he walked into the hallway, only to catch his toe on the edge of a skinny oriental rug. He lost his balance and went sprawling, saving himself from falling by slamming into the wall with a tremendous thud.

"Son of a gun," he shouted. He righted himself and thanked God the gun hadn't gone off. Rubbing his sore shoulder, he stalked the rest of the way to the door and the infernal ringing.

He didn't care if the person on the other side was there to bust his kneecaps. He aimed to give him a mouthful for waking him up so rudely. He flung open the door.

"You unreliable lout!"

The voice yelling insults didn't belong to Mitch, because he was struck speechless. Standing on the doorstep of his brother's fancy Tradd Street sublet was the most desirable woman he had ever seen.

Her eyes were a smidgen too close together, her nose a hair too long and her mouth centimeters too wide, but the net effect slammed into him with a sensual punch. Her short blond hair was cut in haphazard, flyaway layers that framed an oval face with the highest cheekbones he'd ever seen. The eyes that glared up at him were the color of Coca-Cola, which happened to be his favorite beverage.

He wasn't quite through admiring her figure, which tended toward the very lushness he preferred, when she thumped him once in the chest. Hard enough to make him gasp.

"You are the biggest, most irresponsible jerk I have ever had the displeasure to meet." He even liked her voice. If she sang, she'd be an alto. Maybe a tenor. "I can't believe I was stupid enough to believe you."

"Uh, I'm sure you're not stupid," Mitch stammered, unwilling to listen to this captivating creature belittle herself.

"How dare you disagree with me after what you did?"

"What did I do?" Mitch asked. Stupidly, he instantly realized. Her full mouth narrowed in a thin line, and her dark eyes flashed.

"Now you have the incredible gall to ask what you did. Why, oh why, did I ever get involved with you?"

"You're involved with me?" Mitch gaped at her. For an instant, he felt as though he'd won the lottery. Cary teased him about his dearth of dates, but the reason was because Mitch seldom ran across a woman he wanted to ask out. For this woman, though, he would have braved a minefield. Then the reality of what was happening crashed down on his sleep-addled mind.

This enchanting blonde wasn't involved with him. She was involved with Cary, who'd told him not much more than twenty-four hours ago that he didn't have a girlfriend.

Knowing Cary, of course, maybe she wasn't his girlfriend. Maybe she was the latest in the long string of women he'd wronged.

"I swear, Cary Mitchell—"

"Mitch," he interrupted. She was looking at him as though he were crazy, which he probably was for agreeing to impersonate his brother in the first place. But he wasn't going through the next two weeks answering to a name that wasn't his. "Call me Mitch."

"Mitch?" She shook her head, and the strands of her short hair danced. "You're saying you want me to call you Mitch when I yell at you?"

Mitch couldn't help smiling. Even spouting venom, she was so darned cute. "I don't want you to yell at me at all. I want you to call me Mitch all the time."

The space between her eyebrows narrowed. "Why didn't you tell me this before?"

"You didn't ask."

"You're trying to distract me."

"No, I'm not." Something that sounded like a horse whinnying broke the morning quiet, and Mitch looked out at the narrow street in front of the house. It *was* a horse whinnying. A large horse that was attached to a small cart loaded with tourists staring at them.

"Did you know," Mitch said, inclining his head toward the carriage, "that we have an audience?"

She gave a long-suffering sigh. It was then Mitch

noticed that the white shirt she wore with khaki shorts was imprinted with the logo, "Dixieland Carriage Tours."

The blonde was a tour guide.

"When I saw your car in the driveway, I told them this building was a classic example of the French Huguenot style of architecture," she said.

Mitch frowned. "Really? It looks like a simple row house to me."

"It is," she said, all but hissing at him. "See what you made me do."

"Listen. . . ." He was about to call her by name when he realized he didn't know what it was. And he couldn't ask her. As spitting mad as she was, he couldn't ask what he'd done either. As much as he hated to do it, he had only one option remaining.

"Would you excuse me?"

"Excuse you? I'm in the middle of yelling at you."

"You can start again when I come back. Promise. But there's something I have to do." He backed away from the door so she wouldn't see the gun tucked into the waistband of his pants.

Disregarding that he hadn't asked her in, she trailed after him into his brother's place. Great. How was he supposed to get information out of Cary while she was listening in on the conversation? His gaze ping-ponged around the house. How was he going to call him at all when he couldn't find the phone?

"You are doing something," she sputtered, looking more adorable by the second. "You're being yelled at by me."

"Where's the phone?" he asked before realizing why he shouldn't.

With a puzzled nod, she indicated a phone perched on an end table in the living room. He snatched it up, relieved it had a portable receiver.

"Excuse me," he said again, careful not to turn his back to the fetching blonde, then ducked into the half-bathroom off the hall and locked the door. She immediately pounded on it.

"You're acting strange even for you, Cary," she yelled through the ornate door as he navigated the discarded clothes and towels Cary had left scattered on the floor. He sat down on the closed wooden lid of the toilet.

"Cary. Did you hear me?"

"Mitch. Call me Mitch," he corrected absently as he hid the gun in one of the drawers next to the sink and then hurriedly punched in the numbers of his home telephone. He didn't use his given name of Grant. Especially when he was with Cary. Mitch liked the old-time actor who'd been the source of their names. His mother's sense of humor, he didn't like.

"What are you doing in there?" The blonde pounded louder as the phone rang at his Atlanta apartment.

"I'll be just a minute," Mitch answered, then figured he'd better embellish his answer. "Nature calls."

"You're not calling nature on that telephone," she yelled back. "What do you think I am? A nitwit?"

"Of course I don't think you're a nitwit," Mitch answered just as Cary picked up the phone.

"I don't think I'm a nitwit, either," Cary said. "But thanks for letting me know."

"I wasn't talking to you," Mitch whispered, wondering how much the blonde could hear through the door. "For you, I'd use stronger language. Like inconsiderate and irresponsible."

"What'd I do now? And why are you whispering?"

"Come out of there this instant," the blonde demanded loudly before Mitch could answer.

"Who's there with you?" Cary asked.

Mitch gritted his teeth to keep from yelling. "That's what I was going to ask you."

"How would I know? I'm in Atlanta, bro. I can't see who's yelling at you."

"She's yelling at you. Only she doesn't know I'm not you, and I don't know who she is."

Three quick raps sounded on the door. Mitch held the receiver out so his brother could identify the voice. "This hiding in the bathroom is not going to work," the blonde yelled.

"Almost through," Mitch yelled back, then brought the receiver back to his ear and whispered. "Did you recognize her voice?"

"You're hiding in the bathroom?" Cary asked.

"Never mind that. I need to know who this blonde is and why she's yelling at me. I had to come in here. I couldn't have her listening in on the conversation."

"What's she look like?"

"She's gorgeous. About five feet six with short blond hair and freckles." Mitch thought. "Oh, yeah. She drives a horse and carriage."

"That has to be Peyton, although I've never thought of her as gorgeous." Cary sounded thoughtful. "Attractive, for sure. But not gorgeous."

"Who exactly is Peyton to you?"

"My girlfriend," Cary answered, and Mitch's stomach fell so hard he thought it would hit the floor. No. It couldn't be. The delectable blonde couldn't belong to his brother. Not when he'd taken one mouthwatering look at her and had his body overheat.

"You said you didn't have a girlfriend," Mitch protested. Cary especially hadn't said he had a girlfriend who looked like the embodiment of everything Mitch wanted in a woman.

On the other end of the line, Cary grimaced. He should have told Mitch about Peyton, but then again he couldn't be expected to think of everything. Besides, the woman was so unpredictable, he never knew what she was going to do next. He'd guessed Splitsville, but there she was in his home.

"I didn't think I'd still have a girlfriend after I failed to show up for dinner with the Ayatollah and his missus last night."

"Peyton knows the Ayatollah Khomeini?"

Cary laughed. "Not the Ayatollah Khomeini. The Ayatollah McDowell. Her father. The solicitor, which is what they call a district attorney around those parts. For some reason, Peyton cares what her parents think. They wanted to meet me, and she wanted me to make a good impression."

"That's why she's so angry."

"That's my best guess," Cary said. In the background, he could hear more pounding. He had to say one thing for Peyton. She was never going to drop dead of a heart attack on account of stifling her emotions.

"She's angry enough to break up with you."

Cary's back stiffened. He wasn't at all sure his big brother could make things right in Charleston, but, if he did, it'd be nice to have a woman waiting for him.

Though truth be told, Peyton wasn't his type. He'd approached her in a Charleston nightspot the month before solely because she had a wild way of dancing. They'd break up eventually, but Cary wasn't yet ready for it to happen. Peyton was oddly appealing, for one thing. For another, he'd yet to discover if that wild part of her nature played out in bed.

"Can you talk her out of it?" Cary asked.

"How am I supposed to do that?"

He thought of Betty Lou Sorenson, a high-school girlfriend who'd caught him making out with Anna somebody or other the summer before their senior year. She'd been ready to rake her nails down his face until Mitch soothed the savage beast with talk of teenage boys and hormones gone haywire.

"You've done it before," Cary said. "You can do it again."

Silence filled the other end of the phone before

Mitch broke it. "She means that much to you?"

She didn't, not really. But if he admitted the truth to Mitch, Peyton was as good as gone from his life. And he didn't want to lose her. Not yet, anyway. He made his voice sound pitiful. "Please, Mitch. Do it for me."

Mitch didn't answer, which meant Cary was once again going to get his way. His brother was being such a good sport about everything that, for an instant, Cary considered telling him about the bag that was packed and waiting beside the door of Mitch's apartment. He might have if he weren't absolutely sure his brother would dream up some reason Cary should stay put with the old folks in Atlanta. Some reason sure to fill Cary with guilt.

He heard more pounding on the bathroom door in the Charleston he'd left behind.

"Sounds like you've gotta go, bro," he said. "You're the best, you know that?"

He hung up without waiting for an answer, then strode purposefully to the door and picked up his suitcase. He had a fleeting thought of Mitch and the mess he'd left him to deal with before he dismissed it and walked out the door.

His brother could handle whatever was thrown at him. It wasn't as though Cary were abandoning him. He'd call him in a couple of days. Whenever he got to where he was going.

Chapter Three

Peyton McDowell stared at the locked door, willing her temper to cool and trying to get her breathing back under control.

Her parents would be mortified if they knew she'd been huffing, puffing, and trying to blow a bathroom door down. They'd drilled into her every day of her life that she had an image to uphold, and it wasn't that of a shrew who needed taming.

Her doting parents, who loved her all the more because they couldn't have other children, only asked that she take her rightful place in Charleston society. They'd sent her to the city's most exclusive school for girls, groomed her into a debutante, and given her everything she wanted.

Their fondest dream was that she one day marry a man with a Charleston lineage as illustrious as their own two-hundred-year legacy. Yet here she was, acting the shrew in the home of somebody her parents would deem most unsuitable. Especially in light of what he'd done last night.

Heck, she'd known he was unsuitable herself from the moment she'd met him. But he'd been fun and good-looking and outrageously flirtatious, all of the things the suitable men of Charleston were not.

She'd never imagined, not for a second, that the relationship would last. She didn't even want it to. She simply wanted to have a little fun with someone less stuffy than the taxidermy specials her parents were always thrusting at her.

Except dating Cary had ceased to be fun.

Expelling a long breath, she turned and walked for the exit just as she heard the bathroom door open. She lifted her chin in the regal manner her mother had taught her and kept moving.

"Peyton, wait."

"Why should I?" she tossed over her shoulder. "I don't know why I got involved with you in the first place. You're egotistical, arrogant, and inconsiderate."

"Give me a chance to explain." Footsteps sounded behind her, and she paused, curious as to what he would say. It wasn't as though she'd wanted him to meet her parents. It was way too early in their relationship for that. But when they'd gotten past date four, her mother had insisted on inviting him to dinner. He shouldn't have accepted if he were going to stand up the whole family.

She stood, waiting.

"I'd rather not explain to your back."

She slowly turned around, which was a mistake. One of the things that had attracted her to Cary was his good looks, but he looked far better today than he ever had.

His dark hair was mussed instead of perfectly groomed, and his blue eyes seemed softer, like the sky on a hazy day. She'd never before seen him anything other than perfectly shaved, and she liked the slightly rumpled air the stubble on his lower face lent him. Even his mouth seemed different: softer, more sensuous.

But it was his chest that commanded her attention. Cary Mitchell's upper torso looked as though it were fit for a god. Light brown hair sparsely covered a broad, muscular road map of perfection. She had the insane desire to swoon. How odd. She'd never reacted this way to him before.

In the background, she heard a honking sound, but she couldn't quite place where it was coming from.

"That's better," he said, smiling at her. Funny how that smile had never quite seemed to reach his eyes before now. She steeled herself against him, recalling the embarrassment he'd caused her the night before.

"Don't bother explaining. Absolutely nothing you say will matter. We're through," Peyton said sharply, glaring at him.

Even though Cary had predicted this moments ago on the phone to his brother, Mitch wasn't ready for it. How could they be through when he'd just found her? Not that he was going to let himself, even for one second, think of his brother's girl as his own.

"Breaking up with me is a bad idea." He tried to come up with a reason why. For Cary's sake. "You wouldn't have gone out with me in the first place if you wanted to break up with me."

She put her hands on her sweetly rounded hips. "That's nuts."

Okay. Bad reason. He tried to think of another one, but it was difficult considering all the honking going on outside in the street. Ah, what the heck. If Peyton were his girl and he in danger of losing her, he'd go straight to begging.

"I'm sorry," he said.

"You're sorry?" Peyton blinked her big Coca-Cola eyes. "I thought apologizing went against your grain. Aren't you always saying what's done is done?"

That's right. Cary did often say that. "I do," he agreed. "But in this case, it was done poorly."

"You're not making sense."

She didn't know the half of it. If any of this made sense, he wouldn't be here in Charleston pretending to be someone he wasn't, trying to get a woman who attracted him not to break up with his brother.

"That's because you haven't let me explain," he said.

"How can you possibly explain blowing off dinner with my parents? You must have guessed how humiliating it would be for me when you didn't show up."

Mitch took a breath, relieved that he could utter at least one true sentence. "I'd never deliberately hurt you."

She gazed at him, and he knew she was wondering how much she could believe. How could he blame her? Cary meant well, but he had a habit of putting a spin on a situation so that it suited his purposes. It wasn't lying, exactly, but it wasn't the truth, either.

"Then why didn't you show up for dinner last night?"

He hesitated, not wanting to lie to her, and saw resignation fall over her face. "There was this guy in a harness dangling over the bridge," he blurted out.

"The Cooper River Bridge?" she asked, naming the enormous span that connected peninsular Charleston to Mount Pleasant. He'd been talking about a bridge in Atlanta, but he nodded anyway. The time and place might not be true, but the story was.

"He was up there smoking cigarettes, drinking whiskey, singing old Janis Joplin songs." Mitch snapped his fingers. "Oh. And eating Ho-Hos."

"Ho-Hos?"

"Those little chocolate cakes with the creamy white centers. He said they were delicious." Mitch scratched his chin. "Although I never did figure out what Ho-Hos had to do with Janis Joplin."

"You talked to him?" she asked. Suspicion had replaced the resignation.

"Sure. He was tying up traffic. I was trying to get him to come down."

"*You* were trying to talk the Ho-Ho drunk down?" Her eyebrows lifted, and he realized his mistake. As a cop, Mitch talked to nuts holding up rush-hour traffic. Cary didn't. "Why would *you* of all people be doing that?"

Good question. He made up an answer. "Because I was in front of the line?" Judging by her expression, the answer wasn't good enough. "And he liked me. I told him I believed he was Bobby McGee."

"Who's Bobby McGee?"

"You know. From the song Janis used to sing." He sang an off-key couple of lines. "Bobby McGee used to make her feel good when he sang the blues."

"And making Bobby feel better took all night?" Her voice was steeped in suspicion. "You couldn't break away long enough to call me?"

"Bobby had a knife. I was afraid he was going to cut himself loose."

She scrunched up her nose. She even looked a tad sympathetic, which filled Mitch with fresh guilt. "What happened next?"

"The police sneaked a cable onto his rope and lowered him to the ground. Turned out he was depressed over Janis dying."

"Janis Joplin died thirty years ago."

"Yeah, well, he didn't know that. He hadn't been a fan for long."

She grew silent, which made the incessant honking seem louder. So loud that she had to raise her voice to be heard. "Why didn't you call and explain?"

One of her blond hairs was close to falling in her eye. He reached out and brushed it back, enjoying its silky texture. "It was late by the time I got to a phone," he said. "I didn't want to wake you."

She bit her full lower lip, an action he couldn't fully appreciate because of the honking.

"Why wasn't this in the newspaper?" she asked.

Another good question. Too bad he'd run out of his supply of good answers. "Reporters can't be everywhere?"

"Yeah, right." She took a step backward, breaking the contact. "At least it was more entertaining than your other excuses."

"See, I'm improving." Mitch latched on to the positive and ran with it. "Don't do this to us, Peyton. Give us another chance." Her expression was wavering, so he went for the trump card. "Please."

"I shouldn't." She shook her head as she gazed at him, but the flintiness had gone out of her eyes. He reached across the chasm and took her hand, lazily drawing circles on her palm.

"But you're going to anyway," he said, hoping he was right. She considered their linked hands. For one awful moment, he thought she'd yank her hand from his. Then she raised her head, and he saw the resignation in her face even before she nodded. He smiled. She shook the index finger of her free hand at him.

"One more chance. That's all. If I can count on you to pick me up on time for the Charleston League of Historic Preservation ball tonight. It starts at eight o'clock sharp."

"I'll be there in plenty of time," he promised, moving closer to her. Her lips were so darn delectable that he wanted to kiss them even though he knew he shouldn't. She was Cary's girl, not his.

"Do you promise?" She gazed at him with huge eyes.

"I promise." He told himself to move away. Instead, he edged closer. She smelled sweet, like honeysuckle. He'd always wondered what honeysuckle tasted like.

"I shouldn't believe you, but I do," she said, staring at him with those wide cola-colored eyes. Or, at least that's what he thought she said over the honking.

His traitorous body was about to ignore the warning his mind was issuing when the ringing of Cary's doorbell added to the cacophony. Reluctantly, he straightened and opened the door.

Standing there was a middle-aged woman with a broad-brimmed hat who had to be one of the tourists from the carriage. She gestured out at the one-lane street. The horses hadn't moved, but behind them was a row of cars worthy of a rush-hour traffic jam. All of the drivers seemed to be honking their horns and shaking their fists.

"We got a situation here," the tourist said.

"Jiminy," Peyton exclaimed and sprinted for the road. Mitch stepped onto the small porch, admiring the sway of her hips as she ran.

A few minutes later, he stood in front of the refrigerator, where Cary had posted his work schedule for his dual jobs, and groaned.

His eleven-to-seven shift at the parks and recreation department wouldn't get in the way of him attending the ball, but he hadn't counted on having bartending duty beginning at nine-thirty.

Cripes. He'd have to leave the ball soon after he arrived. If he managed to get there with Peyton in tow, that is.

Considering he didn't know where she lived, that was questionable.

Chapter Four

Mitch swallowed a lump of panic as he stared across the net at a sight bound to cause lasting nightmares.

The half-dozen students enrolled in Tennis for Tots were on the other side of the court. The eldest was wearing a T-shirt sporting a large purple dinosaur. The youngest carried a racket taller than she was.

They were all staring at him expectantly. Mitch liked kids. A lot. Except when they were waiting for him to instruct them on the finer points of tennis, a game he'd played only once or twice in his life. A long, long time ago.

He looked down at the ball-hopper at his feet, which was filled with dozens of fuzzy yellow tennis balls. Bending, he picked one up. As a cop, he'd faced gunfire from criminals. How hard could it be to feed balls to kids?

"Everybody in one line," he said in his best authoritative cop's voice. "Okay. Get ready."

He cocked his arm, but paused in his windup when one little boy disengaged from the group and puttered to the net. His eyes were as big as a doe's. He scuffed a sneaker-clad foot.

"Mister," he said. "You're s'posed to use a racket."

He was? Mitch had no doubt he could whack balls with the racket, but he couldn't vouch for his aim. Considering he'd probably wind up beaning a kid, using a racket wasn't a good idea.

"I'm trying a new way today, sport. How 'bout getting back in line?"

"Dick," the little boy said crossly, his mouth a straight line.

Mitch blanched. Had the kid actually sworn at him? All because he wouldn't use a racket to feed balls to him and his little buddies. "What did you say?"

"Dick," the little boy repeated, louder this time. "You promised to 'member our names. My name's Richard, but everyone calls me Dick."

Sweat broke out on Mitch's forehead. Cary had said a trained monkey could do his parks and recreation department job. Mitch only wished one were handy.

"I'm sorry, Dick. I won't forget again."

The boy gave him an unhappy look and ambled back in line. Mitch checked his watch and chucked the first ball to Dick's racket side. A swing and a miss. Strike one.

This was going to be a long half hour. If the kids didn't boo him off the court before time was up.

Mitch congratulated himself on a job well enough done as he approached the two-story stuccoed brick mansion where Peyton lived with her parents. The breeze off the Charleston Harbor blew through his hair, carrying with it the taste of salt.

He'd spent the entire day living as Cary, and so far nobody was the wiser. Granted, he hadn't covered himself in glory today at the recreation department, especially during the tennis class. Dick's lower lip had trembled a couple of times, but at least none of the tots had bawled. And, sure, Cary's coworkers had been surprised at his ineptitude, but accepted that he was suffering the effects of a rough night.

Discovering where Peyton lived had been more of a problem. The phone book listed no McDowells with the first initial *P,* and Mitch hadn't wanted to arouse suspicion by using his police connections to find her address. He could have asked Cary, but his brother wasn't answering the phone at Mitch's apartment. So he'd tailed Peyton home from work to this prestigious address south of Broad Street, the wide corridor that cut a swath through Charleston's swankiest area. The house was on Murray Boulevard, the street that overlooked Charleston Harbor.

It disconcerted him a little that she lived with her

parents, but he couldn't fault her for it. The house was no doubt a classic example of some sort of architecture or other with its elaborate molding and double-tiered porch that provided a stunning view of the sailboat-dotted harbor. Who could blame Peyton for wanting to live the high life as long as she could?

Now it was twenty minutes before the hour, which would give them plenty of time to get to the ball by eight o'clock. He was dressed for the occasion in the elegant tuxedo he'd found in his brother's closet. It'd been a shock to find it there, considering the state of Cary's finances, but at least he didn't have to rent one. In his left hand was a bouquet of lilies.

Yeah, he thought as he rang the doorbell, things were definitely looking up.

He smiled before the door swung open, anticipating the sight of Peyton dressed for the ball. Instead, a tall, broad man he assumed was her father filled the door frame, his posture so erect it put a ruler to shame. Mitch remembered Cary saying he was a solicitor, but he seemed more like a military man. Mitch resisted the urge to salute.

"What do you want?" the man asked gruffly.

"Hello, Mr. McDowell." Mitch held out his hand. "I'm Cary Mitchell."

The man's brown eyes narrowed as his gaze swept Mitch up and down. He neither smiled nor took Mitch's hand.

"So you're the smooth operator who stood my daughter up last night?" he asked in a drawl that had the ring of Southern aristocracy. Mitch dropped his hand.

"If you knew me better, you'd know I'm about as smooth as a gravel road." Mitch tried a smile Mr. McDowell didn't return. Suspicion lurked in the man's flinty eyes. "Okay, maybe I'm smoother than gravel. Would you believe asphalt?"

"Who is that at the door, dear?"

A petite woman with frosted blond hair, immaculately dressed in a shimmering gold gown that probably cost as much as Mitch made in a week, appeared at the man's side. Peyton's mother, Mitch presumed.

"Some joker comparing himself to highway surfaces."

"How charming," his wife said, sending Mitch a beaming smile. "Did you bring those flowers for me? I absolutely adore lilies."

"Then I guessed right, Mrs. McDowell," Mitch said, holding out the bouquet. She brought the flowers to her face, sniffed and sighed. "I'm Cary Mitchell. The flowers are an apology for last night. Something came up and I couldn't get to a phone. I hope you'll forgive me."

"Of course I will, Cary dear."

"Please call me Mitch."

"Certainly," she said, "and you can call me Amelia."

"Call me sir," Peyton's father intoned.

Amelia McDowell smiled at her husband as though he'd told Mitch to call him lucky to make his acquaintance. She cocked her expertly coifed head and peered around Mitch's shoulder at the red Miata parked at the curb. "You're taking Peyton to the ball, aren't you?"

"I sure am."

"Then where is she?"

"Isn't she inside the house?"

"Why would she be inside?" Mr. McDowell frowned. "She doesn't live here, you know."

Mitch hadn't known. He'd assumed she couldn't bring herself to move out of a home so grand. After meeting her father, he understood why she had. He'd never been good at improvisation, but gave it a shot. "I thought she was meeting me here."

"Asphalt, schmasphalt," Mr. McDowell growled. "First you stand her up. Then you don't pick her up. You're no smoother than cobblestone."

Mrs. McDowell—Amelia—laid a delicate hand on Mitch's arm. "You were supposed to meet her here last night, dear. Not tonight."

"Then you can see why I got confused," Mitch said as cheerfully as he could. His jaw hurt from keeping his smile in place. Mitch didn't get confused about places and times. Ever. But then he typically knew where his dates lived.

"Perhaps you'd better go collect her," Amelia said helpfully.

As far as advice went, it wasn't bad. He probably had time to drive to Peyton's place, pick her up, and get her to the ball by eight. The snag was that he still didn't know where Peyton lived, and he couldn't ask her parents.

"I'm afraid we might miss each other if I did

that," he said, trying to be cheerful in the face of Mr. McDowell's outright hostility. He knew that Cary had never met the McDowells. Then why the chilly reception? "How 'bout I follow you to the ball and catch up with her there."

Mr. McDowell turned to his wife, whispering something that sounded like, "Do we have to let him, magnolia blossom?"

Amelia, his champion, acted as though she hadn't heard her husband. "That sounds like a grand plan, dear," she said, offering Mitch her arm.

They walked to the curb ahead of Peyton's father, but Mitch felt the older man's eyes searing holes in his back.

Peyton gathered up the long skirt of her lacy evening gown, swung her smoothly shaven legs out of the car, stood on her fashionable Ferragamo shoes, and slammed the door with all her might.

Anger pumped through her veins along with the Charleston blue blood her parents constantly reminded her that she had. The problem was she wasn't sure who deserved her anger more. Herself or Cary . . . er, Mitch, as though that made any sense.

Probably herself, she thought as she stamped up the sidewalk to elegant Hibernian Hall. In the month she'd known him, he'd never been anything but completely irresponsible. He was one of those men who didn't bother with the details of life, instead opting to get by on charm and good looks. And she'd let him.

Yesterday, instead of dumping him like she should have, her red-hot fury had burned down to cinders while he spun his ridiculous yarn about the bridge and Bobby McGee.

He'd looked so worried and apologetic that she'd let him bamboozle her into giving him another chance. She'd actually believed he'd turn up on time to escort her to the ball.

She needed one of those support groups for family and friends of marred individuals. Like Al-Anon. Only Cary/Mitch was a charmaholic instead of an alcoholic.

Maybe she should check the phone book to find out if there was a group called Charm-Anon.

Except she wouldn't need the group for much longer, because the next time she saw him she was telling him they were through.

Enough was enough.

The tops of her high heels bit into the soles of her feet, and she realized she was stamping. She consciously slowed her steps as she moved through the iron gates that bracketed the hall. How many times had her parents drilled into her that appearances were everything? It wouldn't do for her to barge into Charleston's classiest ballroom red-faced with anger.

"Peyton McDowell, you have never looked lovelier."

At the sound of the man's voice behind her, Peyton whirled, then relaxed. G. Gaston Gibbs III came through the iron gates, wearing a charming smile and a designer tuxedo. Growing up, Peyton had distrusted Gaston's smooth tongue and smoother manner, but her opinion of him had drastically changed when she began volunteering at the Charleston League of Historic Preservation.

"Why, thank you for the compliment, sir" she said, giving a slight curtsy.

"You're just the woman I was hoping to run into."

Peyton didn't miss a beat. "Please say that's because you wanted to tell me you're buying that historically significant property on Smith Street?"

Gaston chuckled as he closed the distance between them. He was the picture of a Charleston aristocrat, with fair hair and a slim build that made him appear taller than he was. She supposed he was good-looking, but she secretly thought his sharp features made him look a little too much like a fox.

"If you mean that *dilapidated* property, yes, I'm buying it."

Peyton gave an unladylike squeal and squeezed his arm. Gaston worked as a real estate agent at a downtown firm, but his parents, who'd moved to Hilton Head six months before, came from old money. Gaston had spent much of it buying and renovating historic properties slated for demolition.

"I was praying you'd come to the rescue," she said. "It would have been criminal to tear down a house with such classic Italianate styling."

"So you've said." Gaston smiled and took her arm as they walked onto the portico. As always, the grandness of the hall, with its great white columns stretching toward the sky, took Peyton's breath away. She and Gaston strolled under the Irish harp imbedded in the paneling above the door and through the main entrance to the domed rotunda where the event was taking place. "I hoped to run into you so I could be your escort this evening. You *are* here unescorted, are you not?"

Peyton's eyes swept over the milling crowd, and her head halted in mid-nod. No more than ten yards away, Cary/Mitch snagged a glass of punch off a passing waiter's tray and handed it to her mother. Her scowling father watched the transaction. His scowl transformed into a smile when he spotted her.

"Why, Peyton, how good it is to see you," her father said after he'd disengaged himself from the group. He clapped Gaston on the back. "You too, old friend. You restore my faith in my daughter's taste in men."

"Darlings, you both look fabulous." Her mother was right behind her husband, clasping Gaston's hand before kissing the air on either side of her daughter's face. "Peyton, it does my heart good to see you dressed in something other than that dreadful uniform those carriage people make you wear."

Peyton's spirits fell the way they always did whenever her mother disparaged the tour-guide business, but she knew better than to disagree. It never got her anywhere.

"I have to differ, Amelia. I think Peyton looks great in those khaki shorts." Mitch's voice cut into her thoughts, and her ire returned. She'd been brought up far too well to blast him while Gaston and her parents were present, but she could silently communicate her displeasure. She shifted, intending to give him the angry eye. "But then I'm biased. I think she'd look great in anything."

His eyes moved appreciatively over her before he gave her an intimate, heart-tugging smile. "Hello, Peyton."

"Hello, Mitch," she whispered back before she could stop herself. She was afraid her eyes were glowing.

Tarnation. How was she supposed to hiss at him and make her eyes angry when he looked at her like that? Or when he looked as he did? The other men in the room were similarly dressed, but Mitch stood out like a peacock among penguins. The cloth of his tux was obviously expensive but only seemed to draw attention to his broad shoulders and long legs. The stark black color complemented the inky darkness of his hair and set off his blue, blue eyes.

As she got to know what was inside the man, she'd thought she was becoming immune to his good looks. So why, all of a sudden, was he becoming harder and harder to resist?

"I'm Cary Mitchell." Mitch held out a hand to Gaston. "Peyton's date."

"G. Gaston Gibbs III," Gaston said, cutting his eyes at Peyton but taking Mitch's hand. "I was under the impression Peyton was unescorted."

"Only because I thought I was supposed to pick her up at her parents' house," Mitch said before Peyton could respond. His words were as smooth as usual, but something about his voice sounded different. His eyes smiled at her. "Work was so crazy today that I got mixed up. Forgive me?"

Peyton's jaw dropped. That was twice in two days that Mr. What's Done Is Done had apologized. The tilt of his head as he waited for her answer suggested a vulnerability she'd never noticed before, and she figured out what was different about his voice. It was crazy, but he sounded . . . sincere. She shouldn't forgive him. Not this time. But she knew she was going to.

"A woman never truly forgives a man until he grovels, dear," her mother told Mitch, saving Peyton from answering.

"Nor does her father," Mr. McDowell growled.

"I can do groveling," Mitch said. Peyton's disbelieving laugh cut into him until he reminded himself that she thought he was his brother. Cary never groveled.

"That I'd like to see," she said.

"You will," he promised, but he could tell from the look she shot in his direction that she didn't believe it.

"You can grovel later, dear," Amelia said. "Peyton needs to mingle now. I would so love to see her voted Volunteer of the Year."

"Mother, they've already voted me Volunteer of the Year," Peyton whispered. "I'm getting the award tonight. Remember?"

"I know that, dear, but it's never too early to lobby for next year." She turned her attention to Gaston. "Darling, I see Senator Mabry Collins across the room. He and your father are friends, aren't they?"

Gaston nodded. "They were roommates at law school."

"Be a dear and take Peyton over there to introduce her. It can never hurt to make the acquaintance of a senator."

"Mother, I can meet the senator later," Peyton said. Mitch hoped her refusal stemmed from wanting to spend time with him, which may have been optimistic considering she wouldn't meet his eyes.

"Nonsense, Gaston is right here," Mr. McDowell spoke up. "What better time than the present."

"He's right, especially since it would be my pleasure," Gaston said, then regarded Mitch. "You don't mind, do you?"

"Actually, I—"

"Of course he doesn't mind," Amelia interrupted. "It'll give us a chance to dance and become better acquainted."

She bestowed a beatific smile on Mitch as she took his arm and turned him in the direction of the dance floor. Mitch liked Amelia, but he felt rather like a pawn in a chess game. Right now, it seemed as though she wanted to maneuver him away from Peyton.

An hour later, Mitch was positive that Amelia McDowell was keeping him away from her daughter. She was like a football player with a nose for the ball, and he was the ball. She was worse than the young women who kept trying to make his acquaintance. Whenever Mitch moved a step in

Peyton's direction, Amelia intercepted him. Considering that Peyton was now dancing with Gaston, it had become a serious problem.

"Mitch, could you be a dear and get me a few of those artichoke hors d'oeuvres across the room." Amelia kissed her fingertips. "They're simply divine."

Mitch's eyes followed Gaston and Peyton as they moved in tandem across the dance floor. The phrase Beauty and the Beast sprang to mind. Peyton looked like a princess in her lacy gown, with her delicate neck exposed by the upsweep of her blond hair and the lights of the ballroom illuminating the beauty of her face. Gaston Gibbs wasn't bad looking, but his smile had a beastly quality Mitch distrusted.

"I'll get you some later, Amelia," Mitch said. "Right now, I'm going to dance with Peyton."

"But, dear, there are plenty of other women in the room who would love to dance with you. You needn't bother Peyton."

Bother her? Mitch's brow creased. "You're forgetting I'm here with Peyton."

"How could I possibly forget that, dear? But surely you realize you're not from her world the way Gaston is. Look at them out on the dance floor. They make a lovely couple, don't you think?"

So there it was. Out in the open. Mitch already suspected Amelia was trying to match Peyton with Gaston, but he hadn't expected her to be so candid about it.

"No, I don't think so," he said, giving her one of

the sugary smiles she specialized in. "I think Peyton and I make a better couple."

She tilted back her small chin and laughed a tinkling laugh. "You *are* charming, dear, and quite handsome. Understand, I have absolutely nothing against you. But the truth of the matter is Peyton is a Charlestonian and so is Gaston. She might dally with you, but in the end blood will win out. Gaston will win out."

Mitch wanted to dress her down for her snobbery, but it wouldn't do any good. She lived in an insulated world he couldn't begin to understand, a world of class and privilege where blood lines were more important than character.

Then again, he wasn't in a position to speak up for his character while he was passing himself off as his brother. His brother, he thought. He couldn't forget he was here because of his brother. That it was his brother's girl, and not his, they were discussing.

"If you'll excuse me," he said, giving her a slight bow.

"Where are you going?" A note of panic tinged her voice.

"To dally," he answered, because it was what his brother would say. Then he walked away from her and toward Peyton.

He would have enjoyed the way Peyton's eyes widened when she spotted him if he didn't know she thought she was looking at Cary. He tapped Gaston on the shoulder.

"May I cut in?"

Gaston turned, his sharp features pinched. "What if I said no?"

"Then I might have to hurt you." Mitch uttered another Cary-like line. Then he smiled.

"Not funny," Gaston said. "But we can talk about that later."

A moment later, Peyton was in his arms, her scent going to his head like a fine scotch. *His* head. Not Cary's. "What's that you're wearing?"

"A gown."

"Not your gown. Your perfume."

"I don't wear perfume," Peyton said. "You must mean my moisturizer. It's scented. Jasmine."

"I like it." He put his nose against her skin and breathed. How could this be, that the smell of his brother's girl went straight to his head? He couldn't stop the truth from escaping his lips. "I like you."

She turned her face away from him. "You have a funny way of showing it. You promised to be on time tonight."

"I was on time."

"You know what I mean, Mitch. I waited for you, and you didn't show up. I can't. . . ." He took her hand and planted a soft kiss on her palm. "Would you stop it? I can't think when you do things like that."

"I don't want you to think."

"That's because you know you're bad for me."

"It's because I don't want you to break up with me."

Reaching out a hand, he caressed her cheek. He

saw the indecision in her eyes before she closed them and shook her head. Please, he prayed. Please don't let her say she never wants to see me again. Her eyes opened after a moment, and he couldn't read anything at all in them.

"Why, Mitch? Why would it matter? Plenty of women would love to go out with you. I saw them flocking around you tonight. It's like you're a sheikh, and they're a harem."

Pleasure skittered through him. "So you were watching me?"

She cast her eyes downward, giving herself away. "Don't change the subject. I didn't see you turning them away so you could be with me."

"Then you didn't see your mother cutting me off every time I headed in your direction."

"She knows as well as I do that it would take you only minutes to replace me."

"You're wrong," Mitch whispered, meaning every word. Hoo boy. He was in trouble here. He traced the line of her jaw with his fingertip, letting it come to rest on her lips. "I couldn't replace you. You're irreplaceable."

He could tell she thought he was lying, and his heart sank like bricks in quicksand. Because she was right to distrust him. No matter how sincere the words, he was trying to win her for his brother.

"Oh, Mitch. Not only don't I believe you, but I can't trust you. I need a man I can rely on."

"You can rely on me," he said.

The soft strands of the slow song faded away, and Mitch reluctantly let Peyton back out of his arms. Her brows drew together. "Do you really mean it, Mitch?" she asked. "Can I really rely on you?"

"Yes," he said again, and her lips curved into a slight smile. A voice came over a microphone, announcing it was time for the awards ceremony and calling the winners to the front of the room.

"Then I'll see you later," she said almost shyly. "After my speech."

"Later," he agreed.

She wasn't gone five minutes when he glanced at his watch and realized it was nearly time for bartending duty.

Peyton would give her acceptance speech in the next half hour, but he couldn't wait. He drew in a frustrated breath, remembering he'd told her mere minutes ago that she could rely on him.

But hadn't he said the same thing to Cary, whose future depended upon whether or not he could gather enough evidence to put Flash Gorman behind bars?

Much as he hated to, he had to leave. He walked through the doors, under the crest of the Irish harp and past the great white columns, feeling like the louse Peyton was going to think he was.

Chapter Five

If Mitch was asked to pick his favorite part of the female anatomy, he'd dodge the question by pointing out that women were much more than a collection of parts.

When he met a female, he was careful to look her in the eye. He never, ever tried to get a woman in bed before getting to know her first. What was on the inside was much more important than what was on the outside.

But the truth was that Mitch had a weakness for breasts, which usually didn't come into play in his everyday existence. After all, most women covered theirs.

That wasn't true at the Epidermis. He couldn't turn his head without getting an eyeful of breast flesh. Big and small. Round and firm. Dark-skinned and light-skinned. They were everywhere.

The few women seated at the bar wore tops with plunging necklines. The cocktail waitresses who came to him with their drink orders were nearly spilling out of their tiny tops. And the dancers on stage let it all hang out.

Mitch should have been in breast bliss, but he wasn't.

He was too angry at his brother, who hadn't bothered to tell him he bartended at a strip club.

Come to think of it, he was also angry at Cary for putting him in a position where the breasts he most wanted to see belonged to Peyton, a woman he couldn't have.

Mitch filled a beer mug from the tap and slammed it down on the bar in front of an aging, overweight man. The beer sloshed over the rim, but the man wasn't paying attention to anything but the breasts on stage.

"Careful you don't provoke the customers, sugar."

A woman with a bosom the size of Kilimanjaro sidled up to the bar and bared her teeth in a smile. Even though her lipstick was thick and ruby red, her teeth looked more yellow than white. Her skin was slathered in makeup, her dark hair teased to towering proportions. She looked like an aging hooker, which would have been preferable to what she was. Millie Bellini. The club manager.

"What'd I tell you about wearing shirts like that, baby?" Her eyes ran over him, making him want to put on a jacket.

He'd made a quick stop at Cary's apartment to change out of his tux, and he looked down at his collarless shirt. "What's wrong with my shirt?"

"It doesn't cling. You're s'posed to wear one of them black shirts that cling. I got a stash of 'em in the back room. Go put one on."

"Why?" The Epidermis was visited mostly by men. Mitch couldn't imagine they cared what he wore.

Millie rolled her mascara-coated eyes. "Why you think I keep you around? Eye candy. With all these girls in here, I need something for me." She reached across the bar and pinched his cheek. "Now go change, baby."

She leered at him, giving him yet another reason to be angry at Cary. He was doubling for his brother at a strip club where the women were nude but he was the one being sexually harassed.

Even as he wondered why he'd let Cary talk him into this, he knew the answer. His brother needed rescuing, and it was Mitch's duty to save him.

"What you waiting for, sugar buns?" Millie asked. "You want me to come help?"

"I've been dressing myself for a long time now, Millie. I can do it," he said easily although his inclination was to refuse. But he couldn't risk alerting Millie that he wasn't Cary, who should be grateful he wasn't in throttling range. Brotherly love wouldn't have saved him.

As soon as he was back at his station, a scantily clad woman hopped off a bar stool and drew him aside. For the last half hour, she'd been flirting outrageously with a middle-aged businessman.

"What's your problem, Cary?" she hissed. As a beat cop, Mitch had seen plenty of girls like her walking the Atlanta streets. She wasn't much older in years than the legal drinking age, but she had the hard edge of experience.

"Call me Mitch," he said.

"How 'bout I call you asshole? What do you think you're doing? Giving me champagne?"

"You ordered champagne," he pointed out.

"I order champagne all the time. You're supposed to give me ginger ale."

"But that guy's paying for champagne." Mitch knew he was missing something.

"How do you think I make my money, asshole? I'm gonna let it go this time, but you give me any more champagne, I'm tellin' Millie. Got it?"

She sauntered back to the bar stool. The businessman was waiting, and she made a point of leaning over and straightening his tie. The man's bloodshot eyes focused squarely on her cleavage.

Mitch could have kicked himself for not noticing she was trying to get the man to drop as much money as she could. No doubt she got a cut for her efforts. If the mark got drunk enough, she probably reached inside his wallet and helped herself to a tip. If he didn't, she most likely offered sex for money.

He might be able to prove that Flash Gorman ran a prostitution ring out of Epidermis, but Mitch wasn't sure he should direct his efforts that way. He surveyed the dark, smoky bar, trying to pinpoint Flash Gorman so he could decide upon the best course of action. Nobody seemed the wiser about Cary skimming money from the cash register, but Mitch figured he didn't have long before somebody figured it out.

He took another drink order, searching his memory as to whether a New Orleans Fizz contained gin or whiskey. He settled on gin, not that it would have made any difference to the man at the bar—whose attention was on a statuesque blonde on stage, wearing nothing but a G-string and a smile. Her figure was centerfold material, but Mitch's mind still turned to Peyton.

He was pretty sure Cary hadn't told her about his second job and he didn't think he should either. What would Peyton think about him serving drinks in the shadow of the naked ladies on stage? Not much, he'd bet.

"Hey, sugar buns," Millie sidled up to the bar and leaned across it. He tried really hard not to look at her cleavage. "Flash wants to see you in the back room."

"He's here?" Mitch asked in surprise. "I didn't sec him come in."

"You know he never steps foot in this part of the club. It's not good for his reputation. He's waitin'. I'll cover for you." Millie's lipstick-red mouth curved into a leering smile and she winked. "Love the black shirt, baby."

The look in Millie's eyes had Mitch beating a hasty retreat through the smoke, the customers ogling the strippers on stage, and the maze of tables. He jerked open the door to the back room, shut it behind him, and tried to recover from shock. The place was awash in red velvet, from the carpeting to the wallpaper border, but the decor was to be expected considering they were inside a strip club.

No, the surprise wasn't the interior decorating. The surprise was sitting behind the desk.

"I suppose I should thank you for pretending you didn't know me earlier tonight," G. Gaston Gibbs III said, leaning back in his chair. The strands of his blond hair barely moved. "The McDowells are too uptight to condone ownership of a strip club. Even if I am a shadow owner."

"That's what I figured," Mitch said, trying to stop his brain from reeling. The G. in G. Gaston Gibbs obviously stood for Gorman. As in Flash Gorman. "I'm nothing if not discreet."

"Of course, I'm sure you wouldn't want Peyton to hear about your indiscretions. Starting with your weakness for strippers and ending with your unfortunate gambling problem."

"You're right about that," Mitch said.

"Then I'm glad we understand each other." Gaston picked up a rubber ball from his desk, the kind meant to relieve tension. His sharp features tightened. "Remember what you said earlier when Peyton and I were dancing? About hurting me if I didn't let you cut in."

"Yeah?"

Gaston squeezed the ball. Hard. "You were kidding, right?"

Mitch hadn't been, but it wasn't a good time to

say so. He was sure he could beat Gaston if it came down to hand-to-hand combat, but they were involved in another kind of struggle.

"Because I'm willing to overlook this little thing you're carrying on with Peyton. But make no mistake about it. When it comes time for me to take a wife, she's the one I'll choose."

Mitch cleared his throat while he recoiled at the thought of Gibbs so much as touching Peyton. "I think she'll have something to say about that."

"Peyton does what her parents want her to do, and her parents want her to marry me. I have the right background."

"But why would you want to marry her? You can't expect me to believe that you love her."

Gaston laughed, a rasping, unpleasant sound. "Of course I don't love her, but she has the right background too. She'll provide me with the perfect cover. Never mind that—this conversation is boring me. I didn't call you back here to talk about Peyton."

"Then why did you call me here?"

"I have your first assignment."

The culture was gone from his voice, and he sounded almost cruel. He rubbed his smooth cheek. He didn't speak above a whisper, and his voice was all the more menacing because of it. "Guy by the name of Cooper Barnes works at a restaurant in North Charleston. He owes me money. If he doesn't give it to you, I want you to break something."

"Break something?" Mitch blinked.

"Yeah. A leg, a finger, an arm. I don't care which. Just get the money out of him. I don't want him messing with me any more."

Mitch stared. It didn't seem possible, but he knew it was. His brother was a debt collector for a bookie.

"Nobody messes with me, Mitchell. You'd do well to remember that."

Thirty minutes later, Mitch was at a pay phone outside the club listening to the phone ring unanswered at his Atlanta apartment. Impotent anger welled up in him, because he wasn't going to get the chance to blast Cary for the mess his brother'd thrust him into.

His brother owed him a lot of answers, but at the moment one question was more important than the rest.

Where the devil was Cary?

Chapter Six

Lizabeth Drinkmiller sat alone outside a Key West cafe at a table built for two, chastising herself for not being able to go through with her grand plan.

She glanced down at the fancy alcoholic concoction with the colorful paper umbrella floating on its surface. *A rum-ba,* the menu had called it. *Sure to make you want to shed your inhibitions and dance.* But the drink had been sitting in front of her for thirty minutes, and Lizabeth still couldn't bring herself to take a sip.

What had made her think she'd act any differently on a two-week vacation than she did the rest of her life?

She was what she was. A research librarian more at home with books and computers than people. No wonder she hadn't had a date in almost two years.

She was as boring as heat in the tropics. Like the chameleon that attached itself to a leafy green bush, she faded into the scenery so well nobody noticed her.

She might as well start going by the name Lizabeth the Lizard. Even the dye job she'd done on her mousy brown hair didn't make a difference. Of course, at the last second, she'd put down the bottle of Yowlin' Yellow and gone with Barely Brunette.

She'd been more daring while shopping for a vacation wardrobe, choosing outfits that showed so much of her skin she'd nearly fainted dead away when she saw herself in the dressing-room mirror. But what good was a mini skirt when she had her legs tucked under the table? Or a plunging tank top when she'd covered it with a sweater buttoned to the chin?

Determined to live it up, she began unbuttoning her sweater. And stopped at the second button. Okay. Exhibitionism wasn't going to fly, but she could at least imbibe. She picked up her drink. And managed a single sip before putting it down.

She propped her chin on her hands, watching the tourists walk by as they enjoyed an evening in Key West. A woman, plain except for her smile, strolled by with a hunk of a man on her arm. Lizabeth bet *she* was secure in her own skin. That woman wouldn't have a problem going to her boss and demanding a raise. Or getting a date.

She watched the parade of tourists with growing despondence. They all looked happy and well adjusted. The kind of people who went after what they wanted and got it.

Unlike Lizabeth, who sat on the sidelines while life passed her by.

A man on the other side of the street snagged her attention, and Lizabeth's entire body went rigid. Even from a distance, she could tell that he was gorgeous. Taller than most of the other passersby, he had thick hair the color of night and a broad-shouldered, long-legged physique that commanded attention.

As he got nearer, he passed under a streetlight that lit his features. She took in the cleft in his square jaw, the generous width of his mouth, the tilt of his nose. A shock of recognition passed through her, and her breath seized in her chest, the way it used to whenever he passed her in the hall at Hatfield High.

Grant Mitchell. The hunk across the street was Grant Mitchell, the boy who'd sent her schoolgirl heart palpitating.

She made herself breathe as her eyes devoured him. His body had filled out, but he still favored worn jeans and denim shirts. He'd been wearing a cap and gown the last time she'd seen him, striding across the stage in the high school auditorium to receive his diploma. She remembered her hot tears of frustration as she watched him. Even though she feared she'd never see him again, she'd known she wouldn't approach him.

Now, ten years later, he was the width of a street rather than the width of an auditorium away. In another few moments, he'd be gone. Again.

"No," Lizabeth said aloud, the word emerging from deep in her soul. She couldn't let Grant disappear. Not this time. Not when she'd come to Key West with the express purpose of shedding her retiring personality and going after what she wanted.

She wanted Grant.

She looked down the length of her body. She also wanted Grant to notice her, the way he never had in high school. Before she could change her mind, she fluffed her barely brunette hair, pulled off her sweater, and gulped a big portion of her drink.

Then she dashed across the street toward her fate, forgetting that the heels she wore with her short skirt were much higher than she was used to. The driver of one of the rental scooters that darted through the narrow Key West streets honked his horn, and Lizabeth panicked.

She lunged for the sidewalk, her heel catching on the curb. Grant turned toward her at the same time she squealed, and his arms shot out to save her from falling.

The sensation of his large, well-formed hands on her bare arms sent warmth pouring over her, like the cascade from a waterfall in the tropics. Her heart pounded a heavy beat as she met his blue eyes, and she knew the drumming wasn't because of the scooter that had nearly run her over. He was looking at her in a way he'd never looked at her in high school, with an appreciative gleam that heated her entire body.

"Wait a minute," he said, grinning. "I'm the one who could fall for you."

He righted her, his warm hands secure on her hot flesh. She blinked up at him, unable to look away from his eyes. They were blue. So very blue. Like the water surrounding the Keys that had looked so inviting from the window of the 747 that had flown her here.

"Did you know that, other than humans, black lemurs are the only primate that can have blue eyes?"

She nearly closed her own boring brown eyes in mortification when she realized what she'd said. What had possessed her to spew that piece of useless trivia?

His eyes smiled at her, as though he hadn't noticed how hopelessly gauche she was. "A lemur couldn't appreciate someone who looks like you. I do."

She gulped. Was Grant Mitchell actually flirting with her? It was such an impossible dream that she figured she must have misinterpreted him.

"You didn't appreciate me in high school," she blurted out. Darn. Why had she said that? In order to masquerade as a self-confident woman, she needed to act like one.

"We went to high school together?" he asked as he released his grip on her shoulders. He cocked his head, scrutinizing her.

Lizabeth's disappointment was swift and all-consuming. Of course he didn't remember her. She forced herself to smile. "You grew up in Richmond, didn't you?"

"Sure did," he said, continuing to stare at her. Then he smiled, and the beauty of it sent her heart to pounding the way it always used to. He snapped his fingers. "I remember now. You were in my biology class, weren't you?"

"No," Lizabeth answered. "You were two years ahead of me, so I wasn't in any of your classes."

"I'll be sure to remember if you tell me your name," he said, but she was sure he wouldn't. Their paths had crossed only once, at a high school dance when the boy she'd been dancing with had cut in on his partner. Grant had graciously finished the dance with her, but she'd been too tongue-tied by the feel of his hands on her waist to say a word.

She started to tell him her name was Lizabeth, but stopped. It was such a boring name, not in keeping with her new image at all. She made a snap decision. "It's Leeza. Leeza Drinkmiller."

"Leeza," Cary repeated, wondering why he didn't remember her. His taste in women hadn't changed much since high school. With her curvy body and revealing clothing, she looked exactly like the kind of woman he usually dated. So how had he missed her?

"You still don't remember me, do you?" The corners of her mouth turned downward, and he found himself thinking that mouth would be prettier if she weren't wearing so much lipstick. "I'm not surprised. I blended into the scenery in high school."

"You could never blend into the scenery," Cary

said. Her tank top was cut low, revealing the most gorgeous breasts he'd ever seen. In her heels, she could look him straight in the eye, which meant her legs went on and on. He even liked her face, which had a big-eyed, gamin quality to it. The net effect was wildly appealing. "If I didn't notice you, I must've been blind."

"I doubt that." Her smile looked forced. "You struck me as someone who had his eyes wide open. You seemed like you knew exactly where you were going."

"I did?" Cary asked, amazed that she'd had this view of him Then again, he had been a star pitcher at Americana High with a swing so potent he was the team's best hitter. Anybody could have seen that he had the talent to make it to the pros.

"Definitely," she said, sounding like a one-woman fan club. "Anybody could see you had the brains to achieve whatever you set your mind to."

"They could?" All Cary's mind had been on in high school was scoring—both on the field and off it. Truth be told, that's the direction his mind was headed now. He had a feeling scoring with Leeza would be more thrilling than hitting a home run.

"So, Grant, what did you set your mind to?"

Grant. She'd called him Grant, which was what people called Mitch when they weren't well enough acquainted with him to know he preferred a nickname.

It caused everything about their strange conversation to fall into place. No wonder he hadn't recognized her. Because their parents wanted them to establish themselves as individuals, they'd sent Cary and Mitch to different schools, where they'd developed separate sets of friends. Leeza had obviously attended Hatfield High with his brother, not Americana with him.

Still, she must not have been very well acquainted with Mitch. Even though they were identical twins, people who knew them didn't generally confuse them. They had different styles, both in speech and dress. Except Cary hadn't packed warm-weather clothes when he'd headed for Atlanta, so he'd borrowed his brother's.

"You don't understand," he said, "I'm not. . . ."

Something in her eyes stopped him from finishing. She was looking at him as though she admired him. He'd already guessed she'd had an unrequited thing for his brother in high school, and the remnants of it shone in her eyes.

"You're not what?" she asked.

He'd been about to say he wasn't Mitch, but that no longer seemed like such a good idea. Despite the way they looked, he was as different from his brother as salsa from ketchup. If Leeza admired his twin, she wouldn't admire him.

"I'm not as successful as you think I am."

"I find that hard to believe. What do you do?"

"I'm a cop in Atlanta," Cary said, making his decision.

If it was Grant Mitchell she admired, it was Grant Mitchell she was going to get.

Chapter Seven

Lizabeth had goosebumps, which wouldn't have been so obvious if the sun wasn't beating down on the deck of the twenty-four-foot cabin cruiser. Or if she'd been wearing more clothes.

She shifted and artfully arranged the sarong that she'd tied loosely at her waist the way the saleslady back in Richmond had shown her—the saleslady who had convinced her she had the figure to wear the itty bitty red bikini that left so much of her pale skin exposed. Lizabeth wasn't so sure. Especially now, when the love of her teen years was sitting across the boat, smiling at her.

She'd been so flabbergasted the night before when he invited her to have a drink that she invented a prior engagement and asked for a raincheck. She simply wasn't prepared to try out her bold new persona on so luscious a man until she rehearsed.

So she'd spent hours alone in her hotel room in front of a mirror, tossing her hair, perfecting her laugh, and practicing to be Leeza. She'd even walked across the room over and over until the book on top of her head stopped falling off.

This morning, when Grant had phoned her hotel room asking if she'd like to snorkel the coral reef, she'd let loose a tinkling laugh and said, "That would be utterly divine."

Lizabeth was to swimming what lead was to liquid, but Leeza could fake it. To keep Grant's interest, Leeza could fake anything.

"It's too bad you forgot to pack your diving certification," Grant called over the hum of the outboard motor. "I hear the scuba diving around here is awesome."

"It can't be better than it was in Aruba," she said, hoping she sounded worldly and sophisticated. "The water's so clear there the fish can see their reflection."

He laughed. "You get around, don't you?"

"Hmmmm," she said, because she didn't want to lie. Not that she was lying. Exactly. She wasn't a world traveler, but she had been to Aruba. Granted, it was the site of the only exotic vacation she'd ever taken. And yes, she'd spent six of her seven days there in a darkened hotel room recovering from the horrific sunburn she'd gotten the first day.

But one of the college roommates who'd been

with her had gone diving and raved about it. Lizabeth herself couldn't dive. It wasn't her fault Grant had misinterpreted her declaration that she didn't have her diving certification to mean she forgot to pack it. That was perfectly fine with her, because Leeza would know how to dive.

Oh, she wasn't so far gone that she believed herself to be Sybil reincarnated. She understood she wasn't two separate beings, but on this trip, she couldn't act like herself. Grant wouldn't have chartered a boat for boring, ordinary Lizabeth. He wouldn't have wanted to share the blue skies and the azure seas with someone as colorless as Lizabeth.

She tossed her head the way she imagined a practiced flirt might, but the wind caught her hair when she turned her chin. Long strands flew into her eyes and all over her face until she imagined she looked like an overgrown Yorkshire terrier.

She frantically swiped at her face, trying to clear the hair, trying to maintain her sophisticated image.

"Let me help." Grant slid across the bench seat until he was next to her. She heard something tear and then able hands were in her hair, pulling the messy mop back from her face.

He smiled at her, a heartthrob's grin that illuminated his eyes so she couldn't tell whether the sparkle was the sun's reflection or simply Grant's inner light. He was wearing a short-sleeved plaid shirt he'd left unbuttoned over his swim trunks, and his glorious, hair-roughened chest was within drooling range.

Be cool, she told herself, even as heat enveloped her. He was even more of a hunk than he'd been in high school. His hair was a rich ebony and a lock of it swirled to the left. Funny, in her mental picture of him, his hair curled right. No matter. As long as he was here beside her, she wouldn't care if he shaved his hair off. Even bald, he'd be gorgeous.

"Here, let me." He turned her by her bare shoulders so that her back was to him. Lizabeth closed her eyes as her goosebump count doubled. Masculine fingers grazed her scalp as he gathered her hair at her nape and secured it. She prayed he wouldn't notice the blush she felt creeping up her neck.

"There," he said, and she felt his breath on her newly bare neck. He rubbed at the goosebumps on her shoulders, and she gritted her teeth against the sensations dancing through her. "Are you cold?"

Cold? She was so hot she ought to jump into the water to cool off. She gave her head one of the airy tosses she'd practiced in front of the mirror. Say something sophisticated, she told herself.

"Did you know that the Star of Africa is the largest cut diamond in existence?"

"Huh?"

Shut up, she told herself, but her mouth didn't obey. "Could you imagine trying to wear something like that on your finger? I suppose that's why it's set in the British royal scepter instead of any of the Queen's rings."

His hands were still on her shoulders and he turned her so she had to look at him. She bravely met his eyes and saw amusement dancing there.

She silently cursed herself. As a research librarian, her mind was full of stray facts. That didn't mean she had to spew them like a geyser gone amok. He must think her a total fool.

"You're a gem, Leeza Drinkmiller," he said, leaning forward slightly to kiss her nose. The sensation was so vivid she could feel the imprint of his lips even when he removed them.

Giddy with relief that her gaucherie hadn't ruined things with him, she managed a cool smile. "I try to be on the cutting edge," she said, and his hands dropped from her shoulders. Gathering her poise, she patted the back of her head. "What did you use to tie my hair?"

He held up his shirt, which was newly frayed at the bottom.

"You ripped your shirt? But it looks brand new!"

"It was worth it to get that hair out of your beautiful face," he said, then glanced down at the shirt. She was right. It did look new, but it wasn't as though he liked it. Plaids weren't his style. Then again, Leeza didn't know that. She thought he was his brother, who'd probably choose to be buried in muted plaid. "I'd give you the shirt off my back if you asked me."

A soft, shy light appeared in her eyes that charmed him, but then she tossed her head and gave a tinkling laugh, so he thought he might have imagined the shyness. Her lips curved upward. "Then remind me to ask you later."

It was a siren's line, one that should have him

anticipating what she had in mind for later. Instead, it filled him with a vague disappointment. He liked it better when she was nervously spouting stray facts about industrial-sized diamonds than when she was tossing out flirtatious lines with practiced ease.

"Oh, you can bet I will," he said, staring into her eyes until she looked away. Again, he thought he detected that hint of shyness. But maybe shyness wasn't why she'd looked away at all. Maybe she was disappointed he'd used so obvious a line. She'd fallen for his twin in high school, and Cary was sure the Boy Scout wouldn't say something like that.

He leaned back against the leather bench seat that lined the front of the boat, letting the wind whip through his hair. If he wanted to keep Leeza's interest, he'd have to do better than this.

But why was a woman like her interested in his brother anyway? With her flamboyant wardrobe and worldly air, she was more his type than his twin's. Aside from the anomaly back in Charleston that was Peyton, Cary'd always stuck to women who were more keen on style than substance.

In her red bikini and sarong with her toenails painted a matching color, Leeza was nothing if not stylish.

"Your reef's over there," their charter boat captain yelled, pointing to a spot in the distance where a pair of boats bobbed on the sea.

Other outfits had fancier boats and better prices, but Cary couldn't pass up the USS *Surprise* when he found out the charter captain's name was Turk.

Granted, he was a tiny bit freaked when he discovered that Captain Turk had a dog named Questie. And the floor-to-ceiling poster of Sprock in his cabin was a little spooky.

But, hey, it was working out. The good captain wasn't charging them for the trip. In exchange for the charter and a couple hundred bucks, Cary had agreed to transport crates of goods for him from Key West to Miami. The caveat was that he not ask what the crates contained. He didn't want to know, anyway.

"Don't ya think it would be neat if I could beam you over there?" Captain Turk called.

"What does he mean? Beam us there?" Leeza asked as she put on a pair of trendy sunglasses that had points vaguely reminiscent of Sprock's ears.

"He's one of those *Star Quest* fanatics," Cary said in a low voice.

"Don't you mean *Star Trek?*"

"Nah. Turk's not too fond of *Star Trek,* but he's nuts about *Star Quest,* which was one of those rip-off series that only lasted for three or four years. His real name's not even Turk. Under interrogation, he confessed it was Irving."

"How fascinating," Leeza said, crossing one long leg over the other. If Cary hadn't been so focused on her shapely calf, he might have thought to get out of the way.

"Ow," he said when the toe of her high-heeled sandal collided with his shin.

Her hands flew to her cheeks, "I'm so sorry. I am such a klutz."

Her off-the-cuff reaction charmed him, as did the way her mouth formed a perfect, distressed O. He was about to reassure her that he liked her just the way she was, klutzy or not, when she prevaricated.

"I didn't mean that. I'm not usually clumsy at all. I'm actually quite . . . poised."

The smile pulling at his lips faded. He'd kind of liked the thought of her with a flaw, because, as far as he could see, she didn't have one. But then, he knew next to nothing about her. Usually, that didn't matter. With Leeza, it did.

"Don't tell me you're a dancer on a chorus line."

"A dancer?" Lizabeth wet her lips nervously. "Why would you think that?"

He rubbed his shin again. "Because you kick like a pro."

She laughed. "I'm not a dancer."

"Then what do you do for a living?"

"I'm a . . ." Lizabeth stopped short of revealing the mind-numbing truth. She couldn't tell him she spent her life with her nose buried in books and computer databases, searching for information.

"Doctor?" he guessed.

She shook her head, content to have him supply her with a profession. With her limited imagination, she was sure he'd come up with something better than she could.

"Lawyer?"

Another shake of the head.

"Indian chief?"

She dissolved into laughter. "Be serious."

"Okay." He considered her carefully. "It has to

be something that takes style, panache, brains." He snapped his fingers. "I know. You're a buyer for a department store. You have such good taste in clothes that you're constantly traveling to New York."

It was so far removed from what she actually did that Lizabeth nearly let out a big, fat chortle. She started to shake her head, then stopped. Nobody had ever looked at her the way Grant was looking at her. As though he found her exciting and interesting. What would it hurt to let him think she was?

"You're amazing," she said. "That's exactly right."

His eyes widened. "Man, I'm good."

The motor on the *Surprise* slowed, then sputtered to a stop, leaving the boat bobbing on its own wake. Captain Turk hopped down from his seat behind the wheel, picked up an anchor, and hoisted it overboard. Now that the boat wasn't generating a breeze, the sun felt hot on her skin.

"This is it," Captain Turk said, smoothing back immovable hair that looked eerily familiar. Lizabeth squinted. Was that a toupee? And what about the too-tight shirt he was wearing with those unfashionable black pants? She'd never watched *Star Quest,* but his ensemble looked scarily reminiscent of the one the *Star Trek* captain had worn. Except for the chartreuse color of his shirt.

"Some people are diving," Captain Turk continued, "but the reef's so close to the surface, snorkeling does just fine."

Grant rose and held out a hand for her foot, making her feel like Cinderella to his Prince Charming. Only Grant was holding out a black flipper instead of a glass slipper. "Let me help you put this on," he said.

Lizabeth tried a smile, which wasn't so difficult considering he was looking at her with that charming half-grin. But no way was she taking off her sarong and jumping into that water, no matter how blue and inviting it looked.

"The sun feels so heavenly I'd like to sit here and bask in it for a while," she said. "You go ahead. I'll watch."

His smile faded. "You sure?"

Sure? She could barely swim. Besides, she'd seen *Jaws.* Of course she was sure. "Positively certain," she said.

"Okay, but it would be more fun if you were with me," Grant said a moment before he stripped the shirt off his well-shaped shoulders. A muscular chest rippled at the stomach. Lizabeth's breath snagged, and her mouth dropped open. Glory hallelujah. The man was glorious.

In seconds, well before she got in her fair share of ogling, he sat on the edge of the boat and plunged into the water. She watched the sleek muscles in his back as he paddled over to the coral reef.

"You know what I always wonder?"

She was so focused on the rippling glory of Grant's back that Captain Turk's voice came as a surprise. She was vaguely aware of him sitting beside her and putting up his feet.

"Hmmm?" she asked, her attention riveted on

Grant. He'd gotten the Most Likely to Succeed award in high school, but personally she would have come up with a new accolade just for him. Most Watchable.

"Why didn't the captain and his crew encounter marine life in outer space? I mean, they met just about every other life form. Why not fish people?"

Lizabeth reluctantly pulled her eyes from Grant and focused on the strange little captain. "Pardon me?"

"Okay, maybe fish people is too far out there. I mean, how could they walk? But why not a race of Lobstermen? They could get around on pincers."

He seemed to be settling in for a long chat, which motivated Lizabeth to reach for a pair of flippers. She quickly kicked off her high-heeled sandals and tugged them on.

"Their eyes could be on the ends of stalks coming out of their foreheads," Captain Turk said, "and if you got on their bad side . . . Pow! They'd clamp down on you with those sharp pincers."

The mask went on next. As soon as it was snugly in place, Lizabeth grabbed for a snorkel and scurried over to the side of the boat.

"They could call the episode 'Long Live the Lobstermen.' "

Lizabeth swung her legs over the side of the boat, took a deep breath and plunged. The water was a cool bath after the heat, but within seconds her body was acclimatized to it.

"Hey. You didn't tell me what you thought of the lobstermen." Captain Turk's voice followed her into the water, but she paddled away from it. She hadn't been in the water for years, not since the YMCA classes she took as a child. Even then, she hadn't been much good at swimming.

Still her arms cut through the water, propelling her forward toward the coral reef. She was actually swimming. Except she couldn't swim. Not really. No sooner did she have the thought than her arms flailed and her legs went dead. Her head dipped once under the clear blue sea.

"Help! Help!" she cried when she surfaced.

Before she ducked under the water a second time, strong hands were holding her up. Grant looked down at her with concern furrowing his brow. My hero, she thought. My salvation.

"You saved my life," she breathed.

A few days ago, Cary wouldn't have thought twice about taking credit where none was due. But a few days ago, he hadn't met Leeza. A few days ago, he had no reason to act the way he thought Mitch would in the same situation.

"You can stand up here," he said, reluctantly admitting that he hadn't rescued her from danger.

"I can?" Surprise lit her dark eyes. She struggled to right her body and planted her flipper-clad feet on the bottom of the sea. "You're right. I can!"

He could pick out the instant embarrassment washed over her skin. She should have looked silly with the big black mask pulled tight over her features, but instead she looked endearingly contrite. She wasn't quite as comfortable in the water as she pretended to be, but he couldn't hold that against her. Not when he wasn't the man he was pretending to be.

"I don't know what came over me. It must've been that hot sun." She placed the back of her hand on her forehead. "Did you know the sun is more than 330,000 times larger than the earth?"

"Can't say that I did." Oddly charmed, Cary took her hand firmly in his. Just holding it made him feel good, like a man who'd finally made the connection that would help the rest of his life snap in place. Where have you been all my life, Leeza Drinkmiller, he thought. "You better stick by me. That way, I can show you the wonders of the sea."

For the next few hours, that's exactly what he did. They floated together, the water sleek and silky against their flesh, as their eyes feasted on the reef's dazzling display. Coral in rich jewel tones provided a stunning backdrop for tropical fish so beautiful they seemed unreal, like paintings from a master artist's vivid imagination.

For the most part, Cary lived in the moment, but a fleeting thought of his brother got in the way of his enjoyment of a sea anemone. Damn Mitch anyway. Why was he worried about what his brother would think of his agreement to transport those crates for Captain Turk?

With the measly thousand dwindling fast, how else was he supposed to romance a woman like Leeza in style? He could have made some quick cash by placing a couple of bets, but the Boy Scout had made him promise not to. So what else was he supposed to do?

He squeezed Leeza's hand and stubbornly refused to give another thought to anything except the radiant coral, the shimmering sea, and the dazzling woman at his side.

He certainly wasn't going to think about what was inside those crates, especially when he didn't *know* they'd contain illegal goods.

Suspecting didn't count.

Chapter Eight

Peyton stalked toward the ballfield, imagining that dating Cary Mitchell must be like performing acrobatics on the flying trapeze.

The exhilaration of twisting, turning, and leaping into the air couldn't be any more thrilling than the way he'd sent her heart into palpitations the last few times she'd been with him.

Unfortunately, Peyton could also relate to crashing to the earth. Flying-trapeze artists used a safety net. She didn't have one.

How could Mitch have walked out of the Preservation League's ball before she'd gotten her Volunteer of the Year award? She'd stepped up to the podium, eagerly searched the crowd for his face, and came up empty.

She'd hardly been able to give her acceptance

speech as the knowledge that he'd fooled her again had penetrated her thick skull. She couldn't count on him. Not even a little bit. No matter what he said.

The anger had come swiftly, as it always did. But this time something that felt far too much like pain had accompanied it. Somehow, in the last few days, Mitch had pierced her heart and begun to creep inside.

The knowledge that she had to shove him out of her heart was the reason she was traipsing through the fields like a pointer directed at its prey. A couple of men had tried to make conversation as she passed, but she'd waved them off. She probably looked like a female commando on a mission.

She wouldn't be in this position if he hadn't had the audacity to turn off his answering machine so she couldn't break up with him over the phone. Or if he'd been at home instead of at work when she came knocking at his door.

Well, she'd show him. She'd had more than a day to think about it, and she wasn't going to be put off this time. She was breaking up with him. Right here. Right now.

She spotted him before she was halfway across the field. He was surrounded by teenage boys, some taller than he was, but Mitch was the one who commanded attention. In a green shirt and gym shorts, he was dressed like other parks and rec employees she'd seen, but no one else looked as good.

The sun was low in the sky, adding a burnished quality to his skin. His dark hair gleamed, like sun-washed coal. It was only when she got closer that she noticed that distress coated his handsome face and that the boys surrounding him were upset.

There were an awful lot of them, too. Boys dressed in red baseball uniforms. Boys dressed in yellow uniforms. In black and in blue. All of them yelling at Mitch.

"We're supposed to be on Field One. It says so on the schedule." A boy in red with a five o'clock shadow shouted to be heard above the rest. "The Red Eyes versus the Blue Moons."

"But I called today and Mitch said we were on Field One," a boy in blue piped up. "And he said we're not playing you. We're playing the White Heads."

"No, we're on Field One," one of the yellow-shirted team members said. "And we're playing the Black Death."

"Death to Mitch, I say," a black-shirted boy said, glaring. "He's the one who screwed up."

"Killing me won't help." Mitch backed up a step as the group advanced. "How 'bout we all get along? We have a field, right. Why don't you guys combine teams?" He snapped his fingers. "I've got it. Black and Blue versus Heads and Eyes."

The team members' voices erupted into angry chaos. If they'd been aboard a ship, Mitch would have a full-fledged mutiny on his hands. Unfortunately for him, there was no deck to jump off. He pinched the bridge of his nose, and Peyton's heart sank. He looked beleaguered. And out of his element.

The boy in black, who took his team name of Death a little too seriously, yelled something resembling a battle cry. That did it.

"Quiet!" Peyton yelled, but nobody heard her. She stepped into the fray, clearing a path through the noisy boys. Mitch's head jerked up and his eyebrows rose when she got to him, but she didn't waste time with explanations. She stood in front of him and yelled. "I said *quiet!*"

This time, they quieted. She looked over the sea of faces.

"Shame on you." She shook her index finger at the lot of them. "What would your mothers say if they saw you behaving like this? Haven't you ever heard of compromise?"

"Compromise?" One angry voice rose above the rest. "We paid our league fee. We shouldn't have to compromise."

"This never happened before," said one of the White Heads, whose skin was so full of them he could have been his team's poster boy. "There have always been plenty of fields."

"Fields?" Peyton asked. "You mean there are more than one?"

"There are lots of fields," a Red Eye answered, gesturing around them.

"Then what are you waiting for? Go see if all of them are being used."

"Hey, good idea," one of the Blue Moons cried and raced off between a Head and an Eye.

Peyton was careful not to look at Mitch for the next several minutes, instead deflecting the mild flirting from the scary boy in black. Things happened quickly when the trio of boys came back to announce that Field Four was empty.

Peyton assigned the Death to play the Heads, hoping the frightening boy wouldn't demand platters of them if they lost. The Moons and the Eyes she instructed to stay where they were, and they happily started their game. Quite suddenly, she and Mitch were alone on the sideline.

Finally, she hazarded a look at him. The last vestiges of the sun had disappeared from the sky, and the overhead lights were flickering to life. His eyes were smiling, with a light all their own.

"Thank you." His mouth kicked up in that half-grin that made her stomach do crazy things. "That's about the nicest thing anybody ever did for me."

Peyton's stomach flipped so hard that for an insane moment she wanted to grin back at him. But she couldn't. She wouldn't.

"Don't you dare accuse me of being nice to you," she hissed.

His eyebrows knotted. "But you were."

"I wasn't being nice. I was being . . . humane. That crowd was about to turn on you."

"Then thanks for being humane to me."

"Oh." She let out an angry sound and balled her hands into fists. "Can't I do anything without it being about you?"

"What?"

"In case you haven't noticed, I'm angry."

"I had noticed," he said, and he sounded resigned. He ran his hands through his hair, giving it a tousled, just-out-of-bed quality. Peyton could have flogged herself for thinking along those lines. "This is about the ball, isn't it? I tried calling you a bunch of times yesterday to apologize, but you weren't home."

"Yeah, right. Then why didn't you leave a message?"

"I wanted to apologize to you, not to an answering machine."

"Because you care about me so much you forgot that I spend all day every Sunday with my parents?" she asked, letting her sarcasm show. "Give it up, Mitch. You and I are through."

"Then what are you doing here?"

"Telling you we're through."

"Why the personal visit? Why didn't you just call and say we were through?"

"Because you don't have your answering machine turned on!"

"I don't?" he said, as though that came as a surprise to him. Then he focused on her, squinted his eyes, and shook his head. "That's not it. I think you wanted to see me in person."

"Why would I want that?"

"So I could talk you out of breaking up with me."

"That's ridiculous," she said even as she noticed the way a lock of his dark hair swirled right across his forehead. That was strange. She thought it usually swirled the other way. She started to brush it back from his face, then stopped herself. "I don't want you to talk me out of breaking up with you."

He cocked his head. "You don't want to hear why I had to leave the ball early?"

"Of course not," Peyton refuted, then paused. She was already here. What would it hurt to listen to his explanation? "Why?"

"Because—"

"You just better not say anything about Ho-Hos or dead rock stars."

"Are you going to let me explain or not?"

She put her hands on her hips, giving him some attitude. "Go ahead. Talk."

"I have a second job tending bar." He looked her straight in the eyes. "If I hadn't showed up for work, I would've been fired."

Of all the things she'd expected him to say, that wasn't one of them. Then again, it explained so much. Since they'd started dating, he'd been about as reliable as the tour-guide business in the dead of winter.

"How long has this been going on?"

He seemed to be mentally adding up days. "About a month."

A month. All of a sudden, the broken dates and early exits made sense. Why hadn't she seen it before? Because he hadn't told her, that's why. He'd merely let her think he was either irresponsible, heedless of her feelings, or fooling around with another woman.

"You're such a jerk, Mitch."

"For having a second job?"

"For not telling me you had a second job." She

glared at him. "Did you think I'd know by osmosis?"

"I didn't want you to know."

"Why not?"

"Because it's not easy for a guy to admit to his girl that he's having money trouble."

She digested that. Surprisingly, it made sense. Men were odd creatures who got their priorities mixed up all the time. She valued honesty above pride, but that didn't mean he did.

"You could have told me," she muttered.

He leaned his head closer to hers. "I am telling you."

She cut her eyes at him. "I thought you knew that money doesn't matter much to me."

"Good," he said, "because I don't have a whole lot of it."

"So, if I dump you now, I guess I'd seem pretty cold-blooded."

"Ice would run through your veins." A corner of his mouth turned up. "You'd have to go to Antarctica and hang out with the polar bears."

"I suppose I could give you another chance," she said, scuffing the toe of her tennis shoe in the dirt.

"Sounds like the only humane thing to do."

She waited for him to point out that by talking her out of breaking up with him, he'd done exactly what he'd claimed she wanted him to do. But he did nothing but stand there, grinning at her. What was a girl to do but give in?

"So where are you taking me for dinner?"

His grin grew wider. He couldn't help it. Every

minute he stopped Peyton from walking away from him was a minute longer he had her in his life.

"Anywhere you want to go," he said.

She rattled off a list of suggestions, all of which sounded fine to him, and he began to look forward to the evening. Out of necessity, he'd spent yesterday gathering information on Gibbs instead of making amends to Peyton, but maybe he could still salvage the relationship.

He wouldn't have to rush off like he had Saturday night, because Gibbs had given him the night off. Mitch shut his eyes. Right. Gibbs had given him time off because tonight was the night he was supposed to go to North Charleston and break some bones.

How could he romance Peyton and terrorize Cooper Barnes, delinquent debtor, at the same time? He rubbed his jaw.

"Peyton, stop," he said in the middle of her description of a new restaurant she wanted to try in downtown Charleston. "I need to—"

"You're backing out, aren't you?" She shook her head back and forth so that her blond hair swayed. Resignation fell over her face, and she seemed disgusted at herself. "I should have known not to trust you. You've given me ample reason."

"I'm not backing out," Mitch refuted, his mind working as hard as it had when he'd taken college calculus.

She ignored him. "But did I listen to my common sense? No. You start spouting your pretty words and I listened to them instead. All because you're easy on the eyes."

He grabbed her gently by the shoulders. Cooper Barnes worked as a waiter at a North Charleston restaurant. If he took Peyton there, maybe he could accomplish both tasks at once. "Peyton, I'm not backing out."

Finally, that seemed to get through to her. The eyes that raised to his were full of hope. "You're not backing out?"

"No. I'm not. There's nothing I'd like more than spending the evening with you."

He hadn't yet figured out how to eat dinner and terrorize at the same time, but he'd lose Peyton if he didn't take her out tonight. He frowned. He meant Cary would lose Peyton. "I interrupted because I want to pick the restaurant."

"I thought you said we could go anywhere I want."

"I did, but then I remembered this special place I wanted to take you." The name of the restaurant where Cooper worked was The Carriage House, which conjured up a picture of elegant Old Charleston charm. "It's very romantic."

"Okay," she said, smiling. "I can live with that."

He heard the crack of a bat, and his head swung toward the game in process. A ball was heading straight for them.

"Watch out," he yelled.

He and Peyton ducked, and the ball sailed over their heads. The kid in black, the one who'd tried to start the battle cry "Death to Mitch," was at the plate.

The ball had missed his head by inches, but Mitch thought he probably should have let it bean him. Death by a foul ball was preferable to death by an irate woman, which might happen to Mitch if Peyton discovered exactly what else he was doing on their date tonight.

Chapter Nine

By the time Mitch drove Cary's jazzy little red Miata down Rivers Avenue later that evening, he was cursing himself for not thinking to look before he leaped into what promised to be another fiasco.

He was a cop who knew to case out unfamiliar areas. It shouldn't have come as a surprise that the North Charleston landscape was drastically different from the southern tip of the Charleston peninsula.

He should have expected the used car lots, the strip shopping malls, and the tattoo parlors. He should have known that The Carriage House would have all the old-world elegance of a stable, which is what it reminded him of as he pulled into the gravel parking lot and shut off the car engine. The restaurant had a clapboard face with gray, weathered wood and windows so grimy they wouldn't afford a Peeping Tom any fun.

"This is the romantic restaurant you were talking about?" Peyton slanted him a dubious glance. She was dressed in a form-hugging blouse and slinky dark pants suitable for a night out on the town. If the night didn't include a dive on Rivers Avenue.

"This is the one," Mitch said cheerfully, determined to make the best of the situation. He got out of the car and came around to the passenger side to open her door. As he circled the car, he prayed she wouldn't refuse to budge.

She surprised him, letting him take her hand and chuckling softly. "That's what I like about you, Mitch. You're full of surprises."

"It's supposed to be nicer inside," he mumbled.

But when they entered The Carriage House, what they could see of the interior wasn't any more impressive than the exterior. The lighting was dim, probably to camouflage the shabbiness of the tables and chairs.

A smattering of patrons turned toward them, and Mitch was acutely aware of how overdressed they were. He had on another of Cary's elegant suits, this one a deep shade of chocolate. Cary's silk tie alone probably cost more than any one of the diners made in a day's work.

He shifted uncomfortably, aware of Peyton at his side. Unlike him, she didn't seem at all uncomfortable.

"What do you want to bet they don't have a hostess?" she whispered.

"Seat yourself," a tall, barrel-chested waiter called from across the room. Peyton lifted an I-told-you-so eyebrow and sauntered to a vacant table. He wouldn't have blamed her had she dusted off the seat before sitting, but she didn't.

Mitch was afraid to ask what she thought so far, but he had to say something. "Somebody at work recommended this place. I expected something different."

"You never know about recommendations. But this place is obviously called The Carriage House because it used to be one."

The large waiter appeared at their table, throwing down two worn menus. "I'm Cooper," he said in a voice deeper than the Atlantic Ocean. "Give me a holler when you're ready."

That was Cooper Barnes? Mitch took in the other man's wide shoulders, thick forearms, and harsh features. With a body like that, he could be playing football Sunday afternoons on national television. It'd probably take a crowbar to break one of his bones.

"Did your friend tell you the food was good here?" Peyton asked.

"What friend?" he asked, the bulk of his attention still on the massive waiter.

"The one who recommended the restaurant."

He pulled his gaze from his problem and focused on Peyton. "Why would one of my friends recommend this restaurant?"

"You're the one who said somebody at work recommended this place. I don't know why. That's why I was asking."

"Oh, yeah." Mitch needed to do better at this. He perused the menu. Ordering fish or chicken, which could be easily undercooked, seemed dicey at best. "He said the meatloaf was good. Why don't we get that?"

"You're joking, right?"

"Well, yeah," he said even though he hadn't been.

"Because I'm an ovo-lacto vegetarian, remember?"

"Of course I remember," he bluffed. "I was checking to see if you were paying attention."

Her wide, pretty mouth frowned as she gazed at him over the menu. "You've been acting sort of strange the past couple days. Is everything all right?"

As right as things could be while he was dining in a dive with his brother's very tempting girlfriend while the man he was supposed to maim waited on them. He thought about how Cary would answer her.

"What could be wrong when I'm with you?"

Her frown deepened. "Is it work? You seemed a little frazzled the other day at the park."

A *little* frazzled? That was putting it mildly, considering he was as hopeless at recreational supervision as Cary was at gambling. He longed to confide to Peyton his worries about the early morning bird watch he was supposed to lead tomorrow, but he couldn't. Cary wouldn't be stressing out because he couldn't tell a pine warbler from a tree swallow. Heck, Cary knew birds. If he didn't, he'd make up a species rather than admit he couldn't recognize an existing one.

"I've got it under control."

She blew out a breath through her nose and went back to studying the menu. "Fine. Don't talk to me about it if you don't want to."

Smooth, Mitchell, real smooth, he thought to himself in disgust, and spent the next forty-five minutes trying to make up for his gaffe.

He wanted to tell her stories about being a cop in Atlanta but settled for talking about growing up in Richmond. By the time her plate of spaghetti—the only thing on the menu that didn't contain fish, meat, or poultry—arrived she was smiling at him again.

"I bet all those girls in high school were after you."

Mitch shook his head. "No way. Teenage girls know instinctively who's the jock and who's the boy who plays in the marching band. They pick the jock every time."

She paused in the process of bringing a forkful of spaghetti to her mouth. "But you *were* the jock. Didn't you tell me you were a star pitcher?"

Of course Cary had told her that. His brother's sense of self-worth was so tied up with the past that everyone who knew him even a little had heard the story. Why hadn't he remembered that?

"Well, yeah," he answered, then figured he couldn't weasel out of this one without providing an explanation. "But I played trumpet in the band, too. I was half cool, half not."

"I think playing the trumpet is way cool."

"You do?" he asked in surprise.

"Yeah, I do," she said, smiling at him. "Maybe you'll play for me sometime."

Pleasure spiraled through him, far out of proportion to her offhand comment. He couldn't practice as much as he liked because the senior citizens in his apartment building didn't like loud noise, but he was the twin who played the trumpet. Cary couldn't blow a single note.

"Although don't get me wrong," she continued, "because I like baseball, too. I'd have loved to see you pitch."

To see Cary pitch, she meant. The pleasure evaporated like mist on a sunny day. She scrunched up her forehead, as though something had occurred to her and gestured to the piece of meatloaf on his fork.

"Why are you using that hand?"

He wondered if it was a trick question. "Because that's what it's there for?"

"But it's your right hand. When we started talking about pitching, I remembered you're a lefty."

"I'm ambidextrous, actually." He swiftly switched the fork to his off hand and shoveled some meatloaf into his mouth. It was so cold, he instantly wished he'd missed the mark. Glancing down at his plate, he noticed the inside of the meat was red. Ah, hell. He'd heard of ordering hamburgers rare, but not meatloaf.

"Is something wrong, Mitch?"

"It's the meatloaf," he said wryly. "I think it might still be alive."

She made a horrified face, and he figured she'd probably become a vegetarian because she couldn't bear the thought of animals being slaughtered for her culinary pleasure.

"You should have the waiter take it back then." She half raised her arm to signal Cooper Barnes, the massive reason Mitch was eating raw meatloaf in the first place.

"No." He reached across the table to lay a hand on her arm, felt something like an electric charge, and immediately released her out of loyalty to his brother. "Don't call the waiter over."

She obediently dropped her arm but her sick expression returned. "Even if you're not going to eat that, you have to let him know the kitchen's serving raw ground beef. People could get sick."

"I know that." Mitch turned in his seat to watch Barnes push through the swinging kitchen door so forcefully that it bounced back like a boomerang. If he didn't approach Barnes now, he might not get another chance. He brought his attention back to Peyton. "But I'd rather skip the waiter and go straight to the cook."

"You can't just walk in the kitchen!"

"Why not?" Mitch asked as he stood and picked up his plate of meatloaf. Something in her incredulous expression as she gazed up at him reminded him of Amelia, her oh-so-proper mother.

"Because it's simply not done," she said, sounding like Amelia too.

"After I do it," he said, winking at her, "I'll tell you all about it."

As he entered the kitchen, he held his breath to delay breathing in the nose-curling smells that bad cooking gave off. But the kitchen didn't look like he'd expected. It was all stainless steel counters and freshly mopped tile. The rosy-cheeked man pulling a casserole out of the industrial-sized oven was dressed entirely in white. Atop his head sat a tall, flouncy chef's hat.

"Allez! Allez!" Mitch didn't have any trouble understanding the Frenchman's outrage. "In my kitchen there should not be a customer!"

Mitch finally had to inhale, and the air didn't smell rank at all. He breathed in the scent of sauces and spice while he located Cooper Barnes, who was beside the grill fixing himself a cheeseburger.

Mitch held up his plate. "The meatloaf's undercooked."

"Il n'est pas." The chef strode across the kitchen and took the plate from Mitch. "Any gourmand knows the rare ground beef makes the flavorable loaf."

"I'm not a gourmand," Mitch said, "but I'm not going to eat raw meatloaf."

"It is not raw. It is rare," the chef said before he plucked off his hat and threw it to the floor. He was bald under the hat, his pristine clothing causing him to resemble Mr. Clean. "This abuse I do not need to take."

The chef huffed once, then stormed out of the kitchen, leaving Mitch alone with Cooper Barnes. The big man finished his bite of cheeseburger and sighed.

"Did you have to set him off? Couldn't you tell he was temperamental?" Barnes groaned. "I'm gonna have to go after him again."

"Not until I talk to you, you're not." Mitch walked over to the other man, who topped him by a good three inches.

"Hey, I don't cook the food," Barnes said roughly. "I only serve it."

"This isn't about the food. It's about Flash Gorman and the money you owe him."

For a big man with a large, fleshy face, the waiter had small eyes. They narrowed as he inspected Mitch. "You're telling me Flash sent a dandy in a flashy suit to bleed money out of me?"

"I'm not as civilized as I look," Mitch said, using his gruff cop's voice. He hardened his jaw and stuck out a hand. "Let's have the money."

He waited for Barnes to laugh, but instead the big man got a mouse-cornered-by-a-cat look and backed up a step. "What are you going to do if I don't have it?"

Mitch made his eyes mean, and bluffed. "I'll have to hurt you."

The waiter's beefy hands shook when he covered his face with them. "Please don't."

"Don't what?"

"Hurt me," the cowering big man squealed. "I got a low threshold of pain. I got a splinter last week, and it about killed me. I can't stand pain."

He sounded so frightened that Mitch's stomach lurched. He was a cop. He was supposed to protect people, not terrify them. He sighed. No matter what Gibbs had ordered and how much trouble his brother was in, he couldn't hurt Cooper Barnes. And it had nothing to do with the fact that Mitch's hand would probably hurt more than the big man's face if he punched him. Mitch's conscience wouldn't let him act like a thug. "Relax. I'm only here for the money."

"But I don't have the money."

"It's only five hundred dollars. Can't you borrow it?"

"Not in the next five minutes." The giant closed his eyes and held out his right hand. When he spoke, he was almost crying. "Go ahead. Get it over with. How 'bout you break my pinky? I don't use it too much."

"I'm not going to break your pinky," Mitch said in disgust.

"Not my index finger. I need that one to point," Barnes said, pulling it to his mouth.

"I'm not going to break any of your fingers!"

"What kind of debt collector are you? If the mark doesn't pay, you got to break something. Didn't they tell you that?"

Mitch screwed up his features, wondering how he'd gotten in this predicament and how he was going to get out of it. Clearly Cooper Barnes wasn't going to fork over the five hundred dollars he owed tonight.

"What if I lend you the five hundred," Mitch said after a minute. "Then you can pay me back."

Barnes looked dubious. "Is this a trick? How much interest you charging?"

"No interest," Mitch said, disgusted at himself for making the offer. If Barnes owed Gibbs money, he undoubtedly owed others, too. "Do you want the deal or not?"

"Sure do." Barnes stopped sniffling and brightened. "Hey, while you're at it, could you lend me an extra hundred?"

"No," Mitch yelled, but Barnes still smiled with relief. And why shouldn't he be relieved, Mitch thought as the waiter went off to hunt down the temperamental chef.

Mitch was probably the only debt collector in history who would end up owing more than he collected.

Chapter Ten

Peyton's nerve endings tingled and her stomach muscles clenched in anticipation as Mitch walked her up the stairs leading to her apartment on the second floor of a charming old Rutledge Avenue home.

Not once in the weeks that she'd dated Mitch had she looked forward to the end of an evening more.

It wasn't because the night had been a bust. Sure, it should have turned into one after Mitch's complaint about the rare meatloaf had sent the chef scurrying into the dining room ranting about unsophisticated palates.

But the muscle-bound waiter who'd served them had understood and presented them with a complimentary desert of dry, inedible cheesecake.

Mitch had seemed to relax after that, shaking off whatever had been bothering him.

No. The reason she was so full of nervous anticipation was because this was the critical point in the date when she got to decide whether to take their relationship to a new level.

In previous weeks, Mitch had already let her know by word and deed that he wanted to be her lover, but she'd repeatedly put him off.

She hadn't been ready. Until now.

She took in the way the moonlight gleamed on his dark hair and cast his handsome features in a kind of golden aura, and her pulse jumped. What was happening to her? She'd always found Mitch attractive, but now he was darn near irresistible.

She hoped, for once, that he'd ignore her often-stated plea that they take things slow. She hoped he'd try to change her mind with his kiss, the way he always did.

At the top of the stairs was a small verandah leading to the front door of her apartment. She stopped and turned toward him, expecting his hands to reach out for her, his mouth to seek hers.

"You're not going to hold tonight against me, are you?" His hands were jammed in his pockets, his mouth too far from hers to do any seeking. "Because I swear I'll make it up to you if you give me a chance."

"What's to make up?" Peyton asked, as frustrated as she was confused. The foot that separated them seemed like a mile.

"The restaurant was a dive, the chef was a kook, and the food was awful."

"That's true," Peyton said, moving forward a step. Somebody had to close the gap. "But the company was good."

His smile was slow and all the more devastating because of it. "Yeah," he said, reaching out to stroke her cheek. "The company was darn good."

Their eyes locked and Peyton held her breath. After a pregnant moment, he moved forward and she took a relieved breath. She liked the way he smelled tonight, of soap and shampoo instead of the cologne he usually wore. Her heart beat heavily as she waited for the feel of his mouth on hers.

Instead she got the feel of his mouth on her cheek.

"G'night, Peyton," he said, drawing back and starting to turn away.

"Good night?" she blurted out in frustration. "What kind of a thing is that to say at the end of a date?"

What was wrong with her, she wondered as he turned back to regard her with obvious confusion. For weeks, she'd been trying to get him to take things slow. Now that he finally was, she wanted to slug him. No, that wasn't right. She wanted to kiss him. Badly.

"Would you rather I say good-bye?"

Say yes. Nod. Make some kind of silly comment about good-bye not being forever. Peyton told herself all those things, but she couldn't make herself do any of them.

"I'd rather you kiss me on the lips instead of the cheek."

She bit her bottom lip, aware that wasn't what a proper young lady would say. And if Peyton knew anything, she knew how to be proper. Her mother had made sure of that by enrolling her in etiquette classes and sending her to debutante balls.

But even the boys she'd danced with at the balls had tried to do more than kiss her on the cheek.

He hesitated, looking more unsure of himself than she'd ever seen him. Since when, she wondered, had Cary Mitchell been unsure of whether he should kiss her?

Since you told him he was moving too fast, came the answer. *This is nobody's fault but yours.*

"There's nothing I'd like to do more," he said in that cocky way that used to annoy her. But he stepped toward her hesitantly, the look in the depths of his blue eyes indecisive.

Had he decided she was right to insist that they slow things down? Could she convince him with her kiss that she'd changed her mind?

She didn't wait for him to reach her, but took a step forward and raised her hands so they were tangled in the silky blackness of his hair. She exerted subtle pressure, bringing his head down to hers.

The lips that met hers seemed strangely unfamiliar, as though she were experiencing them for the first time. His mouth seemed somehow softer, the hands that had crept around her back somehow gentler, the body pressed against hers somehow more exciting.

Mitch usually dived right into a kiss, wasting no time in deepening it. It had always seemed to Peyton to be no more than a prelude of things to come, except there had been something so practiced about his kiss that she'd never been swept away by passion.

This kiss was different. There was something almost worshipful in the way his mouth advanced and retreated, placing soft kisses at the center of her mouth, at the left, at the right.

Something else was different, too. His blue eyes were open, gazing into hers, connecting with her in a way he never had before. He seemed to be telling her that he knew who he was kissing, that there was no one else on this earth that he'd rather be kissing.

A strange, warm sensation spread through her, centering in the region of her heart. Much lower the warmth turned to liquid heat, and his kisses, so sweetly satisfying a moment ago, weren't enough.

She pressed against him, wanting to deepen the kiss, wanting to drag him to her bed and lose herself in him. But he was already lifting his mouth from hers, already resting his chin on top of her head.

She could feel the heavy beating of her heart but couldn't hear anything but the rush of blood pounding in her ears.

This, she thought dimly, was what passion felt like. This was what it felt like to be absolutely sure you wanted the man in your arms not only in your bed but in your heart.

She tipped her head back, smiling up at him. He smiled in return, but she could see the strain in it. He wanted her, too. The knowledge was there in his face.

Surely he'd ask to be invited in. When she recovered from the shock of their passion enough to speak, she'd ask him herself.

"I need to get going," he said, his voice hoarse.

She stared, hardly able to believe her ears. She cleared her suddenly clogged throat. "If this is about what I said, about taking things slow, then—"

"That's what it's about," he interrupted. He removed his hands from around her back and stepped away from her. Though the night was warm, she felt a chill creep over her.

"But I—" she began.

"Have to work tomorrow just like I do," he finished for her. "Did I tell you I'm leading a bird walk at seven in the morning?"

She shook her head. Surely he didn't want to talk about birds. Not now when they were at a crossroads of their relationship.

"Yep," he said, backing away, toward the staircase. "Bald eagles and snipe, wild turkeys and wood storks. I'll be looking for them tomorrow."

"Mitch," she said, hearing the plea in her voice. He must have heard it, too, because he stopped retreating and waited, his mouth slightly parted, his eyes intense.

"Yes?"

She was about to ask him to stay and make love

to her, but she held back, suddenly unsure. Days ago, she'd been so fed up with Mitch's lack of responsibility that she'd been ready to break up with him. He seemed different now, but could a person change that much in a matter of days?

Her heart was telling her to take a chance on him, but maybe that was because the moonlight was playing tricks on her. Maybe tomorrow, Mitch would revert to his old ways.

"I hope you see a lot of birds tomorrow," she said finally.

He nodded once and then disappeared down the stairs. For long moments, she stood outside on the verandah, listening to his retreating footsteps, the opening and closing of the car door, the start of the car engine and the sounds of the car fading in the distance.

She could still feel the imprint of his mouth on hers, the way his arms had wound around her and made her feel cherished. Despite her misgivings about his character, she had never been more attracted to him.

She put both hands on her head, walked over to the railing overlooking the street, and looked up at the stars.

She should be glad Mitch was acting like a gentleman who respected her, the way she'd always wanted him to act.

Why then did she want to pick out one of those twinkling stars and wish that Mitch would resume his mission to make love to her?

Chapter Eleven

Lizabeth hurried to keep up with Grant as they dodged an open-air trolley cruising down Duval Street, a necessity because he was holding on to her hand.

Her sandals, fashioned of leather dyed yellow and made to resemble fish scales, were so ridiculously impractical that the man with the parrot shirt beat them across the street. And he was taking measured steps so the lizard perched on his shoulder wouldn't tumble off.

"I didn't know cops jaywalked," she said with a laugh when they stepped onto the curb.

The devil-may-care smile on Grant's face faded faster than an ice cube in the tropical sun.

"I thought the light was red but I must have been mistaken." He got a determined look on his handsome face. "I'll see that it doesn't happen again. Jaywalking is against the law."

Lizabeth felt her smile waver because she hadn't intended to sound disapproving. She'd meant that it had been fun to go with the Key West flow and cross the street against traffic, something she never would have done back home in Richmond. But here in Key West, people did things the way they wanted instead of the way they were supposed to.

The jaywalkers weren't in any real danger, because the drivers on Duval Street expected anarchy. But Grant was a cop who did things by the book. She sighed. She couldn't expect him to rebel.

A man peddling his art from a sidewalk booth called out, "Sunset paintings. Get your sunset paintings here," in the same tone as a hot-dog vendor at a ballpark.

Grant laughed in that unrestrained way he had, with the laugh starting in his stomach and rumbling upward. The jaywalking incident apparently forgotten, he tugged on her hand.

"Let's see the sights, shall we?" he asked with an arch of his dark eyebrows.

She nodded readily and spent the next fifteen minutes happily strolling with him through the zany street. It seemed surreal that she, boring Lizabeth Drinkmiller, was here in this vibrant tropical city with a hunk like Grant Mitchell.

"Hey, look, Leeza." Grant stopped and gestured to a shop across the street called All the Rage. "Isn't that the chain of stores you work for?"

"No, dahling," Lizabeth said, adding the pseudo-endearment in an attempt to sound worldly. "I work for *The* Rage. We're so big that only major cities can contain us. Paris, London, New York, Los Angeles . . . places like that."

"Wow," he said, although he looked more disappointed than impressed. "I got the impression you still lived in Richmond, but you must be based in Manhattan."

She started to confirm his misconception, if only because it fit with the other delusions he had about her, but discovered she couldn't tell him another lie. Especially because she was so unworldly she'd never been to New York City.

"I do live in Richmond." At his confused expression, she added. "It's amazing how air travel can make our vast world such a small place."

He stared at her for long moments, those blue eyes searching hers. She held her breath, waiting for him to yell out that she was phonier than the silicone pads she'd tucked into her bra to increase her bust size by one and a half cups. But instead that wide mouth of his grew wider, and he reached out to cup her cheek.

"Then I'm thankful the last plane you got on took you to Key West." His voice lowered. "And to me."

She was about to tell him that air travel was so safe that more people were killed annually by donkeys than in plane crashes, but she couldn't get the words past her suddenly dry lips.

She wet them and his gaze dropped, his blue eyes heating in the Florida sun. He hadn't tried to kiss her yet, but it was obvious from the way those eyes lingered on her that he found her attractive.

Correction. He found Leeza attractive. Lizabeth would never be seen in public in a short jungle-print sarong festooned with toucans. Lizabeth wouldn't have coordinated it so that her yellow tank top was an exact color match for the toucans' showy feathers. She wouldn't wear anything with a neckline that plunged deeply enough to show her cleavage.

Leeza was self-conscious about the breast-hugging shirt, too, but Leeza was savvy enough not to show it.

She gave that practiced head toss that said she wasn't the least bit disconcerted by his eyelock on her lips. "Shall we continue our stroll?"

"Sure," he said, dropping his hand from her cheek. Unable to bear not having any skin-to-skin contact with him, she took his arm and told her fingers to stop tingling where they touched his bare forearm. It wouldn't do if he felt the vibrations.

Ahead of them, a small crowd blocked the side-walk as a bare-chested young man, his long brown hair tied back in a ponytail, put his soul into his guitar music.

Lizabeth thought Grant might balk if she suggested another go at jaywalking, so she stopped to admire the handcrafted jewelry in the window of a shop called Everything Under the Sea.

Grant's arms came around her from behind and she stood in the circle, hardly daring to breathe in case he changed his mind and let her go. She was wearing her barely brunette hair in a sophisticated upsweep that her hairdresser had taught her, and she felt his breath on the exposed skin of her neck.

"Leeza Drinkmiller," he said, his breath warm and sweet, "I can't seem to keep my hands off you."

Her pulse skittered and her breath caught, which was pretty much how she acted whenever Grant got this near. She should turn and smile at him, maybe say something witty in return, but couldn't risk having him realize she was so unsophisticated that she couldn't handle a simple flirtatious comment.

In the window display, the jeweled eyes of a turtle designed to be worn as a brooch seemed to mock her cowardice.

"Did you know that some ancient people thought the Great Spirit built the Earth on the back of a giant turtle?"

Oh, no, she thought. *Why had she said that?*

"Can't say that I did," he answered, and she felt the breath from his laugh on her neck. "I never thought of turtles as being very strong."

"Oh, they are. There's a legend in India that the earth is held up by four elephants standing on the back of a turtle."

"Who's holding up the turtle?"

"A cobra. When any of the six of them move, the earth trembles and shakes. And, voila, you get an earthquake."

"You don't say," Grant said and she heard the chuckle in his voice. What must he think of her? "Want to go inside?"

The jewelry on display inside the shop was an

eclectic mix, from tasteful pieces in fourteen-carat gold to garish necklaces in an array of bright colors.

A gold-encrusted conch shell hanging from a simple gold chain caught her eye and she gravitated toward the glass case where it was displayed.

"See anything you like?" Grant asked in her ear, his breath soft and exciting against the lobe.

"Yeah, I really like—"

She stopped abruptly, realizing she couldn't tell him the truth. The conch-shell necklace was the most understated piece of jewelry behind the counter. A go-getter who dressed the way she did would never single it out.

She quickly scanned the rest of the items and pointed to the most garish. It was a brooch shaped like an octopus, with the legs extending in all directions. Lizabeth knew well that octopi changed color with their environment, but she couldn't imagine where the person who designed this brooch thought the octopus had been. It was a brilliant, iridescent green with a bright ruby that served as an eye.

"That octopus is quite something," she said. "One of a kind, I'm sure."

Grant motioned to the tiny, elderly woman standing behind the counter and indicated the hideous brooch. "We'd like the octopus."

"Hallelujah." The woman moved to the case with stunning alacrity. "I never thought anybody would buy that thing."

Lizabeth whirled on Grant as horror overtook her. "You can't buy that for me."

"Sure, I can." He shrugged those impossibly wide shoulders and arched those incredibly perfect eyebrows. "You like it. I'd like for you to have it."

"But it's too. . . ." Ugly, she thought. "Expensive," she said.

"Don't worry." He gave her a lopsided grin. "I can afford it."

He took out his wallet and removed a hundred-dollar bill as though he paid cash for ridiculous trinkets every day of the week. But he was a cop, not a tycoon. His Henley shirt and blue jean shorts were modest, but he'd sprung for the charter boat yesterday. Surely he couldn't afford to keep spending this way.

"Really, I don't need the brooch," she said. "You should save your money."

"What good is money if you can't spend it on a beautiful woman?" he asked, and the protest died on her lips.

No man had ever called her beautiful before. Not her brother, not her father, not even her grandfather.

He pinned the octopus brooch to her yellow tank top, his knuckles grazing her breasts.

"Thank you," she said, gazing down at it. "It's lovely."

And just like that, she broke the vow she'd made to herself not to tell him any more lies. Even though the sentiment behind his purchase of the octopus brooch was lovely, she still thought it so hideous that somebody should shuck it to the bottom of the sea.

She resisted the urge to shield her eyes when they exited the shop and the sun's rays hit the iridescent green, but Grant's attention was caught by something else.

He gestured toward a man standing at a booth advertising a sunset cruise on a luxury boat, complete with champagne, hors d'ouevres, and a full-course dinner.

"That cruise has Leeza written all over it," he said, without a clue that Leeza wasn't a real person. "Will you make me a happy man and go with me tonight?"

"That would be delightful," she said, because the bald truth was that she'd go anywhere to be with him.

But she didn't dare tell him that watching the sun go down while dangling her feet in the water at the end of a wooden pier was more her style.

That was what Lizabeth wanted, and she knew from high school that Lizabeth didn't have what it took to arouse his interest.

She smiled her dazzling Leeza smile and he responded in kind. Now Leeza, that was a different story.

Perfect, Cary thought as he watched the glowing sun sink into the horizon like a ball in quicksand.

The romantics hadn't exaggerated the spectacular beauty of a Key West sunset. Atop the shimmering Gulf of Mexico, streaks of oranges, reds, and yellows lit the sky as though it were afire.

Better yet, he and Leeza were watching nature's

show from a table for two on the aft deck of a sixty-foot motor yacht, a setting that made a perfect prelude to seduction.

Cary was about to pretend he was so touched by the sunset that he couldn't help leaning across the table, taking Leeza's face into his hands and planting an impulsive kiss on those delectable lips.

But he couldn't completely forget that he was supposed to be his saintly brother, who wouldn't do that. His twin would probably say something wholesome, like "Wow."

Cary tried to hide his grimace. "Wow," he made himself say.

Leeza's lips were slightly parted, her eyes round and staring, her breath shallow and excited. Cary vowed to make her look at him like that before the night ended, but her reactions were because of the last vestiges of the sunset.

The glowing sun sank lower and lower until the horizon appeared to have swallowed it, leaving the sky streaked in shades of gray.

"Oh, my gosh," Leeza said in a loud, awed voice. She reached across the table and squeezed his hand, and he noticed her eyes glistened with tears. "I've never been so glad in my life that red rays don't scatter as easily as those of the other colors of the visible spectrum."

Cary grinned at her spontaneous reaction. "And I've never seen anyone react to a sunset the way you do," he said.

For some reason, she seemed to take his comment as criticism. She blinked the tears from her eyes, released his hand and lifted her chin.

"I meant to say the sunset was quite pleasing to the eye," she said, once again in complete command of herself. She picked up her champagne glass with her pinky extended. She sipped and he would have sworn her lips pursed in distaste if she hadn't swallowed and emitted a satisfied "aaah."

"Excellent vintage," she said.

It should be, considering how much he was paying for this sunset dinner cruise. Two other couples, whispering seductive nothings to each other at adjacent tables, were on board. But that didn't significantly cut the cost of the trip.

No matter. Leeza was undoubtedly used to being entertained in style, and far be it from him to disappoint her.

Sure, his credit cards were maxed out. And sure, the cash his brother had lent him had dwindled faster than the champagne in his glass. But he had the money Captain Turk had given him for transporting the crates to Miami and a promise of more where that had come from.

And if those crates did contain something they shouldn't, well, it wasn't Cary's fault he'd been put in a position where he had to take any job he could find.

If the Boy Scout hadn't made him give that stupid promise to stop gambling, he could have scored big on tomorrow's college football game between Florida State and Miami.

"There's no champagne like aged champagne," Cary said.

"Don't you mean new champagne?"

"Actually, no. The general public thinks champagne needs to be fresh to be good, but it develops nuance and complexity over time, just like other fine wines. An aged champagne can be exquisite."

She tipped her head and the breeze off the Gulf blew loose some strands of her sophisticated upsweep. "Who would have guessed a cop would know about fine wines?"

Mitch the cop didn't know about wines. The Boy Scout barely drank, as far as Cary knew. But he couldn't very well backtrack now that he'd let the wine out of the cellar.

"You'd find out that I know lots of things if you got to know me better," he said in a soft voice, smiling into her eyes.

"Oh, I already know lots of things about you," she said.

"Like what?"

"I know that you're loyal and dependable and trustworthy."

Liking the sound of those adjectives applied to himself, he asked, "And how do you know that?"

"I know that you're loyal because in high school you always wore the school colors on spirit day."

"I did?" Cary shrugged, not remembering. "Maybe I just liked blue and gold."

"But our school colors were purple and orange."

He grimaced at both the color combination and his gaffe. Americana High's colors had been blue and gold, but of course she was referring to his brother's alma mater, not his.

"Oh, yeah. How could I have forgotten? If I wore that color combination, I must've been loyal."

"Of course you were. And dependable and trustworthy, too."

"I suppose you know those things because of high school, too?"

"Uh, huh." She nodded to emphasize her point. "I know you're trustworthy because you were student council treasurer, and I know you're dependable because you got a perfect attendance award at high school graduation."

"Perfect attendance?" he asked incredulously, although he shouldn't have been surprised that the Boy Scout had never missed a day of school. It was just that he'd missed so many—and not because he had legitimate excuses.

"You were a model student," Leeza said. "Hatfield High would have been the poorer without you."

She meant Hatfield would have been the poorer without his loyal, trustworthy, dependable brother Mitch.

He'd been wondering through dinner how a woman as sophisticated as Leeza could be so hung up on his brother the cop. Hell, she was wearing a rainbow-colored dress in hand-painted silk. Even the Green Monster, which is how he thought of the horrible octopus brooch he'd bought her earlier that day, didn't detract from her air of class.

Now he had the answer.

Her fascination with his twin was rooted in high school, because she'd never gotten over her teenage crush. He wanted to tell her not to put too much stock in the past, because people changed, but in a fundamental sense his brother was still much the same as he had always been.

Trustworthy and dependable and loyal, a triumvirate of qualities that Mitch possessed and Cary lacked.

But, hey, Cary was smart. He was fun. He was a survivor. And, for one of the first times in his life, he was as jealous as hell of his twin brother.

"I wasn't all that great in high school," he groused.

"Sure, you were." She put down her champagne glass, placed her elbows on the table and got a dreamy look on her face. "My heart about melted when you got everybody to round up used sports jerseys and equipment for underprivileged children."

"But that was *my* idea," Cary protested, remembering how he organized the drive after his baseball team had played a squad so poor they'd written numbers in magic marker on the backs of their white T-shirts. His brother had merely joined the effort by putting up a couple of flyers at his high school.

"Of course it was your idea," she said, giving the Boy Scout all the credit.

Not that Cary wanted the credit . . . precisely. At the time, he hadn't wanted anything except for those kids to have shirts that wouldn't shame them and gloves that weren't coming apart at the seams.

But he did want Leeza to know he wasn't a total scoundrel.

"I'm not completely irresponsible," he said.

"I don't think you're irresponsible at all. Didn't I just get finished telling you that you're amazing? I thought so when we were in high school, and I think so now."

Hours later, Cary was still dwelling on her proclamation when he walked with her through the lushly tropical courtyard of the waterfront resort hotel where she was staying.

She thought his twin was amazing.

She smiled at him, her face aglow in the light of the moon, and he ran that thought through his head another time.

She thought his *twin* was amazing.

He almost smacked his forehead to dislodge the cobwebs in his brain. What was wrong with him? He was pretending to be his brother, so that meant she thought *he* was amazing. And if she thought he was amazing, he might get lucky tonight.

They were in a darkened part of the courtyard, a few feet past the whitewashed gazebo but not yet at the lighted waterfall cascading into the dolphin-shaped pool.

His spirits buoyed considerably, he let his arm snake around her shoulders. He heard the quick intake of her breath and congratulated himself on making the right move. Leeza Drinkmiller might be sophisticated but she couldn't hide her attraction to him.

He stopped walking and turned her in his arms,

thinking when she gazed up at him that he'd never seen such extraordinary brown eyes. He'd started to lower his head when she blurted out, "Did you know that, in spite of the urban legend, a duck's quack does echo?"

His head froze in mid-dip as he tried to digest her question. The sensation of having her in his arms was making him lightheaded, but he was sure he'd heard her correctly.

"No," he said, "I'm not up on ducks."

"You've watched Donald Duck cartoons, right?" she rushed on before he could resume the dip. "Disney's technical directors must not be very savvy, because you'll notice that Donald's quack never repeats."

He ran one of his hands up her smooth bare arm and felt the tiny goose bumps his touch caused. Her skin was soft and supple, her breath sweet and warm against his lips.

"Isn't Donald a talking duck instead of a quacking duck?" he asked, looping his hands around her back at her waist.

Her eyes locked on his as though he'd asked a vital question. He could hear water trickling into the pool, and smell the sweet scent of tropical flowers as he waited for her to give him some sign that she was ready for his kiss.

"I . . . I think he quacks, too," she murmured in a low, sexy voice. His body hardened and it took all his restraint not to haul her the rest of the way against him and show her what kind of passion could be between them.

"Why are we talking about ducks?" he asked, telling himself to be patient the way his brother would be, the way she surely wanted him to be.

She blinked up at him, her lips moist and her mouth parted. As though she trusted him.

Before he could think about what that meant, she moved forward and very softly, very sweetly touched her mouth to his. This was his chance to convince her that she wanted him in her bed, buried between her thighs.

He knew the routine. He'd make sure the kiss started slow, coaxing her to open her mouth and allow him access, before he stroked his tongue against hers and inside her mouth until she didn't know her own name.

But then Leeza's hand came up to stroke his cheek as they kissed and *her* tongue came forward, shyly touching his. Blood pounded in his ears as his tongue tangled with hers, his breath mingled with hers and his heart beat against hers.

She tasted sweeter than any woman he'd kissed, sweeter than he'd known a woman could taste. Her arms went around his neck and her soft breasts pressed against him, and he knew she wasn't the only one who would soon be in danger of forgetting her name.

But she surrendered to him so completely, so trustingly, that somewhere in the back of his mind he remembered quite clearly that his name was Cary. And that Leeza thought she was kissing Grant—his loyal, trustworthy, dependable brother. The LTD man.

Ah, hell. With a supreme act of willpower, Cary pulled his mouth from hers. She looked up at him, her breath coming fast, her eyes darkened in passion, her mouth forming a questioning O.

Take what she's offering, a voice yelled inside his head, but another, louder voice drowned it out. *The LTD man wouldn't take advantage of her.*

"Did you know," he asked, dredging up a piece of trivia he'd heard long, long ago, "that Donald Duck comics were once banned in Finland because he doesn't wear pants?"

Leeza's lips, still swollen from his kisses, curved into a smile. Then she laughed and he did the same.

He didn't try anything more than holding her hand as he walked her to the lobby, but he didn't trust himself to escort her all the way to her room.

"G'night, Grant," she said softly, shyly, an instant before the elevator doors closed behind her.

He stood there for a moment, staring at the blinking numbers on the wall as the elevator crawled upward to a room and a bed he wouldn't be sharing with her tonight. Even though he could have.

He swore ripely.

What in the hell was wrong with him?

Chapter Twelve

A dull throbbing began at the backs of Mitch's eyes as he studied the pages of game charts in front of him. After Monday night's fiasco at the softball field, he needed to go over the schedules and make sure he didn't have any more double bookings.

He cross-checked the rows of teams against the fields until the throbbing turned into a full-fledged headache. He was irked at Cary for overstating the simplicity of his job and at himself for not asking more questions.

If he had, he would have learned that Cary was a recreation specialist—with *specialist* being the operative word. His brother not only ran clinics but planned and organized league play in various sports.

Considering there were coed, men's, and

women's leagues in softball, basketball, and tennis, it was a logistical nightmare. And, as far as Mitch could see, his brother was a one-man show.

"Hey, Cary, my man."

A teenage boy with a grin the size of the Charleston harbor bounced into the office, pulled out a chair, and plopped himself down. He was swigging from a Coke he didn't need, because he already vibrated with enough energy to run a small town.

"Call me Mitch," Mitch corrected, even though he had no idea what to call the boy.

"You mean, like, as a nickname?" The boy shrugged. "Sure, Johnny'll call you that if it'll float your boat. But what gives? What're you doing here?"

Wondering who Johnny was, Mitch said, "I work here."

"Not on Tuesdays, you don't. They changed the schedule last week."

And Cary, of course, hadn't bothered to note the change. It was the latest in a long list of details Cary had neglected to mention, like where in the world he'd gotten himself off to.

Mitch had returned home the night before to a message from Cary on his now-functioning answering machine, informing him that he wasn't in Atlanta. His brother hadn't said where he was, preferring instead to spew nonsense about it being safer for Mitch not to know his whereabouts.

Mitch had to concede that keeping him in the dark was safer for Cary, because Mitch wanted to hunt his twin down and vent some frustration.

The strip club, the missing money, and the job as a kneecap-busting debt collector were bad enough. But Mitch was most steamed because he'd been thrust into a situation in which he was having lascivious dreams about his brother's girl, who seemed willing to let him act out those dreams.

She kissed like an angel, which he had no business knowing because he lived by the touch-her-not code when it involved any woman who was or had ever been involved with his brother.

But how could he refuse Peyton when she asked him to kiss her? And how would he summon the will to stop kissing her if she asked him again? Putting a halt to their amorous interlude last night had nearly killed him.

"Earth to Mitch," the kid was saying, telling Mitch he'd missed something. "You didn't say what you were doing here."

With a nod, Mitch indicated his mound of paperwork, yet another reason to be irked at Cary. "I've got schedules to catch up on."

The kid stretched out his long legs, which were bare from the tops of his white socks to the bottom of his baggy, knee-length shorts. "Bummer, but now that you're here, Johnny needs to ask you something."

Again with the ubiquitous Johnny. "Where is he?"

"Where's who?"

"Johnny."

The kid's face split into a grin, which was an astonishing sight because he had a mouth rivaling

Mick Jagger's in size and scope. "Stop messin' with me. You ain't no English major."

Neither, apparently, would the kid be if he chose to attend college.

"Anyway, Six-Pack says lifting weights every day in the off-season is bad for Johnny, but Johnny was like, hey, bigger is better. But Six-Pack wouldn't lay off 'til Johnny said he'd ask you."

The kid looked at him expectantly and it dawned on Mitch that Johnny *was* asking him, because the kid was Johnny. He also had the delusion that Mitch was as much as an authority on weight training as his brother. Sure, Mitch worked out, but he did more running than training in a gym.

"Well, Johnny," he said as he dredged up anything he'd ever been told about weight training. Moderation. Yeah, that was it. "Uh, you don't want to overdo it. Try every other day."

"But what if I work on my gluts one day and my abs the next? Then it's okay, right?"

"Sure," Mitch said, hoping that it was.

A white-haired man in his fifties with bulging gray sideburns and horn-rimmed glasses stuck his head into the office. Although the office was located adjacent to a gymnasium, the man couldn't have been there to exercise. His paunch was reminiscent of a kangaroo with a joey stuffed in its pouch.

"Mitchell, I heard tell you were here. Come walk with me. We need to have a word."

The man was obviously an authority figure used to having his commands obeyed, because he didn't wait for an answer before he lumbered away.

"Oooooo, C.B. seems pissed," the kid said when the other man was out of earshot. "Johnny thinks you must've done something the boss man didn't like."

"Only one way to find out," Mitch said, grateful to Johnny for providing him with the clue. C.B. must be the director of parks.

Armed with the information, he caught up to C.B. halfway between the outdoor basketball and tennis courts. The streaming sunlight illuminated the other man, who had a complexion as pale as Casper's.

"You wanted to see me, sir."

"Yes, yes." C.B. took out a pipe, lit it and set off at a pace so ambling Mitch had a hard time not passing him. "I heard a disturbing story the other day. A lady I'm fond of was out for a long walk rather early in the morning. And, lo and behold, from out of the cover of trees she sees the most magnificent of sights. A bald eagle."

Mitch tensed, because he could guess where the story was heading.

"A young girl, not as knowledgeable about bird life as the lady, was with her," C.B. continued. "The girl turned to the guide to ask what she was seeing. And do you know what he said?" C.B. didn't wait for Mitch to answer. "The guide said, 'What you got there is one big bird.' "

The response, which had seemed pretty clever at the time, sounded less so on repetition.

"Later in the walk, when my lady friend and the

rest of the group chanced upon a ruby-throated hummingbird, the girl again asked the guide to identify it. Care to take a crack at what he said?"

Mitch was hoping he could take a vow of silence, until it became clear C.B. wouldn't continue until he gave an answer. He cleared his throat. "That there's one itty bitty critter?"

"Exactly." C.B. didn't crack a smile. "Now why do you suppose a recreation specialist who can't identify a bald eagle or a hummingbird volunteered to lead a bird walk?"

"I must've overestimated my expertise," Mitch mumbled, his gut clenching. His brother had such a checkered work history that it was important he stay in this job a lot longer than a couple of months. And here Mitch was on the verge of sending him to the unemployment line.

C.B. puffed up his barrel chest, as though fortifying himself with resolve. "The reason I drove over here was to tell you—"

Mitch didn't let him finish. "Please don't fire me. I'll do better. I promise I will."

"What gave you the idea I was going to fire you?"

"Aren't you?"

"Hell, no. What kind of fool fires the man responsible for seeing that his son got a baseball scholarship to UNC?"

Cary had done that? Mitch shook his head. "You're exaggerating. Your son must've got the scholarship on his own talent."

"Darn right he's talented, but what good is talent if nobody notices it? You got him noticed, son, by calling that coach friend of yours. Coach didn't even wait 'til his senior year was over to offer him the scholarship."

Mitch was starting to get the picture. "So you're keeping me on because I helped your son?"

"I'm keeping you on because you're a damn fine recreation specialist," C.B. corrected. "But as a bird man, you stink. How 'bout doing everybody a favor and staying out of the woods?"

"Sure," Mitch said, gratefully sticking out a hand. "Anything to keep the job, C.B."

He took the hand Mitch offered, but his eyebrows, which were as bushy as his sideburns, rose. "Son, I know everybody calls me Cheek Bristles behind my back, but I prefer you call me Albert."

Mitch muttered an apology, wishing as he walked back to his office that he could tell Johnny that impersonation was hard enough without some wise-guy kid feeding him land mines.

Or taking over his desk space, which he discovered was what Johnny had done. "What gives?" Mitch asked, his hands on his hips.

"Johnny's working on these seriously mixed-up schedules. What happened to you over the weekend, man? You never make mistakes like these."

Mitch scratched his head. "I got too much on my plate, that's all."

"Why don't you take off and let Johnny finish the skeds? You got to have dinner with that blond babe's parents tonight, anyway."

"How do you know about that?"

"She called to remind you. She tried you here

when she couldn't get you at home. She made Johnny promise to tell you."

"Thanks," Mitch said, already striding for the door and wondering how to get Peyton's parents to change their opinion of him.

"Hey, wait a minute." Johnny's voice trailed after him. "Are you and Johnny still on for pitching lessons tomorrow?"

Only if Johnny wanted to operate on autopilot.

"Sorry, man," Mitch said, feeling genuinely so when the kid frowned. "This week's crazy, but maybe I can make it up to you next week."

Whether Cary could make amends to Mitch, however, was more doubtful. What kind of a guy was his brother, anyway?

"You know that Johnny still can't afford to pay you anything, right?" The kid asked hesitantly, and Mitch's heart softened.

"Yeah," he said, glad he had the answer to his question.

His brother was the kind of guy who gave free pitching lessons to kids.

Peyton had been listening for the doorbell since she'd joined her parents for predinner drinks in their study, but the sound of it still sent excitement coursing through her.

"Would you get that, dear?"

Her mother needn't have asked, because Peyton was already heading across the highly polished wooden floor for the door, her anticipation high at the thought of seeing Mitch again.

Since their kiss on the verandah last night, and his unexpected gentlemanly restraint, her sexual attraction to him had reached a new high. If he asked her to make love with him tonight, as he had so many times before, she'd rip his clothes off his hard, sexy body.

She was smiling at the thought of herself as a sexual aggressor when she opened the door . . . and saw G. Gaston Gibbs III and a dozen long-stemmed red roses. A salty breeze blew off the harbor, but every blond hair on his finely shaped head was firmly in place.

"Gaston," she said, trying to keep the surprise out of her voice and failing miserably. "What are you doing here?"

"Amelia invited me to dinner," he said, presenting her with the flowers. "I brought the roses for your mother, but they're so lovely they make me think of you. Of course, their beauty still pales next to yours."

She took the flowers, questions filling her mind as she stared at Gaston. But they had nothing to do with the flattery that poured from his mouth as easily as rain from the sky.

Why had her mother invited Gaston when she'd made such a point of insisting she get to know Mitch? And how could Amelia justify breaking her rule that there must always be an even number of diners at the table?

"If you don't invite me in soon, the wind might do it for you," Gaston said.

"Of course. Forgive me. Come in," Peyton said,

stepping back to grant him admittance. He had plenty of room to step around her, but instead he moved close, brushing a kiss against her forehead as he passed into the house. He'd put on his expensive cologne with such a heavy hand that she almost sneezed.

"Gaston, my dear, how lovely it is to see you." Her mother fluttered into the room, the heels of her size-five feet making dainty clicking noises on the hardwood. She took his hands in hers and kissed the air on either side of his cheeks. "Are those roses for me? I cannot tell you how much I adore roses."

"Good evening, Amelia. Yes, the roses are for you." He slanted a pointed look at Peyton, probably to remind her of what he'd said about their beauty. "And I'm as delighted to be here as you are to have me."

"Is that Gaston I hear?" Her father strode into the foyer and clapped the younger man on his shoulder before heartily shaking his hand. "I hear you've been a busy man. Word at City Hall is that your renovation project on Smith Street has expanded to include four of the properties around it."

"Four other properties!" Peyton exclaimed so loudly that both men turned toward her, but she was past caring about propriety. "Is that true, Gaston? Are you going to renovate all of it?"

He laughed and took both of her hands in his, which were curiously cold. "It's true, my sweet. I plan to renovate the houses and then resell them."

"That's great," she said, the wheels in her mind spinning. "If you renovate five buildings, it can only spur surrounding property owners to follow suit. It'll be a real boon for that part of the city."

"That's what I'm aiming for," Gaston said with the smile that never quite seemed to reach his unreadable gray eyes. But why was she thinking about that now? She'd misjudged him so badly when they were teenagers that it was obvious he had layers she didn't know about. He'd seemed like the kind of slick-talking empty charmer all fathers warned their daughters against and he'd turned into a champion for their city.

"If you need any help with the way the properties used to look," she said, "I could dig up some records at one of the historical societies."

"Thanks," Gaston said. "I might ask you to do that."

Despite her excitement, she began to feel uncomfortable that he still held her hands in his. Making sure her smile didn't fade, she slipped her hands out of his grasp. His eyes didn't leave her face.

"Come into the study with me, Gaston, and I'll pour you a sherry," her father said, breaking the uneasy connection between them. "Then you can tell me more about the property." He winked broadly. "And how you hope to make a killing on the resale property."

The men departed amid deep-voiced chatter and laughter, leaving Peyton alone with her mother.

"That Gaston is such a fine young man from such a good family," Amelia said. "He obviously has a head for business on his shoulders, too."

Peyton had been Amelia's daughter long enough

to realize that she'd earmarked Gaston Gibbs as son-in-law material, but it wouldn't do Peyton any good to point out that she wasn't interested. Amelia only heard what she wanted to hear.

"He is a man who could keep his wife in style," Amelia continued. "His wife would not have to diaper horses before carting pushy, noisy tourists around the city."

Peyton held her temper, but couldn't ignore her mother's reference to the diapers the horses wore to assure that the city's lovely streets were free of waste.

"How many times do I have to tell you, Mother, that I'm not the one who changes the diapers?"

"I have told you before, dear, that appearances are what matters. People *assume* you change the diapers."

As she always did, Peyton swallowed the rant that threatened to erupt from the back of her throat.

"I wish you'd told me Gaston would be joining us, Mother. I thought dinner was going to be just the four of us—you, Father, Mitch, and me."

"Whatever gave you that impression, dear?" Amelia laughed her delicate laugh. "The more the merrier, I always say."

"You never say that."

"I could always start. It's a perfectly fine expression."

"A 'third wheel' is a perfectly fine expression, too, which is what Gaston will feel like when Mitch gets here."

"Nonsense, dear. If anyone feels like an outsider, it will be Mitch, who did not have the good fortune to be born in God's Country like the rest of us."

Peyton knew from experience that it was futile to point out that not everyone thought of Charlestonians as God's chosen people, especially because her mother knew that Peyton loved the city as well as anyone on the peninsula.

"You should have stuck with your rule not to invite an uneven number of people to dinner," Peyton said, which was as close as she ever got to criticizing Amelia.

"Who says I did not stick to my rule?" Amelia plucked the roses from Peyton's grasp. "I do hope Barbara can take time out from her cooking to find a vase and put these lovely flowers somewhere we can enjoy them."

She flashed Peyton a beatific smile and hurried away. Peyton checked the urge to rush after her and demand an explanation, but her mother considered both rushing and demanding unladylike.

Peyton was standing in the foyer, trying to figure out the puzzle for herself, when the doorbell rang. She swung open the door, her smile of anticipation again in place, but it wasn't Mitch this time either.

A thirtyish woman with dyed blond hair, tall black boots, a black miniskirt, and a thigh-length black poncho trimmed with silver stars gave her a grin so genuine Peyton couldn't help smiling back.

"I hope I have the right place," she said in a voicc as high as a child's. Her hair wasn't moving in the wind either. "I'm Hattie. Who are you?"

"Peyton McDowell."

No sooner were the words out of Peyton's mouth than Hattie was enthusiastically shaking her hand and proclaiming it nice to meet her. "So you're Amelia's daughter? She invited me to dinner! Oh, she's the nicest woman."

"I thought I knew all of my mother's friends," Peyton said, thinking of the society types her mother usually ran with, "but I don't remember meeting you."

Hattie lightly slapped her shoulder. "That's because Amelia and I met in line in the grocery store this morning. She was so pretty and classy. I about died when she asked if I wanted to come to dinner. I tried to say no, but she didn't want the number of guests at her dinner party to be uneven. And I just couldn't bear the thought of people thinking her odd."

She was clutching something which, on closer inspection, appeared to be a bottle of salad dressing. Hattie must've seen Peyton's gaze fall on the condiment because she held it up.

"There's an ingredient in most salad dressings that makes me break out in hives, so I always bring my own," she explained. "Low-fat, low-cal, oil free. It doesn't taste too good, but at least it doesn't make me red and blotchy."

Before Peyton could think how to reply to that nugget of information, she caught a glimpse of Mitch walking up the sidewalk and didn't know whether she wanted to cheer or moan.

She'd never seen a man look so good in a pair of

dark slacks and a white knit shirt. Although Mitch's clothes were obviously expensive, both Gaston and her father were wearing suits, complete with dress shirt and tie.

She could only imagine what Amelia would make of that.

"I can tell that hunk's off limits by the way you're looking at him," Hattie said in a stage whisper, her black eyebrows arched like a camel's back. "I sure hope Amelia invited someone half as good for me."

Chapter Thirteen

Despite the delicious menu of she-crab soup, salad with raspberry vinaigrette dressing, and sautéed Atlantic Salmon, Mitch wouldn't say that dinner with Peyton's parents was going well.

Not only was one of the guests a lowlife in disguise, but Peyton's mother had drawn up seating cards that had Peyton positioned next to the lowlife and catty-corner from Mitch. Having Peyton too far away to touch should have been a good thing, but not being able to touch her only made him want to touch her more.

And they would be within touching range sooner or later. Unless Peyton's father, who was scowling at him from his place at the head of the table, had anything to say about it.

Mitch gave the solicitor his imitation of Cary's

most charming grin, the better to win him over with. "Would you please pass the butter, Thomas?"

"Call me sir."

Okay, Mitch thought, he wasn't going to do any winning over tonight.

"Daddy," Peyton drew out the syllables like a plea, placing one of her slim-fingered hands on her father's forearm.

"Okay, okay," Peyton's father muttered as he picked up a miniature sterling silver platter. "He can call me Mr. McDowell if it's that important to you."

Hattie "I-can-string-more-sentences-together-than-you-can" Feinstein, who was sitting next to him, gave Mitch a sympathetic look as she passed the butter.

"You can call *me* anything you want, sugar," she whispered so Mitch alone could hear. "Hattie's already short for Henrietta, but Henny or Hen's fine with me. Heck, call me Hat if you want."

"Thanks," Mitch said. Hattie talked way too much but she'd apparently noticed that the solicitor didn't have any trouble with the criminal at his table using his first name.

But then, Flash Gorman was radiating snobbery and wealth in his Gaston Gibbs disguise. Mitch would have loved to expose him, but couldn't very well accuse him of criminal activity when so far his own undercover investigation had been a bust.

"I hear the Footlight Players at the Dock Street Theater are doing a charming production of *Porgy and Bess,*" Gibbs said. "Everybody is saying it's a must-see." He turned to Peyton. "I was hoping that you—"

"Oh my gosh, would you believe I've lived in Charleston for twenty years and I've never seen *Porgy and Bess?*" Hattie interrupted. "And it's supposed to be so heartbreaking when Bess goes to New York at the end and Porgy sings that song." Hattie broke into an off-key rendition of, 'Oh, Bess, oh where's my Bess?' "

Peyton smiled across the table at Hattie. "I've seen it so many times I can take a pass. Why don't you and Gaston go together?"

"One can never see *Porgy and Bess* enough times, Peyton dear," Amelia rushed to interject. "And I do believe Gaston was going to ask if *you* would like to see it with him."

Enough, Mitch thought, *was enough.* "But Gaston knows Peyton and I are dating, Amelia," he said. "Do you really think he'd ask out my girl when I'm sitting right here?"

Gaston sent him a look that only thinly veiled his irritation, making Mitch wonder if he were crazy to provoke the criminal who could send his brother to jail. And, in the process, possibly see to it that he never worked as a cop again.

"Gaston probably figures he's safe," Mr. McDowell intoned dryly. "If you and my daughter had plans for the night, odds are you wouldn't show up anyway."

"Daddy, please," Peyton said in the same pleading tone she'd used a few minutes ago, but a look in Mitch's direction told her he was the one she should have been trying to soothe.

Mitch was glaring at her father, his mouth a tight line. "This isn't any of your—"

"I once dated a guy who never showed up." Salvation came in the form of Hattie's high, cheerful voice. "He'd call me up, ask me out, and say he was going to pick me up at such and such a time, only he wouldn't show. A couple of weeks would go by, he'd call to apologize and ask me out again. Then we'd go through the whole rigmarole all over again."

"But why did you keep saying yes if he kept standing you up?" Peyton asked, eager to pursue any line of conversation that didn't end in Mitch forever ruining any civil relationship he could have had with her father.

"Because he had a harelip," Hattie said. "And one leg two inches shorter than the other. He wore this thick black shoe to even things out, kind of like the ones Herman Munster used to wear, but he was still lopsided."

"Look, Mr. Mc—" Mitch began, obviously still bristling from the insult, but Peyton didn't let him finish.

"I don't understand what his disabilities had to do with you dating him," she said to Hattie.

Hattie put a hand to her chest in drama-queen fashion. "Why, I couldn't let him believe I was prejudiced against men with harelips and lopsided legs. Besides, I'm no dummy. After the first couple times, it's not like I expected him to show."

"This is quite intriguing, dear." Peyton's mother unexpectedly joined the discussion. "So are we to understand that you never told him you did not want to go out with him?"

"Only once. And would you believe that's the only time he showed up? Then he was peeved at me for being in the middle of a dye job. But what did he expect me to do?" She pointed to her platinum-blond hair. "I gotta keep that dye on a long time to cover up all the brown under here."

"I do believe the actress who played the role of Bess in George Gershwin's original operatic production was a brunette," Amelia said, a transparent attempt to draw the conversation back to the point where Gaston was about to ask Peyton out.

Peyton shot a glance at Mitch, hoping he had his temper in check. She tried to tell him with her eyes how important it was to her that he get through this dinner with her parents. He wasn't used to them the way she was. He couldn't know they were only tough on the men she dated because they wanted what was best for her.

"Tough luck for Bess." Hattie speared a miniature tomato with her fork and waved it as she talked. "Peyton over there can tell you that blondes have more fun. That's why I became one. My mama and sisters and grandmama are brunettes and when they get together, woo wee, it is one dark time."

"Where are your people from, dear?" Amelia asked sweetly.

"Here, there, and everywhere in eastern Europe. We Feinsteins started out mostly in New York but we were freezing our buns off so just about all of us took off for points south."

"The McDowells have been in Charleston for more than three hundred years," Amelia said proudly. "And Gaston, is it not so that your branch of the Gibbs family descended from the city's original settlers?"

"That's quite true," Gaston said. "My family and this city date back to 1670 and the original Charles Towne settlement."

Amelia gave Mitch a pointed look. "And where are your people from, dear?"

"My parents live in Richmond, Virginia," Mitch said, no longer sounding peeved. Peyton slanted him a grateful smile and the one he gave her in return was so appealing that her heart went ba-boom.

"I meant where do your ancestors come from? There is quite a bit of history in Virginia. Do your people hail from the state's founders?"

"No," Mitch said slowly. He sounded suspicious and Peyton didn't blame him. Her mother never asked an innocent question. "My father's grandfather came over from Scotland in the early 1920s, but my mother's people are from Poland and Czechoslovakia and Slovenia."

"Here, there, and everywhere then." Amelia's face blossomed into a smile, and Peyton realized what she was getting at even before she made her point. "Just like Hattie's people. It is so important in life to find people with whom we have a common ground. I believe you two also have the recreation industry in common. What is it you do again, Hattie dear?"

"I'm a sales specialist at Jungle's Gym west of the Ashley." Amelia inclined her head, causing Hattie to continue. "I try to talk people into buying memberships. I'm usually successful, too, once I point out how out of shape they are."

"Isn't that lovely? Mitch here is a recreation specialist. I knew when I met you, Hattie, that you and Mitch would have as much in common as Peyton and Gaston."

"You could say that I work in the recreation field, too," Peyton said before her mother could do any more matchmaking. She addressed Hattie, who was the only one in the room who didn't know what she did for a living. "I work for Dixieland Carriage Tours."

"But only for the time being." Amelia waved a hand in dismissal, the way she always did whenever Peyton mentioned her job. She turned to Gaston. "Now, Gaston. What was it you were about to ask Peyton about that production of *Porgy and Bess?*"

The breeze coming off the Charleston Harbor as Mitch strolled with Peyton on the wide sidewalk next to the seawall couldn't quite blow away the tension remaining from dinner with her parents.

Even though late September in Charleston was still balmy, it was an angry night. The moon was full and the tide high, a combination that along with the wind sent water pounding against the seawall and occasionally spraying onto the sidewalk.

The night wasn't ideal for a walk along the bay, but it was all the time alone they were going to get tonight. Mitch was due at Epidermis in a little more than thirty minutes.

"Your parents don't like me much," he said.

"They *will* like you," she countered, squeezing his arm.

"I don't know about that. Your father's main way to communicate with me is by sneering, and your mother pushed Hattie at me so hard I was starting to feel bruised."

"She's nice, isn't she? Hattie, I mean. We made a lunch date for later in the week."

"That won't go over well with your parents. They wanted me to make a date with her so I'd get out of your life."

"They need time to get to know you better, that's all."

"They don't want to get to know me better. They want to know Gaston Gibbs better."

She stopped walking and grinned up at him. The wind whipped her short blond hair around her head so that it looked like a golden halo. Her cream-colored cocktail dress, which had appeared so sedate and proper in her parents' house, was plastered against her body, showing off her shapely curves.

"This is unbelievable," she said.

"What's unbelievable?"

Her brown eyes sparkled. "That you, Cary Mitchell, are jealous."

He was jealous. He could feel it coursing through

his veins like a thick green stream. He tried to make his voice light. "Assuming for a moment that I am jealous, which I'm not admitting to, why is that so unbelievable?"

"Oh, come on. Don't you remember what you said to me last week when you saw me dancing with Arthur at City Slickers?"

"Not exactly," Mitch hedged.

She seemed as though she were enjoying herself immensely. "You said that you didn't do jealousy because it wasn't worth it to get jealous over any woman who couldn't appreciate the good fortune of dating you."

"I said that?" Mitch barely kept himself from cringing at his brother's line.

"Yes," she said, tapping him on the nose, "you did."

"So, um, do you and this Arthur have a thing going?"

She let out a short laugh and shook her head. "I swear, Mitch. Is your memory really so shot that you don't remember that Arthur is gay?"

He shrugged, trying not to let on how relieved he was. "It's hard to keep track of things like that."

"But he told you that you were a hot papa. He asked you to dance and invited you to the Gay Charleston Ball."

"Did I accept?"

She laughed and swatted his arm. "No! But you were so flattered it was embarrassing."

"Gibbs isn't gay," he said, trying to get back to their original subject.

"No," she agreed, "he isn't."

"How do you know that?" Mitch asked and she burst into laughter.

"You *are* jealous," she said.

"Do I have reason to be?"

"Oh, I don't know," she said with a grin and put on a southern accent both thicker and more refined than her own. "You can not discount the fact, dear, that he is from a very fine South of Broad family. He not only beautifies the city by renovating historic properties but makes oodles of money. And he is easy on the eyes to boot."

Mitch felt his mouth tug downward at her description of a man who, after all, owned a strip club. But he needed to tread lightly here, because he wasn't ready to confess the only reason he knew Gibbs owned Epidermis was because he worked there.

"I didn't know you were such a fan," he said.

She rolled her eyes. "I'm not. You heard me tell him no to *Porgy and Bess,* didn't you? I was imitating my mother. She's the one whose ambition is to get me married off to a Charlestonian who will keep me in the lap of luxury so I no longer have to diaper horses."

Surprise seized him. "You diaper the horses?"

She shook her head, looking bemused. "Of course I don't diaper the horses. I drive the carriages."

"I thought you liked driving them. I never figured you for someone who'd quit working when you got married."

"I don't want that. My mother wants that. I want to use my trust fund to buy the carriage company." She stopped abruptly and put her fingers to her lips. "I can't believe I told you that. That's the first time I've said it aloud."

"Why haven't you said it aloud before?"

"Are you kidding me? How do you think my parents would react if they found out I wanted to buy the carriage company?"

"Badly, I take it?"

"Yes, badly."

"Do you need their permission?"

She frowned. "Well, no. Legally the trust fund became available to me earlier this year when I turned twenty-five, but I can't bring myself to use the money on something they don't approve of."

Before he could question her further about the feasibility of her dream, she walked closer to him, staring up at him with brown eyes that looked golden in the moonlight. She reached up and slowly traced his lower lip with her index finger so that he felt a little dizzy.

"I can think of better things for us to do than talk about horses and carriages," she said in a low, husky voice.

It was a moment before he could speak. "What did you have in mind?"

She turned from sultry to playful in an eye blink as she grabbed his hand and tugged. "Come on and I'll show you."

He didn't figure out her intention until they reached a wet place on the sidewalk and she stopped. Before he could move, she looped her hands around his neck and grinned up at him.

"You can't mean to do what I think you mean," he said.

"Oh, yes I do," she said a moment before the wind whipped the salty water into the seawall with such ferocity that it shot upward into a wet arc that showered golden spray down on them.

In an instant they were drenched, but Peyton didn't seem to care that she'd very likely ruined her expensive dress. She swiped the wet hair off her forehead, threw back her head, and laughed.

She looked so alive and beautiful in that instant that something sweet broke loose in Mitch's chest.

She rose on tiptoe, plastering herself even closer to him. "For the record, you don't have any reason to be jealous of Gaston," she said when her mouth was very close to his, "because you're the one I want."

She meant she wanted his brother, but his brother wasn't the one who was holding her in his arms. Cary was God-only-knew-where, and Mitch was here. How could he be expected to resist the mad pounding of his heart and the beautiful woman in his arms?

But still he had to try. For his brother's sake.

Her eyes were closed, her mouth lifted for his kiss, her body straining to get closer to his. Mitch was soaking wet but every part of him felt hot, from the heart that was beating so heavily to the erection straining against his pants.

He'd kissed her the other night on the verandah,

an experience so potent it had convinced him he couldn't risk kissing her again. Especially when his defenses against her were so low he knew instinctively that this kiss would forever change their relationship so that making love to her would be a foregone conclusion.

His will warred with his mind and body, but it was no use. He wanted this woman, wanted her as he had wanted no other.

At that moment it didn't matter that she thought he was Cary. It didn't matter that anyone could drive by and see them. Nothing mattered but the moment and the woman.

Listening to his heart, he gave up the fight and started to lower his head toward the sweet temptation of her lips. "Ah, Peyton," he murmured before he claimed her mouth. "I want—"

He never finished the sentence. A second wave of water far bigger than the first rained down on them like a torrent, splashing cool water into his face and down his overheated body.

The shock of it immobilized him, enabling him to return to his senses. What was he doing with Peyton in his arms? How could a man who valued loyalty and honor justify taking what was his brother's?

Mitch groaned, putting Peyton away from him and walking away from the spot on the sidewalk where the water rained. She stood there for a moment, looking as dazed as he felt, before she took a few tentative steps toward him.

"Come to my place tonight after work, Mitch,"

she said, and it sounded like a plea. Her voice was strained, as though it had been hard for her to speak the words.

He was tempted to tell her he'd blow off work and come to her place now, but he could think more clearly now that their bodies weren't in close contact. And what he thought about was his brother. He gathered his composure around himself like a cloak and called up his vaunted self-control.

"That's not a good idea, honey," he said, and his gut twisted as he watched the disappointment settle over her.

"Why not?" she whispered.

"Because . . ." he searched his mind, trying to come up with a credible reason that wouldn't reveal he was masquerading as his twin. The trouble was that there wasn't one. "It's just not a good idea."

She nodded once as though she understood but her lower lip trembled. *She thinks I don't want to make love to her,* Mitch thought incredulously. He was tempted to drag her back in his arms, capture that lip between his, and kiss her until her doubts vanished.

But he didn't do anything except stand there, his hands tied as surely as if they'd been bound by rope.

Mitch was still berating himself as an idiot a few hours later as he poured ginger ale into a champagne flute for Honey B. Goode, one of the voluptuous women working the bar crowd.

Honey, who wore a solid triple-D cup, took the stage on a strict three-times-a-week schedule, although Millie Bellini was constantly after her to become a full-time stripper. Honey wouldn't hear of it. Get naked too often, she said, and nobody's gonna look.

"You okay, sugar? You look like something's bothering you," Honey said as she took the pseudo-champagne from him. Normally she'd be too busy flirting to say even that much, but the poor sap next to her had his head resting on the bar. The tune he was singing was the drunken man's snore.

"I need a woman's opinion," Mitch said impulsively, resting his elbows on the bar. The hurt he'd seen in Peyton's eyes down by the bay was eating at him. "Can a woman tell for sure when a man wants her?"

Honey's eyes grew so big it was nearly impossible to see the blue eye shadow caked on her lids. "Oh, sugar, you're cute and all, but I'm married. And I got two head of youngun and a daddy who's a minister."

Mitch waved a hand. "I wasn't talking about you. I was talking about the woman I'm dating."

"You better not be dating one of the strippers." She shook a finger at him. "Debbie Darling won't take kindly to that seeing as to how you didn't date her when you were sleeping with her."

The information struck so hard that Mitch felt bruised. Could his brother actually have been stupid enough to two-time Peyton? "How long ago was this?" he asked.

"You don't remember?" Honey shook her head. "Gawd, Cary, it couldn't have been more than three or four weeks ago."

Mitch was too busy wondering when his brother had started dating Peyton to correct Honey's use of his twin's name. But even if the interlude with the stripper had happened before Cary had met Peyton, he still wanted to pulverize his brother for his bad judgment.

"Well, is she?" Honey wanted to know.

"Is who what?"

She tipped her head inquisitively. "Is the woman you want a stripper?"

"No." He shook his head. "She's not anyone you know."

"And why exactly do you want to know if she can tell whether you want her?"

He sighed. "It's complicated. Bottom line is I don't want her thinking I don't want her."

She reached across the bar to pat his cheek. "This isn't advanced algebra, sugar. If you want the girl, make love to her. That'll give her a pretty good clue."

He frowned at her advice, because of course he couldn't make love to Peyton. He needed to make her feel wanted without betraying his brother, who'd probably betrayed Peyton with a stripper.

Oh, brother.

The drunk beside Honey let out a loud belch, which woke him up enough that he could raise his head. Honey drew in a deep breath, expanding her chest to eye-popping proportions, and turned on the charm. Within moments, Mitch heard the man ask Honey how much she'd charge to have sex with him.

"I don't do that kind of thing, sugar," she said, patting the man's cheek. "I'm not that kind of girl."

And that was another problem, Mitch thought as he poured a customer a shot of whiskey. The entire purpose of the bait and switch was to gather evidence on Gibbs's illegal activities, but so far proof was in short supply.

Epidermis seemed to be full of women who got paid to take off their clothes in public, but not in private. If any prostitution was going on, it wasn't of the organized variety.

Neither was there any tangible proof that Gibbs was running a bookmaking operation, which was most puzzling of all. Mitch knew Gibbs was a bookie because of his dealings with Cary and Cooper Barnes, but he'd seen none of the trappings of the business. There was no separate phone line that always rang, no television tuned in to sporting events, no employee whose job consisted of answering phones.

"Hey, baby doll, how 'bout you do me a favor?" Millie Bellini was at the counter, beckoning to him with a gnarled, long-nailed finger. Her lipstick today was a bright pink that clashed with her leopard-skin top.

"You're not going to start with the black shirt again, are you?" Mitch asked, trying to inject some of Cary's charm in his voice. "Because it's not my color."

"Any color would look good on a hunk of burning love like you," she said, waggling her thick, dark eyebrows.

Think, Mitch told himself. What would Cary say to that?

"Aw, Millie, flattery will get you everywhere. What is it you need?"

She laughed. "Aside from you, I need somebody tall to get down the box of pasties from the high shelf in Gibbs's office. Some of the girls say the ones they're wearing are falling apart."

"You'll cover for me?"

"I'd let you wear me as a cover if you wanted," Millie said, then laughed so hard at her joke that some of her pink lipstick rubbed off on her yellowed teeth.

Mitch didn't waste any time in taking the key from Millie and unlocking the door to Gibbs's office. He recognized an opportunity when it presented itself and this one was too good to waste. If Gibbs were running a bookmaking operation, there had to be a record of it.

Nearly naked women gyrated to an inaudible beat on the screen of Gibbs's computer, but Mitch didn't linger over the images. He pressed the space bar, vanquishing the screensaver, and waited for a prompt to ask for a password.

Instead, the desktop materialized. Mitch swallowed, hardly believing his luck. Gibbs was many things, arrogant certainly among them, but a computer security expert he wasn't. Mitch hurriedly scanned the desktop, equally surprised at the presence of a file labeled "records."

He clicked twice on it, again expecting password protection, but the screen filled with columns of numbers. It took him only a moment to figure out he was looking at Epidermis's books instead of a gambling log. It took a moment longer to realize the figures made no sense.

Epidermis was no doubt profitable, but Mitch had worked the previous weekend and hadn't seen anywhere near the amount of money moving through the place that was recorded in the ledger.

It seemed his brother was right. Gibbs was laundering the money from his bookmaking business through the club.

The heavy stamp of footsteps sounded outside the door, which Mitch had thought too risky to lock. He closed the file and wheeled the chair backward. He was reaching for a cardboard box when Millie walked in the door.

"I came to see what was taking you so long, sugar buns," she said. From the corner of his eye, Mitch noticed that the desktop was up on the computer instead of the screensaver. If Millie noticed, he was doomed.

He lifted the box off the shelf and stood there with it poised over his head, as though he were Adonis holding up the world. As he intended, she focused on his muscles, which he hoped were rippling.

"It's hard to find boxed pasties," he said as he held the pose. A minute or so had gone by since he touched the computer, but nobody set their screensaver on that short a timer. He had to do something—and fast.

"Next time I'll model 'em for you," Millie said with her familiar leer. Mitch forced himself to smile at the same time he pretended to lose his balance. He juggled the box in the air while managing to bump the computer screen with his hip.

"Look what you've gone and done," Millie said, and Mitch thought she was on to him. He waited, expecting defeat. "You turned off Flash's screensaver."

"Darn," Mitch said, feigning disappointment. "And those women could really dance."

"I knew it," Millie said and again Mitch waited for her accusation. "I knew you were taking so long 'cause you were ogling the naked women."

"Guilty," Mitch said and headed past her for the main part of the bar.

He had work to do. The computer records indicated that Gibbs was moving so much money through Epidermis that his bookmaking operation had to be extremely profitable.

All he needed to do now was uncover proof of that illegal operation so he could put Gibbs in jail and go back to his life.

A lump stuck in his throat that he tried to swallow but couldn't, because Grant Mitchell's life didn't include Peyton McDowell.

Chapter Fourteen

Lizabeth tried her best to focus on the house where Ernest Hemingway once lived as the open-air tour train chugged past it, but Grant was more visually appealing than any Key West attraction.

Sure, the Spanish colonial style home had been constructed with native rock and boasted the first pool ever built on the island. But Grant, too, was one of a kind.

The short-sleeved shirt and navy shorts he wore were too muted for her taste, but she loved the thickness of his dark hair, the breadth of his shoulders, the cleft in his chin.

She also loved the sparkle that came into his eyes when something interested him, the quick way his mind worked, and the appreciative way he looked at her.

She frowned, because technically he was appreciating Leeza. Just like it was Leeza he'd kissed the other night instead of her.

She longed to go back to being Lizabeth if only because she wouldn't have to dress the way she was now. She'd nearly put her eyes out that morning when she'd got a glimpse of herself in the mirror after donning a neon green skort, matching sneakers, and bright yellow tank top.

But if she went back to being Lizabeth, Grant would go back to not noticing her. The way he hadn't noticed her in high school.

"I don't know about you, but I wouldn't want a couple dozen six-toed cats roaming the grounds of my house," Grant said.

"What?"

"Weren't you listening?" He gave her an indulgent look. "About half of the sixty cats living at the Hemingway House have an extra toe. They think most of them are descendants of the six-toed cat Hemingway got from a ship's captain."

"The Norwegian lundehund has six fully developed toes on each foot," she blurted out.

"Is that a cat?"

"A dog."

"Is that right?" he asked, a smile playing at the edges of his mouth.

"They're very rare," she continued as though her mouth was a broken faucet that wouldn't shut off. "They can bend their heads backwards over their shoulders and close their ear canals at will."

His smile grew and she was horrified that she'd

been babbling on about the lundehund. *Say something,* her inner voice screamed. *Say something or he'll think you're obsessed with the lundehund.* "What say you we disembark?" *What say you?* Who did she think she was? The queen of England?

"You mean, get off the train?"

"Yes," she said and remembered to toss her head so that her hair swung. Unfortunately, it hit him in the face. She pretended not to notice. "It's a lovely day for a walk."

She would have preferred hopping off the train, like the rail jumpers of the Old West, but of course cops like Grant didn't leap off trains.

He waited until the train had come to a complete stop at a red light and signaled to the conductor before stepping off and offering Lizabeth his hand. She took it, but a burst of shyness prevented her from looking him full in the face.

He brought their joined hands to his mouth and planted a warm kiss on the back of her hand, which sent her stomach jumping like a Ping-Pong ball. The departing train gave a farewell whistle and a car horn blared in response.

"Did you know that most American cars honk in the key of F?"

She'd done it again. Why, oh why, couldn't she keep the encyclopedia in her head closed? Lizabeth evaded his eyes for fear of what she might see in them but left her hand in his while she prattled on.

"Technically the honk we just heard could have been an F sharp or an F flat. Only the key of C has no sharps or flats."

Grant chuckled. "That's mighty sharp of you to point out."

Was he making fun of her gaucherie? Be calm, she told herself. Project poise.

"I have been blessed with a sharp mind," she said and almost groaned aloud.

She started her shoulders-back, head-high walk, pretending the book she'd practiced with was on her head. The mechanics of her walk were so complicated that it was a full minute before she could concentrate on the scenery.

This part of Key West was a surprise after the tourist-jammed downtown. Paved sidewalks took them past modest stucco houses landscaped with swaying palms, ficus hedges, and red-flowering ixora bushes. Tot lots and the occasional soccer field added to the normalcy of the neighborhood.

Although the heat of the day had passed, the temperature still hovered around eighty. Droplets of perspiration formed above her upper lip and she quickly licked them away.

Don't perspire, she begged herself. Perspiration wasn't sexy.

Maybe she'd been perspiring the night he'd kissed her, because he'd let an entire day pass without contacting her. Maybe he never would have contacted her again if she hadn't called upon her phony bold persona to phone him and set up this day of sightseeing.

"What did you do yesterday?" she asked, completely forgetting until the question was out of her mouth that she'd promised herself not to ask him that.

Just because she wanted to spend every minute of her vacation with him didn't mean he wanted the same thing. A strange look she couldn't decipher passed over his face. Oh, no, she thought. He was seeing another woman.

"I had some business in Miami."

She was so relieved she heard the breath whoosh out of her lungs. From what she knew of Grant, he didn't lie. And if he had business in Miami, it had something to do with law enforcement.

"Did you go up there after a criminal?"

He scuffed his Dockside against the sidewalk. "Something like that."

He opened his mouth as though he intended to say more, but then promptly closed it. He was clearly uncomfortable, a state Lizabeth could lay at her own doorstep.

"I'm sorry, Grant," she said. "I shouldn't have pried. I should have known you can't compromise an investigation by talking about it."

"I'd like to talk about it," he said with what she took as earnestness, "but it's better if I don't say anything."

They walked along in silence with Lizabeth thinking about what Grant couldn't tell her. Was he the kind of cop who was married to his job? The kind who would take time off from his vacation to hunt down a subject? When she thought about it, she realized she didn't know much about him at all.

"Why did you become a cop?" she asked after they had walked another block.

Cary brought a hand to his forehead and massaged it, hoping to stimulate his brain. Why had the Boy Scout become a cop? He'd never asked, but the answer was fairly obvious.

"Because I wanted to help people," he said.

She gave his hand a squeeze, as if to show him she approved of the answer. "And how did you end up in Atlanta?"

He hesitated. If she didn't think the Boy Scout was a saint now, the answer would surely convince her of that fact.

"Well?" she persisted.

"My great-grandmother was getting on in years and didn't want to leave the city," he said reluctantly. "My mom and grandma were worried about her, so I applied for a job in Atlanta straight out of the police academy and moved into her apartment building to keep an eye on her."

"Are you saying you live in a senior citizen's building?"

"Afraid so."

"Is your great-grandmother still in Atlanta?"

"She died suddenly of a heart attack last year," Cary said, and felt the familiar pang of hurt that she was gone. "Eighty-five years old and active 'til the end. It's the way she would have wanted to go."

"And you still live in the same building?"

"Yeah," he said reluctantly.

She was silent for so long that Cary got to hoping

that maybe she hadn't heard his answer. But of course she had.

"You're a good man, Grant Mitchell," she finally said.

Her comment made him feel even more like a fraud than he had when he'd made the decision to impersonate his brother, because he was not a good man.

While his twin had been selflessly pursuing a career in law enforcement and moving to Atlanta to be with their great-grandmother until the end, he was chasing the selfish dream of becoming a pro baseball player.

The only person Cary had ever helped was himself. If his busted elbow was any indication, he wasn't even good at that.

He dropped her hand and shoved both of his in the pockets of his brother's unfashionable shorts. He didn't feel like talking and she seemed happy to walk alongside him. And why not? She probably thought she was in the company of some kind of saint.

He kicked at a pebble, watched it skitter crazily out of sight, and then raised his head. The view that greeted him always had the power to lift his spirits: A baseball field chock full of kids.

"Oh, look, Grant," Leeza said. "I bet they're on a Little League team."

Judging from their gangly arms and legs, the boys couldn't have been more than ten or eleven years old. Some of them were taking infield practice while others were in the outfield warming up their arms. Three of the boys were lined up along one of the foul lines with their backs to the street, while three others threw to them across the field.

Cary slowed his steps, remembering the pure joy he'd gotten from baseball when he was that age. One of the kids heaved a ball over his partner's outstretched glove and it rolled all the way to the sidewalk. Cary picked up the ball and expertly tossed it to the boy who came to retrieve it.

"Thanks, mister," the kid said, snapping his gum.

"Hey, sport. Tell your buddy over there that he's releasing the ball too high," Cary said before the kid turned to go. "If he keeps his chin down and lets go of the ball later, you won't have to do quite so much chasing."

The kid's eyes got wide. "You know something about baseball?"

"I know enough."

He'd barely got the words out before the kid was yelling, "Hey, Dad. Come over here. This guy knows something about baseball!"

Within moments, a potbellied man in his mid-thirties trotted over to the sidewalk. The Florida Marlins baseball cap he was wearing was sizes too small, as though he'd filched it from his kid.

"Please say you're a Key West citizen who can't resist a bunch of kids with a know-nothing coach who only took the team because the real coach got transferred?"

Cary laughed. "Sorry, pal. Normally I'd love to help you out, but neither of us are islanders." He nodded at Leeza, only then realizing she was watching him curiously. Damn. He'd forgotten who he was supposed to be again.

"This here's Leeza Drinkmiller," he told the man. "And I'm . . . Grant Mitchell."

"I'm Sam 'I-never-played-baseball-in-my-life' Johnson." The man stuck out a hand, looking thoughtful. "I don't suppose . . . never mind."

"Go on. What were you going to say?"

"I was going to be presumptuous enough to ask if you'd help out at practices while you're here." He shrugged. "But seeing as to how you're on vacation, I—"

"I'll do it," Cary said.

"You will?" The question had an echo because both Sam Johnson and Leeza asked it at nearly the same time.

Sam, though, could recognize a good thing when he stumbled across it. "Thanks, buddy," he said, slapping Cary on the back. "Practice is the same time and place tomorrow, and we have a game Saturday at noon."

He trotted away, probably because he didn't want to give Cary time to change his mind. Leeza was staring at him.

"I knew you played the trumpet but I didn't know you played baseball," she said.

Ah, hell, he thought, irrationally angry at his brother for not taking up the sport. Mitch would have been a good baseball player, but his interests ran in different directions. Like Peyton's probably did.

"I played Little League a long time ago." He

cleared his throat, feeling guilty for not telling her the entire truth. "But I watched enough of my brother's games that I know baseball pretty well."

"You have a brother?"

"Yeah."

What's his name?"

Cary gritted his teeth. Oh, swell. Now he had to pretend not only that he was his own brother, but that his brother was him. "Cary."

"Cary Mitchell, the pitching star?"

"You've heard of him?"

"Who in Richmond hasn't? The sports pages used to be full of his accomplishments." She screwed up her forehead. "Mitchell's a pretty common last name, but funny I never connected him to you."

"We didn't go to the same high school. Cary went to Americana because it had a better baseball program."

The private school also had better academics, but Cary hadn't cared much about that and Mitch had never complained about being at a public school. Or, come to think of it, how much more attention their parents paid to Cary's athletic accomplishments than to Mitch's good grades.

"Didn't something happen to him?" Leeza screwed up her forehead as though trying to remember. "Some kind of accident that ended his baseball career?"

Cary evaded her eyes while he thought how to answer. In the past, it had been easy. He'd merely engineered a subtle shift of conversation to his shining time on the mound instead of the accident that had ended it all.

But a funny thing was happening. The story that had festered inside of him for so long seemed to be bursting to get out, and he realized he wanted to share what had happened with Leeza. The irony was that she wouldn't know the story was autobiographical.

"He was in a car crash after his sophomore year at the University of Virginia," he said. "He was coming off a fantastic season and was turning over the notion of going pro early."

"Now I remember," Leeza said. "His car spun out and slammed into a tree. It seems to me it wasn't his fault. There was a slick spot on the road or something, right?"

Because it had rained shortly before the accident, Cary had told the cops who wrote the accident report that his car had hit a wet spot and hydroplaned into the unforgiving tree.

"There wasn't any slick spot," he heard himself say.

"There wasn't?" Leeza seemed as surprised by his statement as he was. "Then why did he crash?"

Tell her about the minivan that was going so slow it was crying to be passed, he thought. *Tell her the lie about the car's power steering failing.*

"Because he was speeding and lost control of the car," he said, remembering the night as though it were yesterday. He'd downed a couple of beers at happy hour, then hopped into the new sports car his dad had given him. "He wanted to see how fast he could go. He never thought he'd lose control until he smacked into the tree."

"He broke something, didn't he?"

"Yeah. The elbow on his pitching arm," Cary said, remembering the searing pain. And the disbelief that this could have happened to him.

They'd reached a small playground nestled among the houses. Feeling suddenly weary, Cary sat down on a bench undoubtedly meant for parents who wanted to keep an eye on their children while they played on the jungle gym. But the playground was empty now, just like his life had been since that accident.

Leeza sat down next to him. "Didn't the elbow heal?"

"Sure it did." Cary thought back to the month in a cast and the six months of grueling rehabilitation that followed. "The elbow looks good as new on the outside, like he was never in an accident at all."

"Then why can't he pitch?"

"He can pitch all right. He just can't throw more than ninety miles per hour like he used to. And that's what it takes to get to the majors."

"Losing baseball must have been hard on him," Leeza said softly.

Because Cary was talking about himself in the third person, or possibly because he was talking to Leeza, the truth poured out of him.

"Harder than anything that had ever happened to him in his life." He considered how to put the impact of the accident into words. "Cary was so sure he was going to play pro ball that he never considered doing anything else. He didn't have a contingency plan."

"He graduated from college, didn't he?"

"Oh, yeah, but that wasn't so hard, considering his degree was in physical education."

"That's not a very nice thing to say."

Cary closed his eyes briefly. He'd forgotten again that Boy Scouts didn't bad-mouth anyone, not even their no-good brothers.

"You're right. But, believe me, if anyone coasted through college, it was Cary."

"What did he do after college?"

"Jumped from job to job and from place to place. He's tended bar, worked in a health club, at a community center, at a YMCA. A couple months ago, he moved to Charleston and now he works as a recreation specialist for the parks department."

Unexpectedly, her serious expression brightened. "So he's getting his life back in order?"

Nope, Cary thought wryly. He'd merely stolen his brother's life until he had to return to his own.

"The job in Charleston won't last," he said.

"Why not?"

The reason, which he'd deliberately buried for so very long, was pushing at the back of his throat. It was his deepest secret, one he'd never dared utter and hardly ever allowed himself to think, but quite suddenly he couldn't hold it back.

"Because throwing a baseball is the only thing he's ever been good at."

The truth hung in the air between them, stark and ugly. Cary felt as though there was a gaping wound in his throat from which the secret had spewed.

"Is that what you believe or what Cary believes?" Leeza asked after a moment.

"I think it's what both of us believe."

Leeza gazed at him intently, as though she were seeing into his soul. Considering the state it was probably in, he hoped that wasn't possible.

"You know that the only limitations a person has are the ones he puts on himself, right?" she asked softly.

He thought about that and concluded it was probably the credo by which his brother lived. And no wonder. Mitch had so much going for him that, had he lost one of his talents, he could fill in his life with the others. Mitch was the successful, responsible twin. He always had been.

He answered her the way his brother would have. "I do know that."

"Then you have to tell Cary." She reached across the space separating them and placed her warm hand on top of his cold one. "I only wish for your brother's sake that he were more like you, Grant."

His spirits plummeted as though pitched, like the fastballs he could no longer throw, into an abyss.

Because, aside from their physical appearance, he wasn't anything like the brother she so admired.

Chapter Fifteen

Lizabeth took another sip from her frozen margarita when Grant inched closer to her. That way, she could pretend her shiver was from the cold drink.

Worldly, sophisticated women did not vibrate from sexual awareness when the man causing the vibrating was barely touching them.

"What's it going to take to get you to dance with me?" he said so close to her ear that it set off another torrent of shivers. Of course, he was only trying to make sure she heard him above the blaring music.

The entire nightclub assaulted the senses. Two enormous video screens lined the dance floor, showing dual images of a famous male rock star prancing around a stage so energetically that it was a wonder the seams of his tight pants didn't burst.

His female backup singers, who swayed sensually to the beat, wore slinky red dresses not very different from Lizabeth's.

"I don't dance." Lizabeth was dismayed at how stark and gauche that sounded, so she added, "dahling."

"Did you call me *dahling?*" Grant asked, a corner of his mouth twitching.

"But of course, dahling," she said, and he laughed. A few days ago, she might have feared that he was making fun of her, but now she knew he was simply having fun.

It was crazy, but the talk they'd had that afternoon about his brother Cary's shortened baseball career had made Lizabeth feel closer to Grant. As he'd confided his brother's troubles, she'd felt as though a bond was growing between them, invisible but as strong as steel.

They'd gone back to their respective hotels to freshen up after their walk but had spent the rest of the evening together. Grant had been extravagant as usual, taking her to the island's most expensive restaurant when she would have been as happy to dine at one of the casual open-air spots along Duval Street.

Now they were huddled together at a tall table for two in an art-deco nightclub teeming with people bent on having a good time.

"I find it hard to believe that a woman like you doesn't dance," Grant said.

Actually, she'd used the wrong terminology. She *couldn't* dance. Not well, anyway. Certainly not well enough to fool Grant into thinking she was the sophisticated, adventurous woman she was pretending to be. That woman would surely know how to dance.

"Gyrating isn't my style," she said, and he grinned at her again. The way the grin lit up his features produced such a devastating effect that her stomach did a roll.

The video screens abruptly changed from the dancing, prancing rock star to a close-up of a balladeer who rose to fame in the 1970s on the strength of corny love songs.

"I never thought I'd say this about a Barry Manilow song, but this is more like it." Grant stood up and held out his hand. "For a slow dance, you don't have to gyrate. All you have to do is sway."

Lizabeth wasn't much of a slow dancer either, but the sight of Grant Mitchell standing before her with his hand outstretched was more than she could resist.

For years she had only to close her eyes to bring back the memory of being in his arms for that single dance in high school. She liked to fantasize that he'd begged her to dance with him instead of having her thrust upon him when her partner had cut in on his.

And now here he was, her fantasy come to life.

Wordlessly she put her hand in his and followed him to the dance floor, where he turned her into his arms. Her nerve endings came alive when he placed one hand at her waist and the other at her back.

She'd relived their long-ago dance so often that she was shocked to realize she felt as though she'd never danced with him before. The faint, pleasant scent of his cologne was different than she remembered. So were his smooth, self-assured steps and the very feel of him.

But of course he was different. He was ten years older, a mature man instead of a boy. And she was a grown woman. No wonder the warm, wonderful sensations swirling through her seemed unfamiliar.

She let her arms creep around his neck and felt the warmth at the nape of his neck. His heat spread through her, making her seek closer contact with the hard length of his body. She rested her head against his shoulder as Barry sang about writing the songs that made the whole world sing.

"Ah, Leeza," Grant said against her hair. "I'm always going to remember that we danced our first dance to one of the corniest songs ever sung."

Cold fingers of disappointment settled over Lizabeth, snuffing out the warmth. She drew her head back so she could see his face.

"This isn't the first time we've danced," she said.

"Sure it is."

He didn't remember, which shouldn't have come as a surprise. He hadn't recognized her when they'd met on the street, but some silly part of her had hoped that dancing with him would bring back the memory of that long-ago night when Grant had held Lizabeth instead of Leeza in his arms.

"This is the first time you *asked* me to dance. You were stuck with me in high school when my partner cut in on yours, leaving us stranded in the middle of the floor."

"I hardly think 'stuck with you' is the right expression."

"You didn't ask me for a second dance," Lizabeth pointed out. He hadn't asked her for anything at all after a polite inquiry as to what her name was. He hadn't remembered that either.

"Then it's a good thing I have a chance to make up for my mistake," he said, smiling at her before continuing the dance.

He held her slightly apart from him, as he had at the beginning of the song before she'd plastered herself against him. Lizabeth turned her face toward his shoulder and closed her eyes in horror.

Oh, God. She'd been fooling herself about the way he felt about her for days. Grant hadn't been making the moves. She had. She'd approached him on the street and made it very clear he'd been the object of her affection in high school.

Sure, he'd been willing to spend time with her. But she was the one who initiated the kiss in the courtyard. She was the one who'd called to invite him sightseeing after not receiving a post-kiss phone call.

She'd been so busy pretending to be worldly and sophisticated that she'd made a naive, ridiculous mistake.

Grant didn't want Leeza any more than he wanted Lizabeth. If he had, he would have taken her to bed the other night. And he surely wouldn't be holding her so loosely now.

The song ended and she forced her features into a pantomime of a pleasant expression. She waited until they were back at their table and had finished their drinks before she pleaded a headache and asked if they could leave.

The night was over and so was a romance that had existed only in her mind.

Cary trailed Leeza down the corridor leading to her hotel room, his gaze barely lingering on the way her slinky red dress hugged her shapely rear end. He was too busy puzzling over her behavior.

"How's the head?" he asked.

"Still pounding," she answered without breaking stride. In view of her stiletto heels, her quick pace was an amazing feat.

"I could go down to the main desk to see if they have ibuprofen," he offered.

"No thank you. I think I may have some in the room."

She'd reached her hotel-room door and was digging in her small evening purse for the key card. Any second now, she would dismiss him, the way she'd tried to at the elevator before he'd insisted on walking her to her door.

The complexion of the evening—hell, the entire day—had changed after they'd danced, and Cary's gut told him that whatever was wrong with her had nothing to do with a headache.

She pulled out the key card.

"Good night, Grant. Thank you for a lovely evening."

The words were devoid of warmth. She turned away from him to insert the card in the slot, her posture screaming that she didn't want to be touched.

"Wait a minute," he said. The green light on the door was blinking, and he thought she was going to shove open the door and slip inside the room, ignoring his request.

Instead her hand stilled and she turned wary eyes to his.

"How 'bout you tell me what's wrong," he said.

Her eyes shifted, not a lot but enough to indicate that he was on to something. "I already told you. I have a headache."

"I don't think you do."

Her chest rose and fell under the slinky material of her dress as she sighed. "Come on, Grant. Can't you see I'm trying to make this easy for you?"

"Make what easy for me?"

She swallowed. "Do you really need me to put it into words?"

"Yeah, I do."

"I'm trying to give you an easy out. There. I said it. You're dismissed, okay? No hard feelings."

He wrinkled his forehead. "What are you talking about?"

She let out another heavy, bewildering sigh. "I'm saving you the trouble of letting me down gently. I get it. I know I'm not your type."

"Why in the hell do you think you're not my type?" he asked, then remembered the damned Boy Scout didn't swear. He cleared his throat. "Sorry.

Make that why in the *heck* do you think you're not my type?"

She gazed at the floor and she seemed . . . embarrassed. He racked his brain, trying to figure out where she'd gotten that impression. The one time they'd kissed, he'd had to exert super-human control so he wouldn't drag her to bed. Especially because she'd made it clear she'd be a willing partner if he tried.

"Wait a minute," he said. "This is about that kiss the other night, isn't it?"

Her eyes lifted briefly before her gaze returned to the floor, but the hurt he'd glimpsed in their brown depths convinced him he'd hit the mark.

"But I only stopped because I was being a damn—ah, hell, I mean a darn—gentleman!"

Her head came up and the indentation between her eyebrows made it seem as though she didn't know whether to believe him. "Really?"

"Really. You'd gotten me so hot I'd have dived in the ocean if the water wasn't so warm. Surely a woman like you could tell."

With a red stain flushing her cheeks, she didn't much resemble the sophisticated woman he was referring to. She was still wearing her sexy red ensemble with her hair done up in an elaborate long braid, but she looked innocent and so damn sweet he could hardly stand it.

"What made you think," she whispered, "that I wanted you to be so gentlemanly?"

He'd thought she wanted him to act like his brother, who was a gentleman down to his bone marrow. Hadn't he gotten into this situation in the first place because he'd wanted her and she'd wanted his twin?

She was waiting for his answer, her dark eyes locked on his. The air around them seemed charged and filled with promise. If only he could bring himself to take what she was offering. And, oh God, how he wanted to take it.

But he forced himself to give her another out. "I want to make sure I understand. Are you saying you don't want me to act like a gentleman?"

Her tongue came out to lick her bottom lip, though he doubted she was aware of how the simple action made his groin tighten. She looked like she was going to say something, but then she simply nodded.

The other night, Cary had been able to resist what she was offering. He should resist it now, but her allure was so powerful that he couldn't.

He was only a man, after all. A weak, imperfect man powerless to fight the need churning in his gut.

"Invite me in," he rasped.

The key card was still in the slot but incredibly her hands were shaking so badly she couldn't grip it. He reached past her, got the door open, and gently pushed her inside the room.

The moment the lock clicked, he gathered her in his arms and put his mouth on hers. Her lips were already parted, asking for him to deepen the kiss, and he thrust his tongue into the opening. She met his passion, stroking her tongue against his, threading her fingers through his hair to cradle his head while she kissed him back.

It took all his restraint not to tumble her to the floor, tear off her clothes, and lose himself inside her.

He ran his hands over her as he kissed her, from the fullness of her hips, to her rounded rear end, up the slim column of her back and around her rib cage to stroke the sides of her breasts.

He was already so hard that his pleasure verged on pain.

Cary prided himself on being a tender, patient lover, but something about Leeza robbed him of any sense of control. She made him feel primitive, like a man whose hunger to mate was so overpowering that nothing else mattered.

But of course it did. Leeza mattered. This would be the first time they made love, and she deserved more than a wild, frantic coupling only steps from the door.

He tore his mouth from the carnal pleasure of hers, hoping he'd be able to slow things down. But her lips landed on other accessible parts of him: the side of his mouth, his cheek, the column of his throat.

She rubbed her lower body against his erection, and he groaned, running his hands up the tight fabric of her dress until he reached the zipper at the back of it. He managed to tug the zipper down far enough so that he could touch her warm, silky skin.

With trembling fingers, he unfastened the clasp of her bra and ran his hands around her body until he reached the softness of her breasts. He squeezed . . . and felt something come loose.

Her mouth, which had been pressing kisses to his neck, stilled against his skin as he pulled a flesh-like substance from her bra. He drew back and held it up quizzically.

"Oh, no," she wailed and shut her eyes tight.

"Did I hurt you?" he asked anxiously.

"No, but you just outed my silicone bra pad," she said miserably, feeling her face, already flushed with passion, turn redder.

She felt the pad in the other cup of her bra slip to her waist, and she buried her face in his shoulder. What must he think of her? How could she ever meet his eyes again? If he laughed, she'd curl up and die.

"Why would you think you needed bra pads?" he asked against her hair.

The answer was so embarrassing she could hardly articulate it. "Because I'm an A cup."

"What's wrong with that?"

"Did you know that only fifteen percent of American women wear an A cup?" she mumbled into his shoulder. "The average cup size is a B."

"Who says I want average?" he asked, grasping her by the shoulders and moving her inches from him so she had to lift her head.

He tipped her chin up with a forefinger so she had to look at him. His eyes lowered as he slipped her dress and then her loosened bra from her shoulders. The garments fell in a heap to the floor, leaving her clad in only high-cut underwear and stiletto heels.

Her hands came up to cover her small breasts, but he captured both of her hands in his and gazed his fill while her stomach roiled in fear that he'd find her lacking. But when he lifted his blue eyes, they'd darkened a few shades.

"I think your breasts are way above average," he whispered, a husky note in his voice. "In fact, I think they're perfect."

She tried to swallow, but couldn't. "You do?"

He nodded. "I do."

Joy flooded her, making her knees weak. "Would you like to, um, see the rest of me?"

"Oh, yeah," he rasped.

She didn't know what had possessed her to ask the question, but now that she had she couldn't very well take the offer back. *Act sophisticated,* she told herself.

She nodded toward the bedroom, which adjoined the small sitting room they were in. "Follow me into my lair," she said.

Her lair, she thought as she tried to move sensually into the next room. Why had she said such a stupid thing? But he followed and she saw when she turned on the light that a smile was playing about his full lips.

He sat down on the bed and waited, obviously expecting her to follow through on her offer. Expecting, she realized with a sinking heart and a sudden flash of self-consciousness, for her to sexily slip off her stilettos and underwear.

"Would it help if I took off my clothes first?" he asked.

He didn't wait for her answer, but quickly pulled his short-sleeved shirt over his head so that his chest was bare. Wonderfully, mouth-wateringly bare. He had an athlete's chest, defined with muscle and sprinkled with dark hair she wanted to run her fingers over.

"Your turn," he said with a sexy grin.

She took a breath for courage, balanced on one of her high heels so she could take the other shoe off, and lost her sense of equilibrium.

"Oh, no," she cried a moment before she tumbled.

Grant was off the bed in a flash, taking the brunt of her weight as she toppled with him to the floor. He grunted as he hit the carpet with her sprawled on top of him. He lay there with his eyes closed, as still as death.

"Grant, Grant," she said, frantically slapping him in the face to revive him. First one blue eye opened, then the other.

"What do you know, now *I* am the one who fell for *you*," he drawled, harkening back to when they'd met on the street and she'd fallen into his arms.

She was so relieved she hadn't ruined things with her clumsiness that she started to laugh and he joined in. The laughter lasted only a moment, until they both realized they were bare chest to bare chest.

Lizabeth didn't know who made the first move,

but their mouths were soon in a lip lock, their hearts beating hard against each other, their hands ridding each other of clothing. From somewhere a condom appeared, and he sheathed himself.

She felt his fingers slide inside her hot, wet center as he kissed her, then she helped as he grabbed her hips and positioned her above him so he could slide her onto him. She cried out at the pain, then bit her lip to stop the sound.

He stopped moving. "Leeza, are you okay?"

She felt her body gradually adjust to the size of him and the pain lessen, just as she'd been told it would.

"I'm wonderful," she said, hoping to convince him. For good measure, she added "dahling" and restlessly moved against him, asking for she hardly knew what.

"Once we get started," he said, his voice a husky purr, "I won't be able to stop."

"I don't want you to stop," she said because pleasure had already started to replace the pain. The only sounds after that were murmurs and sighs and groans as they lost themselves in the wonder of each other.

Lizabeth met his thrusts with her own, feeling closer to him than she had ever felt to anybody as the warm sensation between her legs turned hot and liquid, spreading like a fan inside of her. She cried out again, this time in wonder, a moment before he pumped into her a last time and met his own release.

She lay there on top of him for a long time as

their heart beats slowed and their breathing returned to normal, wishing she could confide in him that this had been the first time she'd made love.

At the same time, she fervently hoped he hadn't been able to tell that she'd been a virgin, because then he'd know that ultra-sophisticated Leeza Drinkmiller was nothing but a fraud.

Somehow she didn't think it would be any compensation to know that boring, colorless Lizabeth was falling in love with him.

Chapter Sixteen

Peyton smoothed the sheer black nylon over one of her long legs until the lacy top hugged her upper thigh, keeping the stocking in place.

When she'd put on its twin, she walked over to the full-length mirror on her wardrobe and presented her back to it. Swiveling her head, she tried to make sure the black seams were straight but got an eye full of naked butt.

She laughed at herself, not because her butt looked bad naked but because her black thong was the most daring thing she'd ever worn. She turned around so that she was facing the mirror and changed her mind about the thong.

The lacy black shelf bra with the boning that strategically uplifted her cleavage but left her nipples and half her breasts bare was definitely more daring.

She went to her closet, where she'd hung the mere slip of a mini dress she'd bought that afternoon at a store miles from the downtown boutiques her mother and her friends frequented. She shimmied into the dress, grateful she hadn't eaten much that afternoon. The black garment was so slinky that even an extra grape would show. She stepped into a pair of equally new three-inch high heels and returned to the mirror.

She posed this way and that, feeling a draft at the open oval at the back of the dress, and giggled. Her mother would faint dead away if she saw her now.

But Peyton hadn't gone to all this trouble to shock her society-conscious mother. She'd put on the sexiest clothes she could find to shock Mitch into action.

After he'd failed to kiss her the other night while they stood under the sea spray, she'd had a crisis of confidence for, oh, maybe two minutes.

Then she'd come to her senses because there was no way Mitch didn't want her.

He'd tried incessantly to get her into bed from the day they'd met until about a week ago. A man's ardor didn't cool that quickly and that completely.

Nope. Mitch wanted her, of that she was sure. But she was equally sure he'd taken too much to heart her previous reluctance to get intimate.

She didn't jump into bed with a man on the first

date or even in the first month, and she was glad Mitch respected that. She was glad he'd decided to act like the gentleman she wanted him to be.

But too much gentlemanly behavior was too much. It was Friday night and she hadn't even seen him since Tuesday, for heaven's sake.

She was ready, willing, and about to leave him with no doubt that she wanted to make love to him. Tonight.

Mitch had asked her, for no reason that made any sense, to meet him at a restaurant across the Cooper River in Mount Pleasant. The location was fortuitous because she wasn't sure she'd have the courage to dress this way if she thought she'd run into someone she knew.

She snatched a miniature black beaded bag from her bed, took out a tube of wild, wet lipstick in a shocking shade of red, and painted her mouth.

She rubbed her lips together, pursed them, and winked at herself. Then she sashayed out the door, practicing her sexiest walk.

She was glad she wasn't particularly hungry. Because if she got her way, they weren't going to get through their appetizers.

She intended to have Mitch before she had her dinner.

Mitch settled at a table with a view of the front of the restaurant so he could keep a lookout for the rest of his party, and informed the hostess he was going to wait to order.

A line of people who hadn't thought ahead to

make reservations packed the entrance, and waitresses and busboys bustled about the room like live wires. A young boy at the next table put two straws in his nostrils and bucked his teeth, making his baby sister laugh so hard she spewed juice onto their mother.

Mitch grinned. Choosing this crowded, family-style restaurant had been a stroke of genius. So had telling Peyton he needed to meet her in Mount Pleasant.

He'd never thought of himself as weak-willed, but his determination not to make love to Peyton was growing more feeble by the moment. It would have died altogether when she offered herself to him on the Charleston Battery if the sea spray hadn't shocked some sense into him.

He was a man of honor, and men of honor didn't sleep with their brother's girlfriends.

Now that he'd determined that Gaston Gibbs was running a bookmaking operation, finding the evidence to convict him was only a matter of time. Until then, he had a plan that would preserve not only his honor but Cary's relationship with Peyton.

He ignored the sharp stab of jealousy that impaled him when he thought of Cary and Peyton together, and resolved to carry out his plan.

It involved making sure that he and Peyton were never alone together. Just as they hadn't been on their separate drives over the Cooper River Bridge to Mount Pleasant. Just as they wouldn't be in this noisy, crowded restaurant.

The plan was beyond brilliant. Mitch could make

sure Peyton knew he found her attractive while having a built-in reason not to act on that attraction.

A cop like him knew that making love in public places was taboo although, with Peyton, even indecent exposure sounded tempting.

Not that he'd give in to temptation. No, siree. He wouldn't. . . .

A va-va-va-voom woman in a black mini dress that molded to her skin like modeling clay approached the hostess's stand, abruptly stopping his mental pep talk.

Because it wasn't just any va-va-va-voom woman. It was Peyton.

The hostess indicated his table and Peyton turned her blond head. Normally, Mitch would have raised a hand in greeting but his hormones were zinging so powerfully about his body that he seemed to have temporarily lost motor control.

Peyton got a mischievous smile on her lips, lowered her eyelids to half mast, and walked slowly toward him. The slow walking was probably a necessity. Her dress was so tight he was pretty sure it would have ripped had she taken a long step.

Her deliberate, unhurried pace gave him far too much time to feast his eyes on her. He'd laid awake nights envisioning what she'd look like naked, and the fit of her hardly-there dress gave him a pretty good idea.

He'd never gone for the emaciated look on a woman, preferring instead soft, rounded curves like Peyton's. Her legs were disproportionately long for her height and her breasts were, in a word, fantastic.

As she got nearer, he could make out the hard pebbles of her nipples under the clinging fabric of her dress. The restaurant wasn't particularly cold, bringing up the possibility that he'd pebbled her nipples simply by staring at her breasts.

Before she'd gotten to within touching range, his throat went Sierra-Nevada-desert dry at the thought. Another lower part of him sprang to attention.

"Hey, there, Mitch," she whispered in a sensuous purr when she reached the table. She posed there for a moment when he couldn't find his voice, then anchored both of her hands on the table and leaned so that he got an eyeful of beautiful breast. "Are you sure it's food you're hungry for?"

Peyton watched Mitch's eyes darken and felt a surge of female power like she'd never felt before. She was right! He wanted her, maybe even more than she'd imagined.

She'd nearly lost her nerve when she pulled up to the restaurant and realized why the owners had named it Cluckers. But in the end the sight of an illuminated clucking chicken hadn't been enough to make her don the jacket she'd brought with her at the last moment.

She'd left it in the car so the G-rated atmosphere of the restaurant didn't dissuade her from completing her mission, and did her best Marilyn Monroe walk to Mitch's table.

She could sense more than one pair of male eyes

on her, but she refused to be cowed by embarrassment. After all, it wasn't as though she and Mitch were staying long.

She deliberately traced her upper lip, then her lower one, with the tip of her tongue.

"There's a motel next door if you don't want to drive all the way home," she purred.

Peyton might have believed the sound of a throat clearing had come from Mitch if his mouth hadn't been hanging open. The noise came again, louder this time, and she realized it was coming from behind her.

She turned slowly and saw sideburns. Puffy gray ones that reminded her of steel wool. The man exhibiting them was peering at her through black horned-rimmed glasses as though he'd never seen a woman in a dress as tight as skin.

The noise came a third time, but the man with the steel-wool sideburns wasn't making it. The throat clearer was the birdlike woman next to him. Her features were delicate and pointed, her small eyes alert and interested, her hair dyed a rich shade of gold.

"Aren't you going to introduce me, Albert?" the woman asked in a voice as high as her arched eyebrows.

Mr. Sideburns opened his mouth. Peyton even thought he moved his lips, but it was Mitch's voice she heard.

"This is Peyton McDowell, and my name's Cary Mitchell, although you can call me Mitch."

Peyton turned toward Mitch in surprise. Did he actually know these people?

"Peyton, this is Albert Parks and his wife." He paused, and the eyes that had contained such heat a few moments ago looked pained. "They're joining us for dinner."

Oh, my goodness. Not only did he know these people, he'd invited them to dinner!

"I go by my maiden name," the small woman interjected. "The name's Grace Kelley, like the princess. Only I spell Kelly with an 'ey' instead of a 'y'."

This time the throat clearing definitely came from Mitch. "Peyton," he said, "Albert is my boss."

His *boss?* Peyton closed her eyes in mortification but instantly realized the action wasn't doing any good. Although she couldn't see Mitch's boss and his wife, they could still see her. And plenty of her, at that.

She snapped her eyes open, tugged downward on her hemline and sucked in her stomach in the hopes that the dress might look a tad less clingy. Then she called upon lessons she'd learned from the etiquette classes her mother had insisted she take.

"I can't tell you how pleased I am to meet you, Mr. Parks, Ms. Kelley," she said. Her smile was so fake she feared her face might crack.

"I'd prefer you call me Grace Kelley instead of Ms. Kelley," Grace said, lifting her chin regally. "You know, like the princess."

"Certainly, Grace," Peyton said.

"Grace Kelley," she corrected with asperity. "I prefer you use the whole name."

"Of course, Grace . . . Kelley." Peyton swept a hand to indicate the table. The sooner they got this over with, the better. "Won't you both sit down?"

Peyton did so hurriedly, taking the seat next to Mitch and figuring the table would at least cover the lower half of her. Grace Kelley wasted no time in joining them, but her husband remained standing. The horned-rimmed glasses obscured much of his face, but Peyton thought he looked uncomfortable.

"We can dine with Mitch and Peyton another time, Grace Kelley. I think we should go."

"Go?" Grace Kelley nearly shouted the word. "We just got here and I'm hungry."

"But I think they'd rather be alone," Albert whispered, raising his eyebrows.

"If they'd rather be alone, they wouldn't have invited us," Grace Kelley turned to Peyton. "Isn't that right, Peyton?"

Mitch was the one who'd invited them, but Peyton wasn't going to quibble over details when she was meeting her boyfriend's boss for the first time. She tried to make her nod enthusiastic and wondered how she could enhance the couple's opinion of Mitch. Rushing home to change clothes to prove he didn't date floozies wasn't an option.

"Absolutely," she said, trying to make her smile wholesome. To show solidarity, she covered Mitch's hand with hers. "We've been looking forward to this dinner all day. Haven't we, Mitch?"

"How could that be?" Albert asked. The glare coming off his glasses was reflecting directly on her breasts. "Mitch only asked me a few hours ago when I ran into him in the parking lot, and I heard you ask him if he was sure it was food—"

Peyton didn't let him finish. "Mitch knows how much I wanted to meet his boss."

"You did?" Surprise tinged Mitch's voice. Peyton and Grace Kelley looked at him, but Albert's glasses were still pointed squarely at Peyton's breasts. Mitch nodded decisively. "I mean, she did. Want to meet the boss."

"I'm very supportive of him," Peyton said and nodded herself. She and Mitch probably looked like a pair of those dashboard bobble-head dolls.

"And I'm very solicitous of her." Mitch shrugged out of his well-cut gray suit jacket and draped it around her bare shoulders. "She tends to get cold in air-conditioned places."

"I do," Peyton said, nodding some more even though embarrassment had spiked her body temperature so high she was roasting. She pulled the lapels of Mitch's suit jacket together, for once glad of his gentlemanly tendencies. "I'm as cold-blooded as a lizard."

"But much prettier," Mitch added.

"Then why didn't you bring a jacket?" Albert asked.

"Oh, leave the poor girl alone, Al," Grace Kelley said, swatting him with one of the menus the hostess had left on the table. "I'm sure we can come up with a more interesting subject."

"Here we go," Albert muttered.

Grace Kelley touched a hand to her golden hair,

fluffing it. "Don't you think it's an amazing coincidence that Grace Kelly once starred in the movie *High Society,* which was a remake of *The Philadelphia Story,* and that I was born in Philadelphia?"

Peyton took Mitch's arm as they walked to the parking lot in the glow of the giant clucking chicken. Even though her body lightly brushed his with every step, he seemed to be holding himself apart from her.

"Bye-bye," Grace Kelley called as she and Albert peeled off in another direction, bestowing them a rotating-wrist wave that harkened to the kind royalty practiced.

"It was very nice to meet you," Peyton called, then addressed Mitch in a softer voice. "That was fun."

Mitch groaned. "Go ahead. I deserve it. So get it over with."

"Get what over with?"

"The yelling."

She tipped her head to get a better look at his face. Thanks to the illuminated chicken, she could tell that he was bracing himself. "Why should I yell at you?"

He let out a short laugh. "Because I didn't tell you I invited Albert and his wife to dinner. Because we just spent an hour and a half with a woman who's fixated on Grace Kelly."

"You should have told me," Peyton said thoughtfully, "but I did have fun. If I hadn't met Albert's wife, I'd never have known that the princess got off her husband's yacht during her honeymoon to have an audience with the pope."

Mitch laughed. "Not exactly what I'd want to do on *my* honeymoon."

Peyton had been wondering how to get the evening back on the sexy track on which it had started, and she seized the opportunity. They'd reached her car, so she stopped, turned to Mitch and looked up at him from under her lashes. "What would you do on your honeymoon?"

She felt his body stiffen, saw his jaw clench, and knew she'd hit her mark. "Uh, you know," he said.

"Maybe I don't know," she whispered and stroked the arm she was holding. Slowly, deliberately, she removed his suit jacket so that she was once again clad in only the barely there black dress. "Maybe I'd like you to show me."

A parking lot, no matter that it was nearly deserted, wasn't the ideal setting for seduction, but Peyton thought she was doing a fairly credible job of it. A muscle worked in the strong column of Mitch's throat, his breathing was shallow, and his voice kept cracking.

He blew out a breath . . . and lifted his watch. "Boy, it's getting late."

"It's nine o'clock," Peyton protested.

"I should be getting home. I don't like to stay out too late when I have to work the next day."

"You always stay out late. You're a bartender."

He shuffled his feet, yawned, stretched his arms. "That's why I need to catch up on my sleep. If you give me your keys, I'll open the car door for you."

He was dismissing her! It didn't make sense considering the way he'd looked at her in the restaurant and the way he'd reacted to her a minute ago. She knew he wanted her. So why was he being so blasted gallant?

He had his hand out for her keys. But if she surrendered them, within minutes they'd be driving off in separate cars to separate locations. She couldn't let that happen. Not when what she wanted was within grabbing distance.

She opened her small beaded bag and made a show of rummaging through it, trying to be careful not to jingle her keys.

"Oh, no," she said with as much drama as she could muster. "My keys aren't in here."

"Are you sure?" he asked, bending over as though to check for himself.

She closed the bag with a decided click and gave him a wide-eyed, innocent look. "I'm sure."

Ten minutes later, after they'd traced and retraced all of Peyton's steps, Mitch had to concede they weren't going to find her keys.

He'd gotten her to cover up her siren's outfit with his jacket as they searched inside the restaurant, but now that they were in the fresh air she'd taken it off again. He quickly averted his eyes but couldn't turn off his mind's eye. And that one was imprinted with how sexy she looked.

"I guess this means *you're* going to take me home," she said brightly.

Take her home? And wreck his plan to never be alone with her? He didn't think so. He whipped

Cary's cell phone out of his pocket. "I bet you dropped the keys inside the car. We can have a locksmith out here in no time to open it for you."

"No!" Her hands were on him again, darn it. Didn't she realize he couldn't think straight while she was touching him? The scent of a perfume that made him think of decadence enveloped him and her soft breasts pressed against his chest.

"I want to go with *you,* Mitch," she said, those Coca-Cola eyes entreating him. "I'll come out here tomorrow and use my spare key to unlock the car. It'll be safe enough 'til then."

"But. . . ."

"Please, Mitch," she said, and he could feel her soft breath on his mouth. Where he wanted her lips to be. Oh, brother. How was he supposed to resist this?

"Sure," he said and stood perfectly motionless when she lifted her lips and pressed them to his. The kiss lasted only a moment, but it underscored what he already knew.

It was going to be a long drive home.

He helped Peyton into the Miata, a mean feat considering she was wearing three-inch heels and the car was slung low to the ground. Then he settled himself behind the driver's seat, released two clips on the windshield header and lifted the top up and over their heads.

"Oh, good. You're putting the top down," Peyton said as he got out to finish the job. "How romantic."

He nearly groaned. It obviously hadn't occurred to her that he was putting down the top so the drive to Charleston over the tall spans of the Cooper River Bridge, which loomed two-hundred fifty feet over the water, would be almost as effective as taking a cold shower.

"Let's go to Sullivans Island," Peyton announced when he got back into the car. "It's such a pretty night I'd love to take a walk on the beach."

"I don't think that's a good—"

"Please, Mitch," she pleaded, leaning over the center armrest so that her extremely sexy attributes were on full display. She reached out to put her right hand on his left thigh. "Please."

You can barely resist her in a car. Think how much worse it'll be on a beach, Mitch thought. *No. Say no.*

"Okay," he said and turned the key in the ignition.

Chapter Seventeen

The dark green sedan loomed large in Mitch's rear-view mirror on the drive to Sullivans Island, causing the hairs on the back of his neck to stand at attention.

His cop instincts could be working overtime, but he didn't think so. He'd noticed the same car, or one very similar, on his way to the restaurant. And he thought he'd seen it last night when he'd made a quick trip to the grocery store to stock Cary's empty refrigerator.

"Something wrong, Mitch?" Peyton's voice traveled on the wind whooshing through the car.

Oh, yeah, something was wrong. Not only had Mitch gotten himself into a heck of a predicament with his brother's girl, but he was pretty sure somebody was following them. But who?

Gaston Gibbs? He'd ordered Mitch to collect a debt from a poor sap who owed so much money Gibbs wanted him roughed up even if he coughed up the dough. Mitch had until tomorrow night to carry out the assignment, but had Gibbs put a tail on him to make sure he followed through?

"What could be wrong?" Mitch answered a second before he gave the steering wheel a sharp tug. Tires screeched on pavement as the car completed a ninety-degree right turn onto a side street.

"What are you doing? The beach isn't this way!"

"It's not?" Mitch said absently as he watched the green sedan take the same turn into the residential neighborhood that he'd made.

"No, it's not," Peyton said as Mitch took a series of left and right turns in an effort to lose their tail. He heard her heavy sigh. "You're doing it again."

"Doing what?" he asked as he pulled the Miata back onto the main highway and sped toward Sullivans Island.

"Acting strange," she answered.

He slanted her a smile, pretending as though she'd given him a compliment, then monitored the rear view mirror. It couldn't be difficult for their tail to figure out they were heading to the islands. Even as he had the thought, he spotted the sedan pull onto the main drag and turn in the opposite direction. The move didn't fool him. The car had been following them. Of that, he was sure.

"That wasn't a compliment," Peyton said as he slowed the car to a more leisurely pace. "The ability to act strange is not a positive trait."

Thinking about his theory that Gaston Gibbs had put a tail on him would have to wait. With Peyton in the car, Mitch found he couldn't focus on anything but her.

"Oh, it isn't, is it? Then what do you call a woman in an expensive cocktail dress who deliberately lets seawater drench her?"

Silence greeted his question but it lasted only a few moments. "Unusual."

"Peculiar," he shot back.

"Unexpected."

"Bizarre."

"Extraordinary," she countered.

They were still laughing at her quick answers after they reached the island and Peyton directed him to pull onto a side road. Abruptly, Mitch's laughter stopped.

He'd strongly suspected he was making a mistake when he agreed to bring Peyton to the beach, but now he was sure of it.

The only South Carolina beaches he'd ever seen were in Myrtle Beach, and those were illuminated by the reflected light of a tourist-jammed city. Like the city, those beaches slept for only a few hours each day.

As he parked the Miata alongside a row of sand dunes, he conceded that this was a very different kind of beach. If not for the glow of the half moon, they wouldn't even be able to see it.

"This is going to be fantastic." Peyton got out of the car and onto her high heels with impressive grace. "I adore the beach at night."

When she grabbed his hand a moment later, even that minimal contact was enough to send a warning screaming through him. But it was too late to heed it.

They took a path in the shadow of the sand dunes and stepped onto the main part of the beach. He stopped abruptly, scanning the expanse of sand and sea that stretched in front of him.

"There's no one here," he said and heard the panic in his voice.

"Of course there isn't," Peyton said laughingly. "That's why I like to come here."

The truth hit him like a brick dropped from the top of a skyscraper. He was alone with his brother's girl, and he was going to have to pay the consequences.

Peyton took off first one shoe, then the other, flinging them aside. She scampered across the beach, leaving Mitch to navigate the soft sand in his brother's fancy loafers. When he felt sand pour into them, he conceded defeat and took off both his socks and shoes before rolling up the cuffs of Cary's expensive slacks.

Ahead of him, Peyton had stopped scampering and was . . . He narrowed his eyes to get a better look in the semidarkness. Oh, Lord, she was hiking up the hem of her dress, hooking her thumbs in the top of one of her thigh-high stockings, and rolling it sensuously down her leg.

By the time she finished removing the second stocking, he was having serious breathing trouble.

"Can you feel that sea breeze?" she asked, raising

both hands to the sky and doing a slow pirouette. The moon bathed her in light, making her glow like an ethereal being.

She gave a low, enchanting laugh and turned toward Mitch.

"Race you to the ocean," she said and took off for the gently breaking waves.

Earlier he'd theorized that her dress would split at the seams if she took so much as a long step, but the dress was made of sterner stuff than he'd suspected. Peyton was a graceful runner. Her long legs dug into the sand, kicking up granules behind her in an arc-shaped spray.

Mitch shouldn't race her. He shouldn't have let her talk him into coming to the beach. And he very definitely shouldn't be alone with her.

He should hang back and convince himself he didn't find a woman in a tight dress racing toward the ocean incredibly intoxicating. He should pretend her joy of life and disregard for her expensive clothes wasn't refreshing. He should ignore the thumping of his heart and quickening of his body.

"Hurry up, slowpoke," she called over her shoulder, barely breaking stride as the wind carried her laughter.

The laughter seemed to seep inside Mitch until he could no more deny her than he could his need to breathe in the sea air.

"Ah, darn," he said and ran after her.

She was ankle deep in water by the time he reached the wet spot on the beach where the water lapped, but she was no longer laughing. He slowed, his eyes locking on hers, as she reached around her back.

Before it fully registered that she was unzipping her dress, she slid it from her shoulders and down her hips, stepping delicately from it.

The breath Mitch had been about to take froze before it got to his lungs. She was wearing a black triangle of cloth where her underwear should have been and a black bra so skimpy it left most of her breasts bare. The wind tousled the blond strands of her hair, making her look like a seductive sea nymph from Greek mythology come to life.

She balled up her dress and tossed it to him, and he was hardly aware of his hand reaching out to snag it.

"Why don't you leave that on the beach with your clothes." It wasn't a question. It was an invitation.

He'd take off his suit jacket, that was all. The night was balmy, no cooler than seventy degrees, and he shouldn't be wearing it anyway.

He shrugged out of the garment and threw it along with her dress to a dry part of the sand. Nope. There was nothing wrong with a man shedding his suit jacket as long as he didn't take off anything else. And that he wasn't going to do.

Neither was he going to make love to his brother's girl. Heck, he wasn't even going to join her in the water.

"Hey, neighbor!" A loud, masculine voice that was much too close for comfort broke the silence. Mitch didn't think. He reacted, striding into the ocean and moving Peyton deeper into the water. He was shielding Peyton's body from view when the man approached them, waving jovially.

"This is the first time all week I've seen anyone else out here," the man called cheerfully. Mitch couldn't make out his features, but his white hair and beard put his age in senior-citizen range.

"Yep," Mitch said, figuring if he kept his answers short the man would go away. Instead, the man's head tipped.

"Hey, are you wearing a dress shirt and a tie? And . . . are those suit pants?"

"Yep."

"But salt water is hell on clothes, young fella. Why, I once ruined my best pair of socks when I forgot to take them off. Salt nearly ate through 'em. You better. . . ." His voice trailed off and Mitch saw him reach down and pick something up off the sand. Something black. "Why, what's that? Oh my gosh, it's a dress."

"It's mine," Mitch heard Peyton pipe up from behind him. There was a moment of sheer silence before she added. "I didn't want to get it salty."

"Oh my gosh," the man sounded stunned. "There are two of you out there. Oh, my. Oh, my. I'll just go now."

He went, mumbling all the way.

"I think we gave him a shock." Mitch's body was still shielding Peyton's, not that the old-timer was looking. He couldn't be moving any faster had a sea monster emerged from the depths and ordered him to scram.

"He'd have gotten more of a shock if you hadn't hidden me," she said.

The thigh-deep water soaked his clothes but he was more aware of Peyton's bare flesh pressed against his back than the wetness.

"When did you get to be such a gentleman?" she whispered in his ear when the man was a speck in the distance. Sensual shivers started at his neck and ran down his body. "You used to try to pressure me into making love to you."

Try? That meant the pressure hadn't resulted in success. *Cary hadn't made love to her,* his mind screamed.

"Remember how I said I'd tell you when I was ready?" she continued.

He knew he shouldn't turn around, but the allure of her voice was impossible to resist. He pivoted slowly until he was facing her. Her eyes seemed to darken, like sinful, rich, addictive chocolate.

"I'm ready, Mitch. I want to make love to you. Tonight."

Mitch's heart was pumping so furiously he could hear its beat in his ears. She was inviting him to live out the erotic dreams that had been keeping him awake nights.

He ached to take her into his arms but thoughts of what would happen if he surrendered to his desires kept his arms at his sides. Could he live with himself if he slept with his brother's girl? On the heels of that question came another. If he refused her, would she still be his brother's girl in the morning?

"This is it, Mitch." She said what he already knew. "Tonight we either take a step toward each other or move a step back."

In other words, if he didn't make love to her, his brother would lose her. And so would he.

He stepped forward, knowing this moment had been inevitable since he'd first seen her on the doorstep of Cary's home. But when his lips closed on hers and he felt her soft body yield to his, all thoughts of his brother fled, so that the only two people on the beach were Peyton and Mitch.

He had no thought to take it slowly, because he had no thought at all. He pulled her against him only to find that she was already there, pressing against him, kissing him as fervently as he was kissing her.

He didn't have to coax her mouth open because she kissed him with open-mouthed abandon, her head slanting to give him greater access, her tongue tangling with his.

The ocean water was cool but every part of Mitch felt hot, from the heart beating so heavily against her to the erection straining against his pants. She rubbed her lower body against his erection and he groaned, running his hands down her back to cup her buttocks and bring her even closer.

He wanted this woman, wanted her as he had wanted no other. At that moment it didn't matter that she thought he was Cary. It didn't matter that somebody else might be walking the beach and see them. Nothing mattered but this moment and this woman.

"Make love to me, Mitch," Peyton said when he moved his attention from her mouth to her neck. Her head was thrown back in abandon, her blond hair blowing in the breeze.

He put one hand behind her knee, intending to sweep her into his arms, but surprisingly she resisted. He released her at once, putting his hands on both of her shoulders and trying to read what was in her eyes.

"Not on the beach," she whispered. "In the ocean."

The heat flared through him again, more insistent this time. Her hands went to his belt buckle and the zipper of his slacks, although her eyes stayed on his, hot and fathomless. Within moments, she had him free of constraints. He could hardly believe his eyes when she ripped open a condom packet and stuffed the wrapper in the pocket of his slacks before she threw them up on the beach.

"Where did that come from?"

"I believe a nearly naked woman who lures a man into the ocean can never be too prepared," she said, then wiped out Mitch's coherent thought by sheathing his erection.

She took his hands, leading him deeper into the ocean until the water was at his waist. Then she put her arms around his neck, pressed her nearly naked breasts against his still-clothed chest and claimed his mouth before wrapping her legs around his waist.

"Ah, Peyton," he said as she rubbed her lower

body against him. "You really are one extraordinary woman."

The material of her black thong was in the way so he reached down to get rid of the obstacle and felt the fabric tear. The fact had barely registered before she was holding him in her hand, guiding him inside her.

For just a moment, he savored the hot, tight feel of her as their mouths fused, but then he wanted, needed more. He cupped her buttocks, moving her up and down on his shaft.

The sea was so calm that the ocean waves were little more than ripples, but the sound of the water hitting the shore roared in his ears along with his blood. The wind screamed a long, tuneless song. Somewhere above them, a night bird soared in the sky.

Mitch soared, too, caught on a wave of ecstasy that had more to do with the woman he was inside than the act he was committing. He held himself back until he heard her moan and felt her inner muscles contract. Then he slid her up and down a final time until the sounds he heard were coming from his own throat.

His release was swift and all-consuming, as though powerful fireworks had been set off inside his body. The pleasure wracked him, more intense than it had ever been before, more meaningful than it had been with any other woman.

As the remnants of his orgasm shook him and he began to think more clearly, a truth more powerful than the love they'd made slammed into him.

He was falling in love with Peyton.

For a moment, the knowledge buoyed him, filling him with incredible happiness. Then a voice in his head that he didn't want to listen to added a qualifier he had to acknowledge.

He was falling in love with Peyton. *His brother's girl.*

And, because he was falling in love with her, he'd have to come clean about who he was.

And then he'd have to let her go.

"I'd understand if you didn't walk me to the door," Peyton said an hour later as Mitch helped her out of the low-slung Miata. "You really should go home and get out of those wet things."

She cast a meaningful look at his sodden, expensive clothes. His beautiful dark hair was standing in salty spikes after the top-down drive over the Cooper River Bridge, and she spotted grains of sand at the open neck of his shirt. She knew how uncomfortable he must be. Her dress was dry inside and out but it was dusted with sand.

Not that it hadn't been worth it. She'd gladly stand naked on the beach in a wind storm if it meant she could make love to Mitch again.

"I will get out of them," he said. "*After* I walk you to the door."

Peyton was about to offer another protest but it would have been hypocritical. She loved that he insisted on walking her to the door instead of riding off into the night, especially in light of the mind-blowing sex they'd had. It made their intimate encounter more meaningful.

Cary Mitchell, it seemed, had character and depths she'd never dreamed possible. He wasn't the man she'd thought he was mere weeks ago.

She kept her hand in his and together they walked up the stairs to her second-floor apartment. When they reached her door, she opened her purse to search for her key ring.

"How are you going to get inside with no keys?" he asked.

Her hand, which was inside her purse clutching her keys, stilled. She'd forgotten she was supposed to have lost her keys. She snapped the purse shut but couldn't shut out her guilt. She should confess that she'd duped him and hope he'd understand the reason.

"Mitch, I . . ." Her voice trailed off at the crucial moment, because she couldn't make the confession. Not when it might ruin what had been a perfect night.

"I have a spare key over here," she finished.

She bent over at the waist to tip back a flower pot and looked at him out of the corner of her eye while in mid-bend. "Aren't you going to tell me I'll hurt my back if I don't bend at the knees?"

"Why should I say that?" he asked, but his mind didn't seem to be on the question. His mouth was slightly parted, and his eyes had darkened. She realized with a burst of feminine power that he was staring at her breasts.

"Because you're a physical-education major. That's what you usually say."

"Yeah," he said in a low voice, "but not when you're bending over in that dress."

She giggled and stood up, holding the key out triumphantly. She expected him to grab her and kiss her the same devastating way he had on the beach, but instead the corners of his mouth turned downward.

"You need to find somewhere else to keep your spare. The first places a burglar looks are in a flower pot, under a door mat, or on the ledge."

"Ah, but mine was *under* the flower pot, not *in* it."

He took a step forward. "Promise me you'll find another place for the spare. Leave it with your parents or a trusted neighbor, but don't leave it under the flower pot."

His expression was full of a steely determination she'd never seen before, reminding her of something. She studied him and it came to her in seconds. He looked like the actors she'd watched on television cop shows.

"If I didn't know better," she said, smiling slightly, "I'd think you were a cop."

His expression faltered, probably because he was surprised she'd said such a thing.

"Peyton," he said, grabbing her by the upper arms, "there's something I need to tell you."

Whatever it was seemed so important to him that she merely waited in silence, watching a play of emotions she couldn't read cross his strong, handsome face.

"I . . ." He faltered, but again she got the impression he was about to say something crucial. A pregnant moment passed before he whispered the rest of the words in a rough, low voice. "I will never go to the beach again without remembering how beautiful you looked standing there in the surf."

She laughed, the heaviness that had descended over her at his serious mood completely dissipating. She took his face in her hands.

"I don't want to forget anything about tonight either," she said, "but I'm all for making new memories."

Then she kissed him and drew him into the apartment. After that, neither of them spoke another word for a very long time.

Chapter Eighteen

The batter ambled up to the plate from the on-deck circle, looking more like a teenager than an eleven-year-old kid. His arms were tree trunks in the making, his upper lip shadowed by the faintest hint of a mustache, his cleats at least a size eleven. He stood a half head taller than the catcher and a full head taller than the pitcher on the mound.

He was batting cleanup and, appropriately, the bases were loaded. One mighty swing like the solo blast he'd hit earlier in the game and he'd swipe the bases clean. But if the skinny, undersized kid on the mound got him out, the game would be over.

Cary rose from his seat on the bench in the pitching team's dugout and gave three hard hand claps.

"C'mon, Little Bit," Cary yelled to the pitcher. "Remember what we worked on yesterday, buddy."

Little Bit, a.k.a. Jimmy Jacobs, looked over to the dugout, met Cary's eyes, and nodded. He reared back and threw a pitch that sailed over the batter's head and hit the backstop on the fly. Fortunately, the ball bounced directly back to the catcher's glove. None of the base runners advanced.

"Remember to follow through," Cary yelled. "Come on. You can do it, pal."

Cary suffered through another called ball before the plate umpire declared the next two pitches strikes. Casey Jr., which is how Mitch thought of the kid at bat, had yet to take a cut.

"That's it, Little Bit," Cary muttered under his breath. "Point the glove at your target before you throw, pull it back to your heart after you release."

His knuckles were white from gripping the chain-link fence shielding the dugout by the time the next pitch missed high for a ball, bringing the count to three balls and two strikes. The next pitch could decide it all.

Little Bit stepped off the mound and gazed directly at Cary, who thumped his heart twice and gave a thumbs-up signal.

"You can do it, kid," he whispered a second before Little Bit let the pitch fly. Casey Jr. cocked his elbow and took a mighty swing.

"Strike three," the umpire yelled after the batter hit nothing but air.

"Yeah!" Cary roared as he pumped the air with his fist.

Little Bit leaped off the mound, jumping up and down like one of those Mexican beans, as his teammates ran at him from their positions on the field.

After a few moments of wild celebration, the boy extricated himself from the crowd and dashed toward Cary. He was waiting on the sidelines with his arms open wide.

"You did it!" Cary yelled as he swung the kid in an arc.

"No. *We* did it," Little Bit said when he was once again on the ground. "I couldn't throw a strike before you came along."

Cary ruffled the kid's dark hair. "Somebody had to give you a couple of pointers, that's all. You're the man of the hour. Now go over there and shake some hands."

Little Bit ran off to join his teammates, who were congregating along the first-base line to shake hands with the opposing players. Cary got at the end of the line, behind a grinning Sam Johnson.

"Best game we've had this season," he said, slapping palms with Cary.

Sam and Cary proceeded to press the flesh with the boys on the other team, who had won the league championship the season before. Last in line was the other team's coach. He was such a large, imposing man that Cary figured he was Casey Jr.'s father.

"You do realize the only reason we played the bottom of the inning was because league rules allow the home team to get its bats even if it's winning," the other coach said slowly, addressing both Sam and Cary.

Cary grinned. "Yeah, we know."

The other coach narrowed his eyes. "So you know your team lost by two runs?"

"Oh, yeah," Sam said. "We know that, too."

The man shook his head, bafflement stamped on his thick features. "Then why are you celebrating?"

"The ump stopped our last two games in the fourth inning because we were behind by more than ten runs," Sam said. "To us, this is one in the win column."

"As long as you know you're not *real* winners," the other coach mumbled before going off to join his team.

Who said he wasn't a winner?, Cary thought as he spotted the woman in the wild, look-at-me outfit hurrying toward him from the stands. Leeza Drinkmiller wouldn't hang around with a loser.

She would if the loser was impersonating his brother, the voice of his conscience whispered. Ruthlessly, he shut it out and appreciated Leeza's approach.

He'd spent the night after they made love, but hadn't seen her since yesterday morning because he'd committed both to Little League practice and Captain Turk. Now he found that he couldn't take his eyes off her. Her lime-green sleeveless shirt paired with matching capri pants and sandals were almost garish, especially with the Green Monster pinned above her heart, but he couldn't help smiling.

He knew her secret. Underneath her flashy clothes, Leeza wasn't flamboyant or sophisticated. She was a charming mixture of naïveté and spontaneity, a woman whose only fault seemed to be that she didn't know she was perfect exactly the way she was.

And he couldn't tell her. Not without risking everything.

Leeza's worldly, urbane incarnation might indulge in a dalliance with Cary Mitchell. But the real Leeza, the down-to-earth Leeza who spouted strange facts when she was flustered, would want somebody loyal, trustworthy, and dependable.

Like the man he was pretending to be.

"What a great game," she said and he opened his arms. She threw herself into them with the kind of abandon he wished she'd surrender to more often. He grabbed her, swung her around as though she weighed no more than Little Bit, and gave her a resounding kiss on the lips.

She thinks she's kissing your brother, his conscience whispered.

"Shut up," he hissed when he broke off the kiss.

"Excuse me," Leeza said, scrunching up her forehead. "Did you tell me to shut up?"

Hell. He hadn't realized he'd spoken the words aloud.

"Sure did," he said, again moving toward her lips. "I said shut up and kiss me."

The second kiss was as chaste as the first, like a public kiss should be, but nobody had told his hormones that. They were raging, like a rampaging river after a heavy rain.

Trying to keep things light and friendly, he threw an arm around her neck and hugged her to him.

"I'd kiss him, too, if I didn't think my wife would get jealous," Sam said, clapping Cary on the back. To Leeza, he said. "Did you know the kids nicknamed him Dumbledore?"

"Dumbledore? Like the wizard in the Harry Potter books?"

"Exactly," Sam said, chuckling. "He's only been with us for a couple of days, but he's already working his magic on the team."

Cary started to say it wasn't magic, just tried-and-true baseball principles that had been drilled into him during his fourteen years of playing, but then noticed the way Leeza was looking at him.

Was that suspicion in her eyes? Was she wondering how a kid who'd played a few seasons of Little League way back when knew so much about baseball?

"Must be magic," he said, " 'cause I'm not sure what I'm talking about."

"What do you mean by—" Sam said, but he was interrupted by a shout from one of his players, a red-headed kid who refused to take off his baseball hat.

"Hey, Dumbledore," the redhead yelled. He had one hand to his head, as though afraid someone would yank off his hat and expose his hated buzz cut. "You still treating us to ice cream?"

"You bet," Cary yelled back. "Just give me a minute."

"I better go keep peace among the troops 'til you're ready to go." Sam tipped his too-small cap to Leeza. "Nice seeing you again."

"You, too, Sam," Leeza said, then turned back to Cary and smiled. The world immediately seemed like a brighter place.

She's only smiling because she thinks you're the Boy Scout, his conscience taunted. *You were trying to fool yourself that she was more your type than his, weren't you? But now that you know her secret, can't you see she's perfect for him?*

Cary pressed his fingers to his temples, trying to shut out the thoughts. He and Leeza were consenting adults. He hadn't done anything wrong.

Except take her virginity under false pretenses. Except pretend to believe she hadn't been a virgin when you knew damn well that wasn't the case.

What was he supposed to do? Ask why she was putting on an act? Tell her he wasn't Mitch?

Yes, the voice said.

No, a louder voice inside his head screamed. He couldn't do it. Not when she wanted loyal and dependable and he was faithless and irresponsible.

"Are you okay, Grant?" Leeza looked sweetly concerned, making him feel like an idiot for carrying on an imaginary conversation with his blasted conscience.

"Couldn't be better," he said. "Say, why don't you come with us? One of the player's dads owns I Scream for Ice Cream. Kid says his dad has a scream machine by the cash register. You buy an ice cream, he records your scream and plays it back for you."

He thought it was a clever sales gimmick and was pretty sure Leeza did too, but instead of agreeing to accompany them she gave one of her elegant shrugs. As though a place with a scream machine wasn't sophisticated enough for her.

"You go along without me," she said. "I only stopped by the field to see if you were available for dinner."

She made the statement as though she were used to issuing men invitations, but Cary noticed the way her jaw clenched, and he wasn't fooled. Leeza was as nervous as a teenager on her first date. Before he could agree, she forged ahead.

"Did you know that the average person eats about sixty thousand pounds of food in their lifetime?"

"Sixty thousand pounds," he repeated and couldn't help smiling at her. Damn, she was cute. "You don't say."

"I do say," she added pertly. "Did you know that sixty thousand pounds is about the weight of six elephants?"

"Sounds appetizing," he said with a laugh.

"Hey, Dumbledore," Little Bit yelled from across the field. "Are you coming or not?"

"Yeah, yeah," Cary yelled back. "I'm coming."

"You should go," Leeza said, and he saw her swallow. For courage, he figured. "But how about dinner? It'll be my treat."

Her mention of money made Cary remember he had very little of it left, which is why he'd agreed to transport another load of crates to Miami for Captain Turk.

"I can't tonight, Leeza."

He hadn't intended to offer an explanation but her crestfallen expression changed his mind. "I have to go back to Miami on that business I was telling you about."

"You mean on the business you haven't told me about?"

"I can't tell you. It's, um, complicated," he said, although it was really quite simple. She thought she was hanging out with his brother the cop. She wouldn't want to fraternize with a gambler who had a hunch he was transporting illegal goods.

"And you have to do this business at night?"

"Afraid so." Captain Turk had insisted that the nighttime hours were safer. Cary hadn't asked safer for what.

"Dumbledore!" Little Bit yelled again.

Cary looked over his shoulder. The team members had packed up their equipment and looked more impatient than four-year-olds waiting in line to see Santa.

"How about I call you tomorrow?" he asked Leeza.

When Leeza nodded, he bent down and gave her a lingering kiss on the lips before he turned and jogged over to the team.

She thinks your brother is going to call her tomorrow.

He sighed. He'd heard the murmuring of his conscience before, of course, but never in a voice so loud and clear.

How, he wondered, did a man go about getting rid of the voice of reason?

Chapter Nineteen

He should have listened to the voice of reason instead of letting his brother rope him into this impossible scheme, Mitch thought as he watched the little man dance in front of him with his fists raised.

If he remembered correctly, the voice—his very own deep, sensible voice—had originally said no.

"Come on, put 'em up," Stu Funderburk cried. He was a diminutive man who could juke and jive, a Muhammad Ali wanna-be in the body of a jockey. "I can take you."

Mitch glanced around the shabby trailer park, which looked depressing in the gathering gloom of twilight. A light rain had begun to fall, keeping whomever else was home inside, but he had no way of knowing if anyone was watching from their windows.

Or if the man in the green sedan, who had followed him on the drive from Charleston to this community on the outskirts of Summerville, was somewhere in the shadows spying on him.

Mitch had changed his mind about confronting his tail earlier that day when he'd gotten a look at the sedan's license plate. A cop friend in Atlanta was going to run the plate when he had the time. Then, when Mitch knew who he was dealing with, he'd decide on a course of action.

"You afraid of me?" the jockey-sized Ali asked, bouncing on the souls of his miniature feet. "You afraid I'm gonna get a piece of you?"

Ah, geez. One punch from Mitch would probably break Stu Funderburk *into* pieces. Which was pretty much what Gaston Gibbs wanted him to do.

"I'm not gonna hit you," Mitch said in a soft voice, hoping nobody—especially the guy tailing him—overheard.

Funderburk stopped dancing but didn't drop his fists. "What do you mean you're not gonna hit me? You're a debt collector, aren't you?"

"I'm a different kind of debt collector." Mitch nodded toward Funderburk's trailer, in front of which he'd surprised the small man five minutes ago. "Let's go inside and talk about this like gentlemen."

"You expect me to invite the enemy in? Unh unh, no way. You think I don't know what'll happen in there? I might not come out alive."

Mitch let out a breath. This guy was really starting to get on his nerves. "Use your head. If I kill you, Flash doesn't get his money."

"Flash isn't getting his money anyway because I don't have it."

That didn't come as a surprise considering where Funderburk lived. As a cop, Mitch ran into cases like this all the time—down-on-their-luck guys like Stu Funderburk who thought they could get something for nothing through theft or gambling.

"We'll work something out," Mitch said. "I'm authorized to accept a down payment."

Funderburk's eyes narrowed. "You're not supposed to tell me that until you've thrashed me."

"I told you I wasn't going to thrash you." Mitch took a few angry steps toward the other man. He had to make it look good if his tail was watching. "Now let me in."

Five minutes later, he was sitting on a worn sofa in a cramped, dark living room counting out the money Funderburk had given him. It was barely a third of what the man owed.

He rubbed his jaw. "Flash isn't going to be happy about this."

"I knew it," Funderburk shrieked, leaping to his feet and into the Ali stance. "I knew you were going to beat me up."

Out of the corner of his eye, Mitch detected a movement outside Funderburk's window. It was probably Gibbs's flunky, making sure he did the job on Funderburk. Good thing the thick coat of grime on the windows would prevent him from getting a good view of what was going on inside.

"How's your scream?" he asked Funderburk.

"You can't make me scream," Funderburk said. "I'm little, but I'm tough."

Mitch stood up, nearly banging the top of his head on the ceiling of the trailer. He made himself loom, made his eyes mean and his voice rough. "If you don't scream in the next three seconds, I'm gonna come over there and make you."

Funderburk screamed, long, loud, and so shrilly Mitch had to cover his ears. When Funderburk was through, he waited, looking as though he expected Mitch to punish him for eardrum damage.

"What you gonna do now?" Funderburk asked.

"What *I'm* gonna do isn't the issue," Mitch said. "Do you have a pair of crutches and some plaster you can put on one of your legs?"

At about the time Mitch determined the green sedan wasn't following him back to Charleston, Cary's car phone rang. The peeling of the phone made him angry at his brother all over again. What kind of extravagant fool put a phone in a convertible? Didn't he know it was a magnet for car thieves?

With the exception of the other night, when Peyton had cross-circuited his brain and parts beyond so he wasn't thinking clearly, Mitch had kept the convertible top up for safety purposes.

The top was up now, the rain drizzling on the vinyl. His sniffles told him he should have had enough sense to put the top up last night after he and Peyton had made love in the waves. But she'd raised her arms to the sky, declared she loved the feel of the wind in her face and, as usual, he'd taken leave of his senses. Why else had he gone against every honorable instinct he had and made love to his brother's girl?

Keeping his eyes on the road, he rummaged for the phone and lifted the receiver. "Yeah," he said.

"Oh, good, you're there." It was Peyton, her voice reminding him of all the intimate things they'd done to each other. His body temperature shot up ten degrees. Yep, he was a goner over her, all right. Evcn if shc wasn't rightfully his. "I tried you at home and at work. I hope this isn't a bad time."

"Not at all," Mitch said. It had been a bad time thirty minutes ago. Stu Funderburk had crutches but they'd called a half-dozen medical supply stores, on Mitch's cell phone no less, before they located something that would approximate a cast. "What's up?"

"I have a carriage tour in a few minutes so I don't have a lot of time, but I need to tell you I can't meet you for dinner tonight."

Relief hit him as hard as the disappointment. He hadn't been able to get the words out the night before, but he'd promised himself he was going to tell her tonight that he wasn't Cary.

The reprieve was only temporary, but it gave him a few more hours to pretend she'd forgive him.

"I want to meet you," she continued in a silky, sexy voice. "Oh, God, I *want* to meet you. But I can't. Can you come over later?"

"I better not," Mitch said reluctantly. "I have to bartend tonight. I won't get off until after two A.M., and neither of us got much sleep last night."

"You're probably right," she said, her voice thick with disappointment. "I'm spending tomorrow afternoon with my parents but I should be able to get away by five or six. Maybe we can do something after that."

"I'll call you," he said.

"Great," she said and he heard somebody shouting her name from a distance. "Listen, I've got to go. I'm sorry about canceling, but it's important that I meet Gaston tonight to talk about his plans for renovating those buildings."

Alarm skittered through him at the mention of Flash Gorman's more common name. "But—"

He didn't get to finish the sentence. "Hold the horses. I'm coming," she yelled, though obviously not to him. "Sorry, Mitch, but I really do have to go."

The line went dead, leaving him holding the receiver while dread reached out its cold fingers and touched every inch of him.

He was probably being unreasonable. Gibbs was so protective of his public face that Peyton wasn't in any danger from him.

But, on the other hand, Peyton didn't know who Gibbs was or what he was capable of doing. She thought of him as a heroic family friend who out of the goodness of his heart rescued her beloved historic properties from demolition.

Mitch was sure renovating those buildings had

nothing to do with goodness, because Gibbs didn't possess any. If he was involved in a project, it was because there was something in it for him. A substantial profit, most likely.

Mitch squelched the urge to call the carriage company and leave a message that Peyton should not meet G. Gaston Gibbs III tonight or any night.

He'd sound like a jealous lover and he couldn't risk that. He couldn't do anything that would make Gibbs seem like the more reasonable man.

Because the last place he wanted Peyton to head for comfort after he confessed his deception was Gibbs's arms.

"The boss wants to see you in the back," Millie Bellini of the towering hair and the Kilimanjaro breasts told Mitch later that night as she thundered up to the bar. She smiled lasciviously at him with her orange lips, then smacked said lips together.

"I want to see you, too," she added. "Much *more* of you."

Oh, brother, Mitch thought as he finished washing a glass. *Here she goes again.* Millie rested her elbows on the counter and leaned forward. Mitch leaned backward.

"I've got a proposition for you," Millie said.

So what else was new? She'd propositioned him in one way or another every night since he'd started working at Epidermis. Because he suspected his brother enjoyed being a sex object, he made himself keep smiling.

"I'm thinking 'bout having a ladies' night at Epidermis once a month with guys up on stage. You interested?"

"In stripping?" Mitch asked.

"You're cute, honey buns, but nobody's gonna pay to see you unless you take off your clothes."

Mitch's immediate impulse was to refuse but then he had a thought. "When would this be?"

"Not for another three or four weeks," Millie said. "I can't get the acts lined up 'til then."

Three or four weeks? By necessity, this masquerade would be long over by then. Mitch had only taken two weeks off from work, and one of them was already gone. Three or four weeks from now, he'd be back in Atlanta patrolling the streets. Cary, hopefully, would have resumed his life in Charleston.

"Pencil me in," Mitch said. "I'd love to strip for the ladies."

"Really?" Millie's heavily mascaraed eyes widened.

"Really. But I want you to promise me one thing. If I'm not working here anymore, hunt me down and remind me I said I'd strip."

"I will," Millie said, rubbing her hands together. Mitch thought she might be salivating. "I can help you pick out your music. I bet you can do a stand-up number to 'You Sexy Thing'."

"Talk to me about it in a couple of weeks," Mitch said as he moved around the counter and away from the bar. "I won't be able to focus on it until then."

"You mean it?" Millie's voice followed him through the music and the smoke.

"Sure do," he called back absently, wishing he could be there to see the look on Cary's face when Millie told him he'd agreed to do a striptease.

Cary was so unpredictable, though, that he might take off all his clothes and boogie. After what Mitch had discovered about his brother in the past week, he wouldn't put anything past him. None of the things he'd learned, however, had made him any less determined to extract Cary from his latest jam.

He frowned as he approached G. Gaston Gibbs's office at the back of the strip club. Unfortunately, Mitch hadn't made much more progress toward rescuing his brother than he had the first time he'd been summoned to Gibbs's office.

He'd been so busy working the two jobs and dealing with Peyton that he hadn't spent as much time delving into Gibbs's personal affairs as he would have liked. Sure, he'd staked out the man's real-estate office and his home, but he hadn't noticed anything criminal going on.

In fact, Gibbs probably knew more about Mitch's actions than vice versa, which was something the two of them were going to talk about.

Gibbs, however, started talking first.

"Do you have my money?" he asked in his smooth, refined voice when Mitch was barely more than a few steps inside his red-velvet sanctuary.

Gibbs was leaning over a pool table that hadn't been there days before, lining up a shot.

"Sure do," Mitch said, taking the envelope Stu

Funderburk had given him out of his pocket. He waited for the thwack of balls smacking into each other, but the cue ball rolled soundlessly to the other side of the table.

Gibbs didn't seem to notice that the ball had hit nothing but air. He walked around the table and made a show of lining up another shot. This time the cue ball grazed one ball, hit another and sent two more bumping off the cushioned sides of the table. The pockets didn't see any action.

"Only the second shot I've missed all day," Gibbs said before leaning the cue stick against the table.

"I hear they're thinking about remaking *The Hustler,*" Mitch said lazily. "Maybe you could play the part of Minnesota Fats."

Gibbs walked over to Mitch, dislike evident in his small eyes. "If I were you, Mitchell, I'd be careful of what I said."

Mitch bristled. It galled him that this man had snowed Peyton into believing he was a respectable citizen. "And if I were you, I'd be careful of what I did and who I did it with."

Gibbs laughed, which thrust his pointed features into prominence. "Jealousy doesn't become you, Mitchell. Especially because you're fighting a battle you can't win."

"I am winning," Mitch said through clenched teeth.

"Oh, really?" He raised his too-thin eyebrows. "So I suppose the McDowells asked you to the get-together they're having tomorrow on their luxury sailboat? No? Oh, that's right. Counting Peyton and me, there are already four of us. Wouldn't want to have an odd number."

Was he telling the truth? Mitch wondered as the smaller man took the envelope from him and started counting his money. Had Gibbs finagled it so Peyton would spend two days straight with him? Mitch wouldn't put it past either Gibbs or the McDowells.

But it wouldn't matter for long, because Peyton would soon know what kind of a man Gibbs was underneath the smooth exterior. Once Mitch told her he wasn't Cary, he'd explain why the masquerade was necessary. If she gave him the chance.

"Where's the rest of the money?" Gibbs asked, raising hard, mean eyes to Mitch. Once again, he was all business. "I told you to collect at least half of what Funderburk owed."

Mitch shrugged. "I couldn't collect what he didn't have. He said he'd try to get the rest by next Saturday."

"Try?" Gibbs's eyes bore into his. "I don't like the sound of that. If you'd done your job right, he wouldn't have said he'd *try* to get the money. He'd have said he *would* get the money."

"You know I did my job right."

Gibbs walked back to the pool table and leaned against it. He crossed his arms over his chest. "And how do I know that?"

"Vincent Carmichael."

Mitch let the name hang between them while he watched Gibbs for a reaction, but the only expression that crossed the other man's face was one of confusion.

"Is that name supposed to mean something to me?"

"He's the private investigator you hired to have me followed. Has an office west of the Ashley in a strip shopping center. But you know that already, don't you?"

Gibbs let out a short laugh which sounded like a bark. "You think I hired a private dick to follow you? Why on earth would I do that?"

"To see whether I'm carrying out your orders."

"If you bring me back my money, I can tell whether you're carrying out my orders."

"Then maybe you wanted to make sure I made Stu Funderburk sorry he couldn't repay all that he owed."

Gibbs's arms uncrossed. He straightened. He did not look happy. "Are you saying this Vincent Carmichael, this *private investigator,* followed you to Funderburk's place?"

When Mitch nodded, Gibbs muttered an oath. He rubbed his brow with a thumb and two fingers as he crossed the room to his desk and sat down. "What kind of a car does Carmichael drive?"

Mitch told him and he fell into a deeper silence. "I haven't noticed a green car but then I wasn't looking for one," he finally said.

"You think this man is investigating you instead of me? Is that it?"

"Of course he's investigating me. If you weren't working for me, you wouldn't be important enough to follow." Gibbs pointed at Mitch. "I need you to find out if he has anything on me."

"How do you expect me to do that?"

"Break into his office and go through his files."

Mitch put both hands up palms out. "I'm not breaking into anyone's office. That's against the law."

"So is stealing money from the cash register," Gibbs said and paused to let the words sink in. Mitch schooled his expression to remain neutral, but inside he was damning his brother.

"Yeah, I know you've been stealing from me, Mitchell," Gibbs continued. "The only reason I haven't had Millie call the cops is because I've found it handy to have you around. If you cease to be handy, I could change my mind."

"You can't prove I stole from you."

"Do you really think I couldn't get an employee to say she saw you stealing? Do you really want to bet a jail sentence on that?" Gibbs stroked his jaw as he considered him. "Because if you don't break into that office and get those records, that's exactly what you'll be doing."

When Mitch didn't answer, Gibbs opened his desk calendar and flipped through it. "Let's see, it's Saturday night, so that gives you all day tomorrow to figure something out. That way, you can have the information to me by Monday."

"I don't work on Monday."

"You do now."

The notion of breaking and entering was so distasteful to Mitch that he couldn't trust himself to say anything else. He simply turned and started to leave.

"Oh, and Mitchell," Gibbs's voice trailed after him, making him stop in his tracks. "If you have any notion of telling Peyton what I do when I'm not buying and selling real estate, I'd get rid of it right now."

Mitch turned and felt as though he was staring into the face of evil.

"If anyone in Charleston society, especially anyone so prominently associated with the Preservation League, got wind of my, uh, extracurricular activities, I'd have to make sure they didn't spread ugly gossip."

A chill settled over Mitch, because it occurred to him that this man was capable of anything. "Is that a threat?"

"A threat?" Gibbs leaned back in his desk chair. "I prefer to think of it as advice on how to keep someone you care about safe."

Mitch whirled and walked out of the office, closing the door behind him with a resounding bang. Now it was himself, and not Cary, who was in a jam.

He wasn't sure how to get out of it, but he was sure of one thing. For Peyton's sake, he had to keep quiet about who he was until Gibbs was safely behind bars.

Chapter Twenty

The sun had barely begun its fiery descent into the horizon, but that didn't matter to the throng that had converged on Mallory Square for the nightly sunset celebration.

The party was already in full swing.

Tourists rubbed elbows with souvenir vendors, street entertainers, and locals out to make a buck selling conch fritters and cold beers from the backs of mobile carts.

Lizabeth kept her hand securely in Grant's as they wove a path into the heart of the square. A sense of anticipation pulsed below the surface of the crowd, anticipation that Lizabeth could identify with.

But Lizabeth was looking forward to something far more exciting than a sunset, no matter how glorious. She was impatient to dive back in bed with Grant and make love with him again. And again. And again.

A shadow fell over them. Lizabeth looked up to see a gorgeous face made up so expertly she'd have guessed she was looking at a supermodel if the body that went with the face weren't about six feet three and two hundred forty pounds.

The drag queen didn't make any secret of the fact he was eyeing Grant instead of Lizabeth. He took a pull from his cigarillo and blew out a plume of blue-gray smoke before finally turning his attention to Lizabeth.

"Some girls have all the luck," he said with a petulant frown before thundering away on a giant pair of women's platform shoes.

"Remind me not to come here alone," Grant said with a raised eyebrow as the drag queen pushed his way through the crowd.

Lizabeth giggled. She knew giggling was undignified but she couldn't help herself. Everything about the last few days seemed magnified. Comments struck her as funnier, the sun seemed brighter, the air sweeter.

And it was all because Grant Mitchell was her lover.

As little as two weeks ago, as she'd sat at the library in Richmond staring into a computer screen, the prospect of any lover seemed a distant possibility. Let alone Grant Mitchell, the star of her youthful daydreams.

"What are you smiling about?" Grant asked.

"Nothing," she fibbed.

Quick as a cheetah, he turned her into his arms and gave her a swift kiss that had her toes curling in her safari-print sandals.

"What was that for?" she asked when he was through and she had her breath back.

His blue eyes twinkled. "Just thought I'd give you something to smile about."

She giggled again as he put an arm around her and steered her through the crowd. When she'd had her desperate crush on him in high school, she'd never have guessed he was the sort of man who'd kiss a woman in public.

Lizabeth had only known Grant from afar, but he'd seemed much too straitlaced for public displays of affection. He'd seemed like a man destined to become, well, a cop.

She'd been attracted to his air of seriousness when she was a teenager, but now that she was an adult his playful side most appealed to her. She only wished he'd show her more than glimpses of it.

They stopped beside a small crowd that had gathered to watch a short, stout, bearded man who resembled an undersized sumo wrestler. He was wearing a black T-shirt and shorts and loudly proclaiming, "I am the Balancing Bob. You give it to me, I balance it."

A ponytailed young woman in a headband, tank top, and long, tight shorts offered him her bicycle. Balancing Bob didn't hesitate. He had two volunteers heave the bicycle overhead by its wheels, then proceeded to balance the bike from a contraption he held in his mouth. He extolled the crowd to cheer him by raising his hands.

"Is magnificent, eh?" asked Balancing Bob when the bicycle was no longer airborne. He was breathing hard, telling Lizabeth that balancing was as hard as it looked. "I balance a motorcycle, an oven, a kitchen table. Who has something else I balance?"

Grant laughed as he put a few dollars in Balancing Bob's tip can, then slung his arm around Lizabeth again. By mutual consent, they moved away from the balancer and toward another small crowd gathered in front of yet another street performer.

This one was wearing something even brasher than Lizabeth's safari-print mini dress: a billowing purple shirt paired with yellow-and-purple striped pantaloons that ended at his knees. He'd paired the whole shebang with yellow knee socks.

"Nice outfit," Grant whispered. Before Lizabeth could giggle again, she put her hand against her mouth to stifle the sound. Enough giggling was enough.

With rare panache, the street performer juggled a trio of two-toned clubs that mimicked the colors of his outfit. Double flips, triple flips, between the legs, behind the back, four clubs instead of three. He could do it all.

"I'd regale you with passing tricks now," the juggler said, tossing back his mane of long, blond hair, "but my partner spent all afternoon at Sloppy Joe's and passed out an hour ago. So I'll get on with the show unless . . ." He cast a laughing glance around the audience, "anyone here can juggle like me."

Lizabeth's hand shot up as she remembered a captivating boy at a long-ago school talent show. "My boyfriend can juggle," she announced.

Grant's shocked blue eyes swung to her face, probably because she'd called him her boyfriend. How unsophisticated was that?

"I would have called you my lover, but I wanted to keep it G-rated," she whispered an aside to him. "There are kids around."

Wearing a disbelieving look, the juggler pointed to Grant. His narrow nose pointed skyward. "You claim you can juggle like the master?"

"I'm not claiming any such thing." Grant said, shaking his head in an adorably modest way.

"I did not think so. Juggling takes great skill and coordination, not to mention a flair for entertaining." The juggler puffed out his purple-draped chest. "Many pretenders brag of their so-called juggling expertise but few can deliver."

Lizabeth stepped forward, her hackles raised. Who gave this arrogant juggle-it-all a monopoly on tossing things in the air and catching them?

"Grant can deliver," she stated firmly.

"Leeza, what are you doing?" Grant tugged at her hand, trying unsuccessfully to draw her back to his side. "I *can't* deliver."

She didn't miss the frantic note in his voice but that was probably because he was shy about showing off his talent. But she'd seen him juggle five balls at once and flip clubs with the best of them. He could teach this bigheaded juggler a lesson.

She gave him an encouraging look over her shoulder. "Don't be modest. I know you can do it."

"How can you know that?" he asked, but Lizabeth didn't have time to tell him how awed she'd been as she sat in the darkened auditorium watching his unexpected talent.

The juggle-it-all was laughing at them. "I do not believe this man is a juggler."

Lizabeth raised her chin and jerked a thumb at Grant. "I'd put his juggling up against your juggling any day."

"Okay," the juggler said. "You're on."

Lizabeth turned to Grant, who looked a little sick. She felt a flash of guilt for pushing him into performing, but it vanished when she heard the juggler's lingering laughter.

"You heard him," she said. "You're on."

"But I don't want to be on," Grant said.

"You have to be on," she whispered. "I told him how well you can juggle."

"I'm still trying to figure out why you told him that."

"Because I saw you at that talent show in high school. You were amazing."

An emotion crossed Grant's face that Lizabeth figured was resignation. But when he spoke, his voice sounded pained.

"That's right," he said. "How could I have forgotten? Wouldn't expect it from good old Grant. But I can juggle. Who would have believed it?"

She squeezed his hand. "I know you're shy about

doing it in front of this crowd, but would you please juggle? For me?"

He let out a long, soft sigh. Finally, he nodded.

Lizabeth clapped, anticipating the show and the look on the juggler's face when he got a load of Grant's talent. She lifted her lips and kissed his cheek. "You won't regret this," she said.

"Oh, yes, I will," Grant muttered before he joined the egotistical juggler in the center of the circle. "What do I do?"

"Catch these." The juggler picked up three brightly colored clubs and tossed one of them to Grant, putting a spin on it that made it rotate three hundred sixty degrees in the air. Then he prepared to throw the second.

"Show him your stuff, Grant," Lizabeth yelled when the first club was still hurtling toward him.

Grant started on a high note. He caught the first club in his left hand and transferred it to his right in time to catch the second club. But when the third came hurtling toward him, he dropped all three.

"I'm a little out of practice," Grant said.

Lizabeth frowned as Grant bent down to pick up the fallen clubs. What was going on? He was an excellent juggler. She'd seen it with her own besotted eyes.

The juggler with the silly pants took the clubs from him. "Perhaps we should try something simpler," he said with a frosty air.

He threw a club that didn't flip it all. Grant nabbed the first one and got it airborne but made the mistake of watching it while the second club was coming toward him. The second club struck him in the forehead.

"Ow," Grant said.

"I was right," the juggler yelled. "This man can't juggle."

"Yes, he can," Lizabeth spoke up. "He's just rusty."

"Yeah, I'm just rusty," Grant said as he rubbed his brow.

The juggler strode over to his box of supplies, pulled out three juggling bags and tossed them to Grant. "Then let's see you juggle these."

"How hard can it be?" Lizabeth heard Grant mutter before he flung the bags into the air. For a few precious moments, he kept all three of them rotating. Then, one by one, with Grant making unsuccessful lunges, they crashed to the pavement.

"Ha," the juggler shouted. "He's an impostor."

Lizabeth stood stock still, gazing at the man with whom she was halfway to falling in love as the juggler's words pierced her consciousness.

An impostor, he'd called Grant.

Grant gave her a wary smile, waved apologetically to the booing crowd, and sauntered back to Lizabeth's side. He flung his arm around her shoulders. "It's like you said, I'm out of practice."

But as they rejoined the milling crowd, Lizabeth was no longer reveling in the excitement of the night. She was thinking about why Grant couldn't juggle. And why she kept seeing flashes of a different man under his surface. And how somebody who hadn't played baseball since Little League could turn a team of losers into instant contenders.

The scenario that occurred to her seemed impossible, but she asked the question anyhow.

"Grant, how old is your brother Cary?"

His smile appeared false around the edges. "What does age matter?"

"How old is he?" she persisted.

Just when she thought he wasn't going to answer, he said, "Twenty-eight."

"Aren't you twenty-eight?"

His Adam's apple jumped before he gave her that charming, carefree smile of his. "We're both twenty-eight. We're twins."

And then Lizabeth's theory was no longer only a theory. Because in that moment she knew that the man she'd made love with, the man she'd been *falling in love with,* wasn't Grant Mitchell.

It was his identical twin brother, Cary, the irresponsible former baseball star.

"Why are you asking about my brother?" asked Grant, who wasn't really Grant at all.

She stared at him, the answer frozen on her lips. Why was Cary Mitchell pretending to be his brother Grant? It made about as much sense as his frequent trips to Miami. Maybe he was on an undercover mission where secrecy was all important. She frowned. That didn't compute, either. Grant was the cop, not Cary.

"Leeza, did you hear me?" he asked. "Why did you ask about Cary?"

Tell him, Lizabeth thought. *Tell him you know*

he's an impostor, exactly as the juggler claimed.

But she couldn't make herself say the words. Not when she didn't know why he was making those suspicious trips to Miami. Not when she herself was pretending to be somebody she wasn't.

"No reason but curiosity," she said, resolving to satisfy hers by following him when he disappeared later that night on another one of his forays.

She recognized the relief on his face before he drew her to him, kissed her on top of the head and pointed to the setting sun.

"It's dropping," he said.

The sunset started exactly like the one they'd seen the other night from the cruise ship, with the glowing sun majestic against a red and orange sky. The night was spectacular, warm and clear with but a single cloud in the sky.

"No, no, no!" someone yelled. A sea of disappointed voices soon joined in. From somewhere nearby, a young girl burst into tears.

Because that single cloud drifted nearer and nearer the sun until it completely obscured the sunset.

"Oh, well," the man who wasn't Grant said amidst the groans of the crowd. "We'll see lots of other sunsets together."

But Lizabeth didn't believe him.

It was as if the cloud was hanging over them, casting an ominous shadow.

Cary heaved another crate into the trunk of his brother's SUV, trying to shut off his brain so he wouldn't worry about what was inside the thick wood.

It was no use. After the sunset they hadn't seen, Leeza had asked why he couldn't spend the rest of the evening with her.

He'd wanted to tell her the truth, especially because he was starting to feel rotten about passing himself off as Mitch, but he'd dodged the question. Just as he'd dodged near disaster earlier that night when Leeza had almost guessed he wasn't the man he claimed to be.

He doubted Leeza would forgive him for impersonating his twin, but he was positive she wouldn't condone the way he was smuggling crates to Miami.

He gulped as it struck him that smuggling was the word for what he was doing. The worst part of it was that he didn't know what he was smuggling.

"You swear these crates don't contain drugs?" he asked Captain Turk, who was bringing the last of the cargo from the USS *Surprise.*

"You insult me," Turk said, his breath coming hard from exertion. "I told you before, man. Turk and his crew don't do drugs."

Turk settled the crate inside the nearly full trunk, and Cary heard something clatter. If not drugs, he wondered, what could be inside the boxes? Cuban cigars wouldn't clatter. Bottles of Cuban liquor would most likely clink. He considered illegal arms, but rejected the idea. Turk would be smuggling arms into Cuba, not out of it.

"What's inside the crates?" he heard himself ask the question he swore he'd never ask.

Turk drew himself to his full height, which was still six inches shy of Cary's. The wind was kicking up from the Gulf, but Turk's hair—or was that a toupee?—didn't so much as rustle. His chartreuse tunic had a ghostly blue gleam in the moonlight.

"Hey, man, you want the money, you keep quiet. The deal was *no questions.* The less you know, the better."

Turk was right. If Cary didn't know what he was helping to smuggle, it wasn't really smuggling. Just as he hadn't really stole money from Flash Gorman because it wasn't stealing if the money was dirty.

Ha!

Cary recognized the sound of his conscience, laughing at him.

"You understand about keeping your mouth shut?" Turk asked and Cary nodded, although he didn't understand what was going on at all.

"Good," Turk said, then instantly changed from resolute to weird. "I've been meaning to ask you. Don't you think it would be cool if there really were Press-on warriors in the galaxy?"

"Don't you mean Klingons?" Cary asked.

"Nah," Turk said in an annoyed voice. "Klingons were in that other show."

"Oh, right," Cary said absently.

"I bet the Press-ons could keep the ozone layer from thinning," Turk said and then droned on about a race of ozone-eating aliens.

Cary was no longer listening. His mind was still

on the crates and whatever was inside them. And on what would happen if he got caught transporting them.

He cast a paranoid glance around the boat landing and his attention snagged on something at the edge of the bushes. Something that had a weird green glow in the moonlight. He squinted, picking out a speck of red in the center of the greenish gleam.

Then, just like that, the glimmer of red was gone.

But Cary heard rustling, followed by the not-so-distant sound of a car engine, and he knew that someone had been watching them.

Someone wearing an ugly brooch of an octopus with a bright ruby-red eye.

Chapter Twenty-one

Peyton massaged her temples as she waited for the red light leading from the City Marina to Lockwood Boulevard to change. The massaging wasn't any more effective than the sea breeze that had billowed the sails of her parents' luxurious boat.

Her headache persisted. It had bloomed during an evening spent trying to ignore the way her mother was pushing Gaston Gibbs at her. Peyton's throbbing head was partly her own fault. She should have been suspicious when her mother had dabbed prettily at her eyes, claiming she didn't understand why Peyton couldn't spend all day Sunday with her parents rather than just part of it, especially when they were planning a sail.

She should have figured out that Amelia McDowell would finagle it so that Gaston was on the sailboat with them while Mitch was on shore.

Peyton checked her watch to discover that it was nearly midnight, which she'd claimed was too late to join Gaston for a drink, but seemed like a fine time to come calling at her lover's door. A few minutes with Mitch should be enough to get rid of her headache. She smiled. Especially if they spent those minutes in bed.

A flash of red caught her eye and she glanced up to see a Miata traveling north on Lockwood Boulevard. The top was up, which made her think Mitch wasn't the driver. Until she caught a glimpse of a profile so stunning it made her pulse skitter. Yes, it was Mitch all right.

She reached for her cell phone to call his car phone, only to realize she didn't have it with her. The light turned green and she swiftly made the decision to follow him. Wherever her lover was going, that's where she wanted to be.

By the time she reached the Ashley River Bridge, the Miata was about five car lengths ahead. Anybody driving at a decent clip would have lost her, but Mitch had developed a strange penchant lately for going only the speed limit.

He'd done a lot of strange things lately, she thought a few minutes later as his car veered off Savannah Highway onto a darkened side street. Not the least of which was taking a midnight drive by himself.

By the time she maneuvered her own car into the turn, she recognized the neighborhood. It was more commercial than residential, with a warehouse of some sort on the left and a strip shopping center she'd visited a few times on the right. The road led to a dead end, which brought up the possibility that Mitch had taken a wrong turn.

But then where was he? She pulled over to a curb, keeping her car idling while she wondered why she couldn't see any tail lights. And what Mitch could be doing here.

Her headlights caught a man in dark clothing walking around the corner of the warehouse. He shrank into the shadows but not before Peyton saw that it was Mitch.

Joy bubbled inside her, making her temporarily forget her questions. She smiled, beeped her horn, and shut off the car. Then she was running across the street to greet Mitch, who seemed frozen in place.

"Peyton? What are you doing here?" he asked before she reached him.

"This," she said and launched herself into his arms. They came around her, his hands fastening at her waist while she pulled his head down and kissed him.

The headache immediately eased as now-familiar sensations assaulted her—the feel of his thick, silky hair; his clean scent; the intoxicating heat that hit her when he returned her kiss.

Even though the passion that flared between them was no longer unexpected, she was still dazed by it. She wondered how she had the strength to remain standing when he finally broke off the kiss, set her from him, and leaned his forehead against hers.

"That was an unexpected pleasure," he said, his breaths coming as rapidly as hers. She laughed.

"It's the only pleasure I've had all night. I spotted your car when I was leaving the marina so I followed you to see what you were up to." She leaned back and gazed into his face, which was cast in shadows. "What *are* you up to?"

She saw his hesitation and wondered at it. "I was taking a walk."

"In this neighborhood? At midnight?"

He shrugged his broad shoulders. "I needed a change of scenery."

She indicated his clothing, which was unremittingly black. "Walking alongside the road when you're dressed like that isn't a good idea. Cars won't be able to see you."

"There aren't many cars out at midnight."

"Sure there are. There's one now," Peyton said as a dark-colored vehicle pulled onto the street. When it got closer, she saw that it was a green sedan.

"Oh, no," Mitch said.

"Oh, yes," Peyton exclaimed at almost the same time. She disentangled herself from his embrace and headed for the car at a quick trot.

"Peyton, don't," Mitch shouted, the puzzling words coming from close behind her. Don't what? Chase after the car? She wouldn't have to if the driver hadn't sped up at her approach.

"Hey in there, slow down," she yelled. She

rapped a tat-tat-tat on the driver's side window as she jogged alongside the car, which was rapidly running out of road.

"Get away from there, Peyton!" It was Mitch again, shouting another nonsensical order. He grabbed her arm, presumably to stop her, but she'd already stopped because she and the car had reached the dead end.

"Really, Mitch." She rolled her eyes at him before transferring her attention to the car. The window rolled down and she leaned forward.

"I thought that was you," she said, beaming at the driver. Even in the darkness, she could detect his five o'clock shadow. He often joked that he had more hair on his lower face than on his head, which was covered with his customary fedora.

"Peyton," he said with a nod.

"You know this man?" Mitch was so close it seemed as though he were standing guard over her. His protective instincts were sweet, but unnecessary.

"I wouldn't have been chasing his car if I didn't know him," Peyton stated the obvious. "Mitch, this is Vincent Carmichael, my uncle. Uncle Vincent, this is Cary Mitchell."

Uncle Vincent, who was usually so polite he did Miss Manners proud, grunted a greeting. Mitch did likewise, leaving Peyton to fill in the conversation.

"Uncle Vincent's my mother's brother," Peyton explained to Mitch. Her mother's black-sheep brother, but she didn't need to delve into that during a midnight curbside conversation. "He has an office around the corner in that strip shopping center."

She beamed at her uncle, trying to communicate that she was proud of his profession even if her mother thought it undignified. "He's a private detective."

"Is that right?" Mitch asked in a considering tone. He put his hands on the top of the car and leaned down to peer at Uncle Vincent. Neither man looked happy. "I wondered why you were following me. Now I have the answer."

"Following you?" Peyton interjected, whirling to face Mitch. "Uncle Vincent's not following you." She whirled back to her uncle. "Tell Mitch you're not following him, Uncle Vincent."

The damning silence coming from the car spoke volumes, and Peyton felt her jaw drop. So it was true? "But why would you be following Mitch?" she asked.

Again her uncle didn't answer, instead pretending great interest in readjusting his wire-rimmed glasses.

"My guess is that your parents hired him," Mitch said.

"My parents?" Peyton shook her head, not able to make sense of it. Her mother barely tolerated her own brother, but her father. . . .

She shoved Mitch aside so she had better access to her uncle. "Did my father hire you to follow Mitch, Uncle Vincent?"

"No," he said, but the word lacked conviction. Anger streamed through Peyton, like lava from an erupting volcano. She reached through the window and grabbed her uncle by his shirt front. "Tell me the truth, Uncle Vincent. Did my father hire you?"

"No," he choked out, his hands going to her wrists. She held tight, her anger fueling her strength.

"Peyton," Mitch said, "maybe you should let him go."

"Not until he tells me the truth," Peyton said, shaking him.

"It wasn't your father. It was your mother," Uncle Vincent said, gurgling. "Now will you let go of me?"

She released his shirt front as she let the information sink into her stunned brain. Her mother might not consider Uncle Vincent's profession respectable, but she'd gone to him to dig up dirt on her daughter's lover.

"Of all the dirty, underhanded tricks," she muttered, turning hurt eyes toward her uncle. "How could you do this to me?"

Uncle Vincent rubbed his brow and sighed. "I needed the cash, honey. And Amelia said it was for your own good. I didn't mean to hurt you."

Peyton swiped at her damp eyes, determined not to let any tears fall. How could her mother and uncle have teamed up on her this way? Without another word, she pivoted and headed down the street for her car.

"Peyton, stop," Mitch called but she kept walking. He reached the car door seconds after she'd settled herself behind the driver's seat. She pressed the button that automatically rolled down the window.

"Where are you going?" he asked gently.

"I don't know," she confessed. "What I should do is wake up my mother and give her hell."

"Are you going to?"

"Not tonight," she admitted, inwardly cursing the ingrained good breeding that wouldn't allow her to pound on her parents' door in the wee hours of the morning.

"Good," he said, reaching into the car and cupping her cheek. In an intangible way, she immediately felt better.

"Don't you want me to give her hell?"

The corners of his mouth lifted. "I sure do, but I'd rather you do it tomorrow."

"Why's that?"

He moved his hand from her cheek to her lips and traced them with a delicate touch that had her shuddering in reaction.

"I have other plans for you tonight," he said before he lowered his head, ducked inside the car window, and gave her a gentle kiss that made her want to weep.

"Follow me?" he asked when he drew back.

The knowledge that she would follow him to hell and beyond hit her hard, but not as hard as another truth. With the words stuck in her throat, all she could do was nod.

"Good," he said, his face creasing into that devastating smile that flipped her insides upside down. "I'm parked behind the warehouse. Wait here until

I get the car and then I'll see you at my place."

He turned and she wanted to call him back, wanted to blurt out her realization. But it was too new, too precious, too extraordinary. She hugged the knowledge to herself, savoring it.

Confronting her mother could wait until tomorrow.

Tonight was reserved for Mitch, the man she'd only now discovered that she loved.

Amelia McDowell took a sip of her mint julep, crossed a silk-clad leg and gave her daughter an unhappy look. "Honestly, darling, I thought you understood that you and your father are the most important people in the world to me. I would never do anything to deliberately hurt either of you."

She and Peyton were sitting on the elegant verandah that wrapped around the second story of the McDowell home and provided an excellent view of the Charleston harbor. Beyond them, white sails billowed in the breeze against the night sky.

When Peyton had showed up at the house after her shift at the carriage company, wanting to talk, her mother had insisted they do so over cocktails. But Peyton's drink, another of the mint juleps she couldn't bring herself to tell her mother she detested, sat neglected on a wicker end table. For the first time in memory, Peyton was tempted to take a swig of the hated liquid.

"You should be grateful you have a mother who cares enough to look out for you," Amelia continued.

"I have a mother who hired her brother to spy on my boyfriend," Peyton said, careful not to show her anger. Her mother and countless hours of etiquette training had taught her never to exhibit wrath.

"Your boyfriend?" Her mother's expertly made-up eyes looked pained. "A few weeks ago, you told me you two were casually dating. And now you're calling him your boyfriend?"

Peyton hesitated, knowing her mother wasn't ready to hear she loved Mitch. She hadn't yet told the man himself, but she'd showed him as they gave themselves to each other the night before.

"Our relationship has taken a turn for the better," she said.

"Oh, dear. I was afraid you two were getting too close too fast." Her mother raised her perfectly groomed eyebrows. "Don't you understand that's why I had to hire your uncle? If Mitch had been from Charleston, there wouldn't have been a need. But we don't know anything about him. Somebody needed to check up on him."

"Mitch can tell me whatever I need to know," Peyton said while she struggled to hold onto her temper.

"But the kinds of things your uncle uncovered are not subjects he's going to be eager to discuss," she said.

Peyton squared her shoulders. "Save your breath, Mother. I'm not interested in hearing what Uncle Vincent found out."

Her mother laid a manicured hand on her arm

and sighed. Fine lines showed on her usually smooth face, making Peyton realize that however misguided her intentions, her mother truly did want what was best for her.

"Oh, darling, you really should hear what's in your uncle's report. Vincent may not be very good at tailing people but he is good at finding the truth. I know it won't be easy for you, especially with Mitch being such a handsome young man, but I'll help you through it."

"Mitch is as handsome inside as out," Peyton declared stubbornly.

"I'm sure you think so, dear. And I don't blame you, really I don't. How could your head not be turned by such a good-looking, charming man? The fact that Mitch is so handsome is one of the reasons I had your uncle look into his affairs. And thank goodness I did."

Her mother took a breath, giving Peyton the opening she needed. Interrupting was impolite, but speaking up before the other person finished their train of thought wasn't quite so grave a sin.

"Mother, I've already told you I don't want to hear what Uncle Vincent found out about Mitch." She folded her arms across her chest. "I trust him."

Her mother took another swallow of her mint julep before setting down the glass, as though fortifying herself. "Then you know about his second job?"

"Of course I do." Even though Peyton did trust Mitch, she was relieved her mother hadn't thrown out a zinger that caught her unawares. "He's a bartender at a club in North Charleston."

"Epidermis," her mother said.

"Excuse me?"

"Epidermis is the name of the club."

Peyton nodded as though that didn't come as a surprise, but her feeling of dread was so powerful she felt as though she'd stepped from the sunlight into the gloom.

"So it doesn't bother you that he's around all those naked women night after night?" her mother asked.

Peyton closed her eyes briefly, because she'd known what sort of club Epidermis was the moment her mother had provided the name. Why hadn't Mitch ever mentioned he bartended at a strip club?

"Of course it doesn't bother me," she managed to answer.

Her mother looked confused. "So you're fine with him being around Debbie Darling?"

All Peyton could manage was a shrug, because her mother obviously knew something she didn't. That Debbie Darling was a stripper was evident. Her relationship with Mitch wasn't.

Her mother shook her head and put a hand to her frosted blond hair. "Oh, Peyton. I don't think you should be this understanding, especially since Mitch didn't stop sleeping with her until about three weeks ago. You were already dating him by then, weren't you?"

Bile rose in Peyton's throat while her gut

churned. It couldn't be true. The man she loved wouldn't sleep with a stripper, especially not while he was dating her.

"I don't believe you," she said.

"Oh, darling, why would I lie to you? I'd rather you choose a man other than Mitch, but I'm not blind to how you feel about him. Telling you this hurts me, too." Her mother rose, smoothing the lines of her elegant silk pantsuit. "I'll get your uncle's report. There are other things you need to know."

Before disappearing into the main part of the house, her mother reached out and stroked Peyton's shoulder, as though she thought her daughter needed comforting.

Peyton stared into the night-dark sky, thinking about what she'd learned. A part of her yearned to reject the news, but another part wanted to know why Mitch hadn't confessed that he worked at a strip club.

Glancing down at her watch, she saw that it was past nine. That meant Mitch was already at work with the naked women. Whom she was sure he never touched.

She bit her lip as she remembered that little more than a week had passed since she'd impulsively hopped out of her carriage, stranding her group of tourists as she'd stalked to Mitch's door, ostensibly to break up with him.

She'd believed him to be self-centered, egotistical, and inconsiderate, exactly the kind of man who might dally with a stripper.

But instead of breaking off their relationship, she'd fallen in love with him. And the man she loved wouldn't cheat on her. She brightened, because there was a way she could prove it.

She went back into the house and nearly ran down the stairs in her eagerness to put her plan in motion. Her hand was on the doorknob when her mother realized she was leaving.

"Peyton." Her mother descended the stairs leading to the foyer, waving Uncle Vincent's report. "I've got the report, darling. Please don't leave until you read it."

"I'm sorry, Mother, but I've got to go," Peyton answered as she opened the heavy oak door and slipped into the night. Before she closed the door, she heard her mother's parting question.

"What could possibly be more important than reading the report?"

"Finding out what's fact and what's fiction," Peyton answered aloud before she got into her car, called information on her cell phone, and asked for the address of Epidermis.

Then she went off in search of the truth.

Chapter Twenty-two

G. Gaston Gibbs III tapped the side of his nose as he regarded Mitch from his seat on the leather armchair in the corner of his office. The room was so quiet it was difficult to believe that only a few feet away women were taking off their clothes to clamorous music and loud whistles.

"You're saying I was right? That Vincent Carmichael is investigating me?" Gibbs asked.

Mitch nodded once, feeling not the least bit guilty for lying. He could have confessed that he himself was the target of Carmichael's investigation, but he wanted to shake things up. Who knew what might lead to the evidence he needed to go to the police about Gibbs?

"Where are the reports?" Gibbs asked.

"I already told you. I'd located the file when I

heard someone coming. I had to get out of there fast or risk getting caught."

Flash let out a harsh, angry breath. "Why didn't you take the file with you?"

"It was too risky. If I'd gotten caught, Carmichael would have known you sent me."

"And you're saying you didn't see enough of the file to know who hired him?"

"I didn't see much of anything," Mitch said, watching Gibbs carefully. Why didn't the man ever give anything away? "Just your name and a couple notations about money laundering and bookmaking."

"Bookmaking?" Gibbs gave a harsh laugh and got up from his chair. He paced the office. "Are you sure that's all you saw?"

What the heck, Mitch thought. It was a shot in the dark, but he might as well give it a try. "I was in a hurry, but there might have been something in there about drugs."

Gibbs stopped pacing. His expression turned to stone and he rubbed the back of his neck. "I don't like the sound of this," he muttered, then looked up so quickly Mitch thought he heard his head snap. "I'm going to need you to take care of Carmichael."

Take care of him?

Mitch's heart pounded, a sound he hoped the tape recorder he'd concealed under his shirt didn't pick up. If he could get Gibbs to say what he really meant, Cary was off the hook.

"I don't know what you mean by that," he said.

"Then you're not too bright." Gibbs fixed him with a glare, driving home to Mitch that a lack of intelligence wasn't one of the man's faults.

"Maybe not," Mitch said, praying he wasn't stretching his luck, "but I still need to know what you mean. Do you want me to break a leg? An arm? What?"

Gibbs walked across the room until he was less than a foot away. Mitch braced himself, expecting the other man to rip open his shirt and expose the taping device. Mitch could smell brandy on the other man's breath when he moved his face close.

"Just take care of him," Gibbs hissed.

Great, Mitch thought sarcastically as he processed the order to do away with Peyton's uncle. *What more could possibly go wrong?*

Three quick raps on the door sounded before it opened and Millie Bellini stuck her head inside the office.

"Sorry 'bout interrupting, boss, but I need Mitch. Some lady's backstage upsetting the strippers."

Gibbs didn't bother to veil his irritation. "Then why don't you get the bouncer?"

"He called in sick. Besides, Mitch'll want to handle this." She frowned like a child whose candy had been confiscated. "The lady says she's his girlfriend."

"I don't know what the problem is." Peyton stood in the dressing room with her hands on her hips, surveying the group of strippers in varying stages of dress. Make that *undress*. "All I want to know is which one of you is Debbie Darling."

"And we want to know why you're askin'," said a willowy redhead who was wearing the briefest tuxedo Peyton had ever seen. It consisted of a G-string, pasties, collar, and cuffs. "We can't be too careful."

"Careful about what?" Peyton asked.

Nobody answered. One of the strippers took out a jar and applied shimmering gold glitter to her stomach and legs. Another fiddled with her flashing belly-button light. Finally, a voluptuous blonde in a leopard-print dress so sheer her breasts were visible took pity on her.

"Every so often, we get a crazy-jealous woman who comes looking for us," the blonde said. "We gotta watch our backs."

"But I'm not a crazy-jealous woman," Peyton denied. "I came here to prove my boyfriend didn't sleep with one of you, not that he did."

The blonde laughed. "Not bloody likely."

"Who's your boyfriend, honey?" The question came from the redhead in the tuxedo.

"Cary Mitchell, the bartender."

The redhead's smile faded. She pulled on a pair of strappy black sandals that added at least four inches to her height and strutted across the room without an ounce of self-consciousness. Then again, with a body like hers, why should she be self-conscious?

"You mean Cary Mitchell, the *snake.*" She gazed down at Peyton with what looked like pity. "I'd compare notes about how he is in bed, sugar, but the audience is out there clamoring to see Debbie's darling new act."

Debbie Darling pivoted with as much grace as a runway model and headed for the stage on her stiletto heels. Peyton's hand went to her heart, which felt as though it had been stomped on.

Mitch wrenched open the front door of Epidermis and headed for the parking lot, nearly felling a tree of a man who was on his way inside the club.

"What's your problem, buster?" the man growled. Mitch wasn't a small man, but this guy had biceps as big around as Mitch's thighs and a snarl meaner than a junkyard dog's.

This isn't my night, Mitch thought. First Gibbs had commanded him to put a hit on Peyton's uncle, then one of the other strippers had told him that Peyton knew about the way Cary had been hitting on Debbie Darling, and now he was probably going to get hit by this behemoth.

Not to mention that he'd needed to do some fast talking to convince Gibbs that Peyton had showed up at Epidermis because Mitch was there and not because she knew Gibbs was.

"I asked you what the problem was," the man barked, louder this time. He took hold of Mitch's shirt collar and growled low in his throat, like thunder from a stormy sky.

Mitch sighed. What the heck. He might as well tell the truth.

"My girl's pissed at me because she thinks I made

it with a stripper," he said. "I'm trying to catch up with her before she drives away."

The giant's menacing expression disappeared like the clothes the strippers cast off the stage. He released Mitch's collar and patted him on the back with a beefy hand.

"I hear ya, man," he said. "The same thing happened to me last week."

"Oh, yeah. What did you do?"

"What else could I do?" The big man shrugged. "First I apologized, then I begged, man. I begged."

"Thanks, buddy," Mitch said as he moved past the sympathetic behemoth. He scanned the parking lot with desperate eyes, finally spotting the back of Peyton's blond head as she got into her car and slammed the door.

He took off for the car at a dead run, reaching the passenger door as she was switching on the ignition. He gripped the door handle and bent at the waist to look into the window just as he saw her go for the automatic door lock.

He was quicker than she was, pulling open the door and jumping into the car before she could lock him out. He closed the door, shutting both of them inside.

"Get out of the car, Mitch."

She was staring straight ahead, her hands gripping the steering wheel. Her posture was rigid, her voice sounded hard.

"Not until you let me explain."

"There's nothing to explain," she said. He heard her take a ragged breath, hinting she wasn't as composed as she seemed. “I didn’t want to believe my mother when she told me you’d had an affair with that stripper, but now I have to.”

He gritted his teeth because he’d known something like this would happen the instant he discovered her uncle was the man who was following him. He’d distracted Peyton from talking to her mother by taking her to bed, but he couldn’t very well have kept her there. Even though he’d wanted to.

“I said get out, Mitch.”

He angled his body toward hers but still she kept staring out the window into the darkness. “And I said I wanted to explain.”

“Debbie Darling already did that.”

“But you don’t know the whole story.” He let out a sigh. “Would you at least look at me, Peyton?”

Her head didn’t move. “Why should I make anything easy on you?”

“Believe me, you’re not.”

“Good.” She did turn then, but it was too dark inside the car to read her expression.

“Debbie Darling doesn’t mean anything to me,” he began.

She didn’t let him get any further. “Are you saying you didn’t sleep with her?”

He faltered, wanting to tell her Cary had been the one who’d slept with Debbie. But then she’d demand an explanation and that explanation would plunge her into danger from Gibbs.

“I’m saying the only woman I want to make love with is you.” He stopped himself before he could add that he’d felt that way since he’d gotten his first look at her. As much as he loved his brother, he hadn't been able to stop wanting her.

"And that's supposed to pacify me?" Peyton's voice spiked. "That right now, at this moment in time, I happen to be your flavor of the day?"

"You'll always be my flavor," he said softly. "You're the only woman I'll ever want."

"Oh, come on, Mitch. How stupid do you think I am? You can do better than that. You obviously didn't feel this way three weeks ago."

"But that was before. . . ." His voice trailed off.

"Before what?"

Before I switched places with my brother, he thought. *Before I saw you standing there on Cary's doorstep, yelling at me. Before I fell in love with you.*

"Before I changed," he said aloud, knowing he couldn't tell her he loved her until she knew exactly who he was, knowing she probably wouldn't listen to him once she did know.

"Changed?" The word seemed to take her aback, to squeeze some of the anger from her voice. "What do you mean?"

He swallowed, wondering how much he could tell her. Even though he was masquerading as his twin, he couldn't have played the role very well. He and Cary might look identical, but they were as different as Millie Bellini and Peyton.

"Knowing you has changed me," he said and took a chance. He reached out and smoothed some of her short blond hairs back from her face. Although she didn't shy away from his touch, she didn't lean into it, either. "In the past week, I've been a different man."

He took his thumb and ran it over her trembling lower lip. He didn't realize she was crying until he felt the splash of her tears. He pressed his advantage, hating himself for doing it, aware that he didn't deserve her any more than his cheating brother did.

"You've noticed the changes, Peyton. I know you have. You've got to believe me when I say you're the only woman for me."

"I want to believe you," she said, her voice cracking.

"Then do," he said and opened his arms. She hesitated for a gut-wrenching moment, but then gave a little sigh and moved into his embrace. Mitch cradled her head against his heart, which she already occupied.

"God help me, Cary, but I don't know whether trusting you is a mistake or not," she whispered.

His heart fell like a cement block in his chest because he was about to give her the answer.

"Mitch," he corrected like a man who couldn't be trusted. "I like to be called Mitch."

Chapter Twenty-three

Lizabeth Drinkmiller sat huddled in a chair in her darkened hotel room, her legs tucked under her. The sun had already risen fifteen minutes ago but she hadn't opened the draperies. It was more appropriate that she be in the dark, which is where she'd been since Cary Mitchell told her he was his twin brother Grant that first night on Duval Street.

If she let in the light, she'd be forced to acknowledge that she was far removed from the confident, flamboyant creature who dressed in the latest fashions and had gotten a dynamic man to fall for her. She'd have to admit she was an embarrassingly naive research librarian who had been played for a fool by an impostor who wanted nothing from her but sex.

She'd been thinking about the reason for Cary's

masquerade all through the sleepless night and hadn't been able to come up with another reason for it. Why else would Cary have pretended he was Grant if not to take advantage of the mortifying crush she had on his brother? It must have been painfully obvious that the torch she carried for Grant still shined so bright that it wouldn't take much effort to get her into bed.

She wiped at a tear that had fallen down her cheek. What kind of man did something like that?

A man who loaded crates into his SUV in the dead of night so he could smuggle their contents to Miami.

No wonder money had seemed to flow from his pockets. She sniffed. To think she believed she had fallen in love with a man like that.

A knock on the door made her jump. She sniffed again and brushed away her tears with the back of her hand, automatically getting out of the chair and heading for the door.

She had her fingers on the doorknob before she gathered her wits about her enough to wonder why somebody would be knocking on the door to her hotel room at seven-thirty in the morning.

She peered out the peephole only to see the handsome, dark-haired, blue-eyed man who had kept her awake all night.

Her traitorous knees went weak at the sight of him and she staggered backward. Again, the knock sounded.

She stood stock still, with only the width of the

door separating her from the man she'd so foolishly believed she loved.

If she ignored him, he'd probably go away. But he'd return because he didn't yet know she was on to him. Without detaching the key chain, she opened the door, and prepared to get rid of him once and for all.

"Leeza, I need to talk to you," he said through the crack before she could speak. He looked terrible. His eyes were blood shot, he needed a shave, and his hair was mussed.

Probably, Lizabeth thought, because he'd spent the night making the round trip to Miami and back with those suspicious crates.

"Do you know what time it is?" she asked, making her voice testy.

"Seven-thirty," he answered and sighed. "I know it's early but I couldn't wait any longer. Will you let me in? Please?"

She steeled herself against his pleading tone and the sorrowful look in his blue eyes. All she had to do was tell him she knew he was Cary, say she never wanted to see him again, and slam the door in his face.

Instead, she unhooked the key chain and let the traitor in.

He was wearing the clothes he'd had on the night before when she'd seen him with Captain Turk: dark pants and a dark short-sleeved shirt, the better to blend into the night. They were as rumpled as he was.

She knew she didn't look any better herself. Instead of her fancy Leeza lingerie, she was wearing the single item of clothing she'd packed that reflected the real Lizabeth. It was a well-worn knee-length Winnie the Pooh night shirt. Her feet were bare, her hair a tangled mess. But for once, she didn't care how she appeared.

"I'm sorry I woke you." He rubbed a hand over the stubble of his lower jaw, looking more uncomfortable than she'd ever seen him.

She didn't bother to correct his misconception but went to the drapes in the bedroom and drew them back, letting in the blazing tropical sunshine. It was time she was out of the dark.

"I'll get right to the point." He hesitated, something else that struck her as uncharacteristic. But what did she really know about him?

"It's like this," he said and hesitated again. She sat on the edge of her unmade bed, where they'd made love just days before, and waited for him to confess his deception.

"I know you saw me last night at the boat landing."

Her lips parted. Was that what this was all about?

"It was your octopus brooch. It glows." He stopped, paced from one side of the room to the other, and dropped into the chair she'd been sitting in before he'd arrived. It was probably still warm from her body heat. "I don't blame you for following me. I should have told you what I was doing, but the truth is that *I* don't know what I'm doing."

He paused and shook his head. "Hell, I usually

don't know what I'm doing. Or why I'm doing it." He let out an unamused laugh. "Do you know that's the first time I've ever admitted that to anybody?"

Lizabeth wanted to believe he considered her important enough to confide in, but she wouldn't let herself. If she meant anything to him, he wouldn't have lied about being his brother. And she wouldn't be hurting this badly.

"I know it looks bad, but it's not what you think." Again, he laughed that cheerless laugh. "Hell, maybe it is what you think. I don't know what's inside those crates, so how would I know?"

"What *are* you doing here?"

He ran his fingers through his disheveled hair and his hands over the lower half of his unshaved face. "I suppose I'm trying to get you to think of me as one of the good guys."

The smile he flashed her was a shadow of its former self but still potent enough to make her heart turn over. She ruthlessly commanded it to stay in place.

"Imagine that," she said, aiming for sarcasm. "And here I was having a hard enough time thinking of you as Grant's identical twin brother."

His smile disappeared, his shoulders dropped, and she heard him expel a heavy breath.

"I know you're Cary, so don't bother to deny it. The juggling was the clincher, but I should have figured it out before then." She would have if she hadn't been so blinded by how she thought she felt about him.

"I wasn't going to deny it," he said softly, but she didn't believe that either.

"I suppose now you're going to say you intended to tell me you were Cary but hadn't gotten around to it." She hated the way her voice cracked but there was no help for it. Not when her heart was cracking, too.

"Nope." He shook his head. "I'm afraid I'm not that noble."

"I don't understand." She swallowed hard. "Aren't you going to deny you pretended to be your brother because you figured out how I felt about him?"

"Why should I deny it when it's the truth?" His blue eyes fastened on hers. "You liked my brother. That was a sure thing. I didn't have any guarantee you'd like me."

"So you admit you used my feelings for your brother to get me into bed?"

He swallowed and an unreadable expression crossed his face. "If I had any sense, I'd say that wasn't my intention. But I won't insult you. Especially because it was probably pretty clear right from the first that I wanted to make love to you."

"But that's. . . ." Lizabeth paused, trying to come up with a word powerful enough to convey her horror.

"Despicable?" He suggested. "Underhanded? Contemptible?"

"Yes," she bit out. "I can't believe you're not trying to defend yourself."

His teeth flashed, but it wasn't really a smile.

"How can I defend myself? I'm not my brother, Leeza. I'm not loyal. I'm not dependable. I'm not trustworthy. Hell, I've spent the last week helping smuggle crates out of Key West. That's what kind of man I am."

"But how could you have lied to me about who you were?"

He got up and walked across the room with a powerful, masculine grace, stopping inches shy of her. He bent down and cupped her cheek, filling her senses with his touch. Her heart hammered and, no matter what he'd done, she was powerless to resist him.

"I lied because I wanted you from the first moment I saw you," he said softly, his gaze intent. "And I knew that if my brother was your type, then I wouldn't be."

Something inside of her softened at his words. She thought of how wonderful he was with the children on the baseball team, of how contagious his smile and spontaneity were, of how self-assured she'd started to feel in his company. She opened her mouth to tell him he should think more of himself, but he placed two fingers against her lips.

"Don't say anything, Leeza. I know I'm not worthy of you. I know I could never be the kind of man you want. The kind of man you want wouldn't do what I'm about to do."

He removed his fingers from her lips, leaned down and brought his mouth to hers. His lips were soft, moving over hers with something that felt like reverence, giving her no choice but to open her mouth and kiss him back. The moment she did, he drew back and gave her a sad smile.

"Good-bye, love," he said, staring into her eyes.

Then he turned and in moments was gone, leaving her sitting there with the Key West sunshine at her back.

He'd claimed he could never be the man she wanted, and he shouldn't be. Not after the elaborate deception he'd pulled off.

So why did she have the suspicion that, despite everything, Cary Mitchell was exactly who and what she wanted?

Cary sucked in a breath and walked through the door to the main Key West police station on Angela Street, in the heart of Key West's historic district.

He might have lost the courage it had taken him all day and half the night to gather and turned back around if the drag queen from last night's sunset celebration hadn't been leaning one of his hard-boned hips against the reception desk. The drag queen let out a loud whistle.

"Will you look at the piece of eye candy the wind just blew in?" he asked the desk sergeant, a paunchy middle-aged man who looked like he'd have been on the verge of pulling his hair out if his head wasn't shaved. "Five'll get you ten you'll listen to *his* complaint."

"Only if he complains about something more substantial than his evening gowns getting ripped off from the clothes hanger in his back yard."

The drag queen harrumphed so powerfully a

piece of paper on the reception counter fluttered into the air and back down again. "Those gowns *are* substantial! Do you know how hard it is to find a stylish dress in a size twenty-two?"

"About as hard as it would be to find a thief to fit into it," the desk sergeant muttered. "Why'd you have those dresses on the clothesline anyway?"

"They were smoky, and smoke isn't sexy. Now what you gonna do about it?"

The sergeant sighed. "I'll send an officer out to take a look. That's all I can do, Bubba."

The drag queen put his broad hands on the counter and leaned forward. His yellow dress was so shiny Cary thought the officer was in danger of being blinded. "I told you not to call me that anymore. The name's Xanadu now."

Xanadu straightened to his full lofty height and clomped to the door, pausing to give Cary a come-hither smile.

"Hey, there, handsome. I'll be performing in about an hour at Club Cockatiel." He blew a kiss out of lips that seemed to have undergone collagen injections. "You don't want to miss it."

Cary could have debated him about that, but there wouldn't have been much point. If the next few minutes went the way he suspected they would, he wouldn't be free to go anywhere tonight but a jail cell.

"How can I help you?" the desk sergeant asked.

Cary hesitated. He didn't have to do this. It wasn't too late to claim he'd made a mistake and disappear into the tropical night. Nobody would blame him. Everybody knew he wasn't the twin who was cut out to be a Boy Scout.

"Actually, I, uh, don't have anything you can help me with." Ignoring the speculation on the sergeant's face, Cary turned around and went back outside, where he expected to be able to breathe again.

But his chest tightened and the glow of the moon reminded him of the night before, when Leeza had spied on him and found out what kind of man he was. He thought about the way she'd looked that morning, her beautiful face cloaked in sadness, her dark eyes filled with disappointment.

"Aw, hell," Cary muttered and turned back around.

"I'm here to report a crime," he told the policeman when he was once more standing in front of the reception desk.

"What kind of a crime?" the sergeant asked.

"I don't know," Cary said.

"What kind of answer is that? How can you not know?"

"I will know," Cary said, then drew in a breath. After this, there would be no going back. "As soon as you open the crates in the trunk of my SUV."

After he popped the trunk, Cary stood between two uniformed cops as the three of them considered the heavy crates he and Captain Turk had loaded into the SUV the night before.

"So you're saying you don't know what's inside?" asked the taller of the two cops, cracking his gum so loudly it sounded as if someone had set off a firecracker.

Cary tried not to jump, although his insides were bouncing. "That's right."

Aside from the traffic noise, the only sound was the officer's teeth coming together as he chomped on his wad of gum. He gave Cary a long look. "And you were supposed to deliver them to a warehouse in Miami last night?"

"Sure was." Cary kept his voice light, as though he wasn't the least concerned that he was about to give up twenty-eight years of freedom. "That's where I took the other crates."

"Why didn't you take these, too?" The question came from the shorter cop, who wasn't nearly as pleasant as his tall buddy. Even though the only light came from a street lamp, his eyes were shaded with the sort of black sunglasses men wore when they'd stayed out too late partying the night before. Cary should know. He'd used that trick plenty enough times himself.

"My conscience wouldn't let me." Cary made himself shrug, as though he discussed his conscience every day.

The little cop snorted and reached for one of the crates, which his partner helped him hoist to the parking-lot pavement. He pulled out a crow bar and looked up at Cary. "Well, Mr. Good Citizen, let's see what your *conscience* has been letting you smuggle into Miami."

The splintering sound of the crate being opened ripped into Cary like the slash of a knife, and he was tempted to use the speed God had given him to dash for his freedom. But then he'd have to add coward to the slate of reasons he didn't deserve Leeza Drinkmiller. Figuring the list was already long enough, he stayed where he was and pretended the contents of his stomach weren't rising with the top of the crate.

At the last second, he closed his eyes against the truth in the crate.

"What are those things?" the tall cop asked.

"Looks like they've been underwater," came the gruff cop's answer, and Cary's stomach fell. He'd driven by the Mel Fisher Maritime Heritage Society and Museum. He knew all about Shipwreck Trail, and about Key West's rich legacy of preserving history through the artifacts found on those unfortunate ships that had gone down in the waters off its coast.

He'd been aiding Captain Turk in plundering history. Maybe even in stripping one of those seventeenth-century Spanish galleons treasure hunters like Fisher had treated with such veneration.

"Looks like action figures to me," the tall cop said, and Cary's eyes snapped open. The officer reached into the crate and pulled out a plastic doll dressed the same way Captain Turk did. "Hey, isn't this the guy from *Star Trek?*"

"Star Quest," Cary corrected. At the officers' puzzled look, he explained, "It was sort of like a spin-off of *Star Trek.*"

"A spin-off? Looks to me like it was a rip-off,"

the gruff cop replied as he pulled out a Sprock doll, complete with pointed ears. He turned to his partner. "Hey, remember that insurance scandal back in the eighties involving a ship carrying a shipment of toys? The cargo was insured for far more than it was worth. Maybe these dolls are from that wreck."

Cary moved closer to make sure there weren't any ancient Spanish coins inside the crate, but all he could see was more plastic, including a replica of the USS *Surprise.*

"Does this mean you're not going to arrest me?" Cary asked.

"For what?" the short cop said, straightening. "Stupidity?"

The tall cop cocked his head, gesturing Cary away from his partner. They walked a few paces before he said, "We'll check the rest of the crates but my guess is they include more of the same. Somebody obviously located a shipwreck, but it doesn't seem to contain anything of historical significance."

"But isn't plundering against the law?"

"Whoever's behind all this should have gotten a permit before he excavated, sure. And I am going to need you to give us his name, but he'll probably get off with a fine." The cop frowned. "If he thinks *Star Quest* action figures are valuable, I'd venture to say this guy is probably not the brightest light in the chandelier."

Cary thought of Captain Turk's theory on the Press-ons who could ingest ozone, and nodded.

"How about me?" Cary asked. "What's going to happen to me?"

"Nothing," the cop said. "You probably would've been okay even if we had found something illegal inside those crates. You came to us before we found you."

Cary thought of the way his brother had advised him to go to the authorities when he'd found out about the mess Cary had created in Charleston. And of the way Cary had refused his advice.

"You guys give credit for things like that?"

"Sure do," the cop said and smiled. "We tend to like guys who do the right thing."

With that, he turned back to his partner, who was ripping open another crate. The cop's parting words rang in Cary's mind.

Do the right thing.

Suddenly, the right thing seemed so simple. Why, Cary wondered, had it taken him so long to figure out what the right thing was?

Chapter Twenty-four

Mitch reluctantly rolled away from Peyton, who was trustingly tucked against him as she slept, to grope for the ringing phone.

Before he opened his eyes, he wondered if masquerading as his brother had resulted in so much bad karma that his punishment was being repeatedly woken up from a sound sleep. But at least this awakening had a different twist. Usually, he was jarred out of dreamland by a doorbell.

"Yeah," he said into the receiver, his eyes still half closed.

"Hey, bro. It's good to finally hear your voice."

"Cary," he said, coming instantly awake. He was about to make a sarcastic comment about who had been wanting to hear from whom when Peyton stirred beside him and turned over on her side. Her eyes came slowly open.

"Who's that?" she asked drowsily.

Oh, no, Mitch thought as his stomach pitched. Had Cary heard Peyton ask the question? Worse, had Peyton heard Mitch greet his brother by name?

"Like I said, this is Cary. Who's calling?" he improvised as Peyton gave him a sleepy smile.

"This is Cary," Cary said. "Are you okay, Mitch?"

"Yes. I mean no." Mitch sat up in bed and rubbed a hand over his eyes. He'd have been perfectly within his rights to blast his brother for talking him into the twin switch and then disappearing—if he hadn't been in bed with his brother's girl. "It's just that you woke me up."

"You're kidding. I waited until ten to call so I wouldn't."

"Since when do you care if you wake me up?" Mitch asked at the same time something else his brother had said registered. "Is it really ten o'clock?"

"Ten o'clock," Peyton repeated, sitting bolt upright so that the bedsheets fell away from her lovely breasts. Mitch pressed the mouthpiece of the phone into his cheek, hoping his skin would muffle Peyton's comments. "I'm supposed to be at work at ten," she said.

"Of course I care if I wake you up. Do you think I don't appreciate this favor you're doing me?" Cary said. "You wound me, bro."

As Peyton scrambled out of bed and headed for

the bathroom, her bare behind about the loveliest thing Mitch had ever seen, he thought his brother couldn't guess exactly how much he was wounding him.

But darn it. Peyton didn't feel like Cary's girl. She felt like Mitch's. He certainly wouldn't cheat on her with a stripper.

"Don't pull that wounded act with me," Mitch said, angry for Peyton's sake. But he couldn't very well take his brother to task for two-timing her, not when he could hear Peyton turning on the shower in the bathroom. "You've been missing for more than a week, then you call me up out of the blue and pretend to be appreciative. How stupid do you think I am?"

"I don't think you're stupid," Cary said. "I think you're a damn fine brother."

Mitch narrowed his eyes as he swung his legs over the side of the bed and pulled on a pair of his brother's sweatpants. Made of a revolutionary lightweight material, the sweatpants were as expensive as everything else in Cary's home. "What kind of game are you playing now?"

"No game."

Mitch got out of bed, walked to the window and drew back the blinds. The day was overcast, with only thin rays of sunlight breaking through the clouds. "They why are you calling?"

"A man can call his brother to say he's sorry, can't he?"

"You never say you're sorry," Mitch reminded him.

"Maybe I do now."

"Where are you and how much money are you trying to get me to send you?"

"I'm in Key West," Cary said.

Typical, Mitch thought. *Here he was risking everything while his brother was living it up in the tropics.*

"But I don't want you to send me money," Cary continued.

Atypical, Mitch thought.

"What do you want then?" Mitch asked.

"I wanted to tell you that you were right in the first place. I've decided to come back to Charleston and turn myself in to the authorities."

"No!" Mitch said. "I was wrong."

"No, you weren't. Turning myself in is the right thing to do."

"Since when are you concerned with doing the right thing?" Mitch heard the shower turn off and knew he didn't have much time to talk his brother out of making a major mistake. "Never mind the answer. Just listen to me. You can't come back right now."

"Why not?"

"Because you're my brother and you're not going to end up in a jail cell if I can help it."

"Maybe a jail cell is where I belong."

"You must be getting too much sun down there in Florida. You sound like you fried your brain."

"I'm serious, Mitch. You're always telling me I should face up to the consequences of my actions. I'm ready to face up to them."

"It's too risky," Mitch hissed. He glanced at the bathroom door, knowing he only had moments before Peyton reappeared. "You were right. Flash Gorman's a bad character but I can't prove it yet. I need a few more days to find out where he's running his bookmaking operation from."

"Flash isn't a bookie," Cary said.

Time seemed to stop for interminable seconds while Mitch tried to process what his brother had said.

"But you told me you were in trouble with him because of your gambling problem," Mitch said slowly.

The door to the bathroom burst open and Peyton rushed out, pulling up the zipper on the dressy pair of black pants she'd worn the night before.

"That's right. I borrowed money from him to pay back my bookie, but I didn't place bets with him."

Mitch's mind whirled as he thought of Cooper Barnes and Stu Funderburk, the two men he'd been sent to harass because they owed Gaston Gibbs money. He'd assumed they were gamblers, like Cary. If they weren't, why did they owe Gibbs money?

The possibility that Gibbs was making the bulk of his money by loan sharking didn't ring true. That was small-time stuff. It wouldn't account for the staggering sum of cash he was laundering through Epidermis. So what was his evil?

"Why didn't you tell me this in the first place?" Mitch asked.

"I thought I had," Cary answered as Mitch

watched Peyton pull a comb through her wet hair and get on her knees to search under the bed for her shoes. "About my coming back—"

"I told you to stay put," Mitch interrupted. "Now is a bad time."

Peyton looked at him quizzically as she pulled on her sandals. He wanted to demand that Cary listen to him but instead deliberately toned down his voice. "Check back with me tomorrow. Maybe things will be different by then."

"But—"

"It's for the best," Mitch said. "Call me tomorrow, okay?"

"Okay," Cary said after a long pause. "But I want you to know I really did mean it when I said I was sorry."

Cary broke the connection, leaving Mitch staring at the receiver, wondering at his brother's serious tone. Cary was never serious, which was one of the hundred reasons Mitch needed to look out for him.

"Who was that?" Peyton asked, moving across the room toward him. Her hair smelled like his shampoo. Check that, like Cary's shampoo.

"My brother," he answered.

"You have a brother? I didn't know that." She looped her arms around his neck and smiled up at him. "You'll have to tell me about him when I have more time."

"Sure," Mitch said as she planted a swift kiss on his lips and drew back from his arms. "I'm already late, but if I don't stop home to change everybody's going to know what we were doing last night."

He smiled despite the fact that his head was crammed with thoughts of Gaston Gibbs and what kind of illegal operation he could be running.

"Hey, I left work last night without telling anyone," Mitch said. "Don't tell me missing work to do what we did isn't worth it."

She laughed and blew him a kiss. "You're bad for me, Cary Mitchell."

She left the room and a few seconds later, Mitch heard the front door shut. He sank to his bed, already feeling a sense of loss. Maybe, he thought, it was a foreshadowing.

He hadn't been entirely honest with his brother. He loved Cary too much to see him thrown into jail, but he was afraid the main reason he'd ordered his twin to stay put had more to do with Peyton than Gaston Gibbs.

As long as Peyton didn't know who he was, Mitch could pretend that it wouldn't matter to her once she found out.

"Fool," he said, because of course it would matter.

With great difficulty, he thrust thoughts of Peyton from his mind and concentrated on his most pressing problem: G. Gaston Gibbs III.

Within minutes he realized his next move was to contact Cooper Barnes and Stu Funderburk to find out exactly why they owed Gibbs money, but it took the better part of the day to accomplish it.

"I ran up my bar tab and couldn't pay it back," said Barnes when Mitch finally got him on the restaurant's phone. "Damn Millie Bellini anyway."

"What's Millie got to do with it?"

"Long as we're going out, she don't give me no trouble. But the minute we're through, she starts jawin' about the bar tab."

Mitch blinked. Cooper Barnes and Millie Bellini an item? He never would have guessed it, but then again he couldn't imagine any man with Millie. Although his advice went against his true thoughts on the subject, he said, "You shouldn't have dumped her."

"I didn't dump her, man. She dumped me." Barnes paused. "Hey, her birthday's comin' up. You think you could lend me a couple hundred so I could get her somethin' nice?"

"You owe me five hundred dollars already," Mitch pointed out with heat.

"What's a couple hundred more among friends?" Barnes asked before Mitch slammed the phone down.

Stu Funderburk, who had neither a telephone nor a job, was more difficult to track down. After Mitch drove to Summerville and found his trailer deserted, one of Funderburk's neighbors pointed him to a rundown pub on the outskirts of town.

Mitch found Funderburk cradling a glass of Jack Daniels, sitting alone at a bar so dark it was hard to believe the sun was still shining outside. Not only didn't Mitch see a pair of crutches leaning against the bar, but the small man wasn't wearing his cast.

"Darnit, Funderburk," Mitch said as he took the stool next to him. "I told you to wear the plaster."

"It itches," Funderburk said. Even though he'd

probably been drinking all afternoon, his eyes were bird-bright. "Not to mention cramps my style."

"Listen to me." Mitch brought his face close to the little man's. He got a whiff of alcohol and perspiration but didn't back away. "After we talk, you're going home and putting on that cast or I'm giving you a real reason to wear it."

"But you said you were a different kind of debt collector," Funderburk whined. "Now you're talking stereotype. Sticks and stones. Break some bones. Jesus, where's your originality?"

"Funderburk?"

"Yeah?"

"Shut up."

"Okay," the little man said. "But I'm telling you right now, I don't got no money. So if you're here for money, we're gonna have to go outside and rumble. I can take you. I know I can."

"Funderburk?"

"Yeah?"

"I thought you were going to shut up."

He shrugged his narrow shoulders. "I forgot. So shoot me." A concerned look descended over his face. "Forget I said that. Don't shoot me."

"I'm not going to shoot you," Mitch said. "I'm not here for money, either. I just want to know *why* you owe Flash."

"That's it?"

"That's it," Mitch said, and the small man seemed to relax.

"I was supposed to do some renovation work for him."

Mitch let out a surprised sound. "You're a renovator?"

"An *aspirin'* renovator," he corrected. "That's why I didn't get 'round to doing the renovating. But some people get touchy 'bout things like that after they give you a deposit."

Mitch rubbed at the indentation between his eyebrows. He'd have thought Gibbs was too careful to mix his criminal life with his philanthropic one, but then again Gibbs had never struck him as the charitable type in the first place. "You're telling me Flash hired you to renovate one of those historic buildings of his?"

"Historic? I heard people call Epidermis a den of iniquity, but I didn't think it was historic."

Mitch sighed. "Did he hire you to renovate those buildings in downtown Charleston or not?"

"Hell, no. I was supposed to put a roof on his strip joint. Not that he hired me himself. I never seen the guy. I been dealing with this scary lookin' woman with a beehive on top of her head."

"Millie Bellini," Mitch provided.

"Yeah, Bellini. I tell ya. That woman got bees in her beehive."

An hour later, Mitch pulled his brother's SUV into a parking place at a strip shopping center on Savannah Highway and cut the engine. He hopped out of the vehicle, walked directly to the office on the end, and pulled open the cookie-cutter door.

The outer office had a secretary's desk but it was deserted, so Mitch gave three hard raps to the inner door and jerked it open.

Vincent Carmichael, his fedora and wire-rimmed glasses in place, glanced up from the file on his desk. Wariness replaced his initial curiosity.

"If you're here for the report I worked up on you, it's too late," he said. "I already gave it to Amelia."

"That's not why I'm here," Mitch said, although Carmichael's comment explained how Peyton had known about Cary's fling with Debbie Darling.

"Then why are you here?"

"You ever heard of Flash Gorman?" Mitch asked.

Carmichael inclined his head almost imperceptibly. "Whispers, mostly. I know he's bad news, but I can't say we're acquainted."

"Are you acquainted with G. Gaston Gibbs III?"

"Not socially, but I've heard Peyton's mother mention him," Carmichael said slowly. "Why?"

"Gibbs and Flash Gorman are the same person."

Carmichael whistled. "I can't imagine he wants that to get around."

"Exactly. In fact, he'd go to great lengths to keep that information secret."

The older man's eyes narrowed. "What's this got to do with me?"

"Gibbs has got it into his head that you're investigating him."

"I was investigating *you,*" Carmichael pointed out.

"He doesn't know that." Mitch stepped deeper into the room. "So he sent me here to take care of you."

Carmichael's eyes widened so that Mitch could

see whites all around the pupils and his hand went to a desk drawer, where he probably kept a gun. "Is that why you're here?"

"Heck, no." Mitch sank into the seat across from Peyton's uncle's desk, then sat forward, his hands on his knees. "I'm here to get you out of trouble."

"I'm not in trouble."

"With Gibbs believing you're investigating him, I'd say you're in a heap of trouble. The next guy he sends to take care of you might not have any qualms about doing it."

He saw Carmichael's Adam's apple bob when he swallowed, but his hand fell away from the desk drawer. "So how are you proposing I get out of this trouble?"

Mitch smiled. "By helping me investigate Gibbs."

Carmichael was shaking his head before Mitch finished the sentence. "That's crazy."

"Not so crazy. If Gibbs didn't have anything to hide, he wouldn't be worried about somebody snooping around. Once we know what he's hiding, we'll have a weapon we can use against him."

"Makes sense, but there's something I don't understand. Why would you be investigating anything?"

Mitch told him, figuring the only way to get Carmichael on his side was to tell him the entire truth, which included the twin switch. When he was through, he sighed.

"Look, I wouldn't be coming to you if I hadn't hit a brick wall. I know Gibbs is laundering money through his club but I don't know where it's coming from. I've staked out his business and his home. And nothing."

Carmichael tapped his chin with the eraser of a pencil. "How do you know I won't hit a brick wall, too?"

"I don't know that," Mitch said, "but I'm betting you're better at snooping than I am. Are you in or not?"

Mitch heard the wall clock tick five times before Carmichael nodded. "I'm in," he said. "But are you sure your information's correct? Gibbs is a model citizen. A philanthropist. He buys up dilapidated properties and renovates them, for God's sake."

"What did you just say?"

"That Gibbs is a model citizen."

Mitch shook his head. "No. The part about the dilapidated buildings."

"He buys them and renovates them," Carmichael said. "He's been doing it for years."

Mitch's mind clicked and whirled. He'd known that, of course. He'd been puzzling over it just that afternoon when he was talking to Stu Funderburk, but it hadn't occurred to him then that the break he was looking for might be linked to Gibbs' motivation for buying the properties.

"Those buildings are abandoned when he purchases them, right?" He was so preoccupied he hardly saw Carmichael's nod. "And they probably stay vacant for at least a couple months, maybe more, until he hires the workers."

"Yeah, so?"

"So I want you to call Peyton and get the addresses of those places," Mitch said. "I think we might have ourselves a lead."

Chapter Twenty-five

As Lizabeth Drinkmiller walked through the historic part of Key West, the late-morning sun was so blindingly hot that the drop of moisture trickling down her cheek could have been perspiration.

By all rights, it should have been.

A woman who pretended to be someone she wasn't and then had the gall to dress down a man for impersonating someone *he* wasn't didn't have the right to cry.

Lizabeth wiped at the offending tear with her forefinger and veered off one of the major shopping streets to take the path that led to the bed and breakfast where Cary Mitchell was staying.

Not only shouldn't she cry, but she shouldn't be nervous. She meant to say what she'd come to say and be done with it. She'd hardly linger long enough for it to seep in that she was never going to see him again.

Cary wouldn't want her to stick around in any event. Not after he realized that self-assured, flamboyant Leeza was gone and in her place remained boring old Lizabeth. A naive, silly woman who hadn't even been bright enough to realize the man she was falling in love with wasn't the object of her high-school crush.

As she walked, she glanced down at the clothing she'd bought the previous afternoon. The lightweight khaki slacks paired with a simple short-sleeved top in white cotton were along the lines of the clothes she normally wore.

She'd packed away her flashy Leeza clothes inside the suitcases she was going to take on her flight back to reality later that day, but she could just as well have pitched them into the Atlantic.

She certainly couldn't wear them again without thinking about Cary, and she already knew that, in the future, thinking about Cary would hurt far too much.

She felt the wetness on her cheeks again and blinked rapidly to dry her eyes. When her vision cleared, the black SUV she'd seen a few nights before on the boat landing came into view. So did the suitcase an achingly familiar dark-haired man was heaving into its trunk.

So Cary was leaving, too.

She stopped where she was on the sidewalk, used her fingers to sweep her cheeks clean of moisture, and tried to wipe the sadness from her face. Then she marched determinedly on.

"Were you going to leave without saying good-bye?" she asked when she was close enough to the SUV for him to hear her.

His head whipped around, and her heart panged at the way his blue eyes seemed to drink her in.

Silly woman, she chided herself. No man looked thirstily at a woman in khakis and white cotton.

"I already said good-bye. I didn't think you'd want me to do it again," he said.

She didn't want him to say good-bye again. She wanted him to say he'd suddenly developed a penchant for colorless research librarians with retiring personalities.

Instead of telling him that, she reverted to her pre-Leeza ways and didn't say anything at all. She must have been staring, though, because he gestured to the open trunk of the SUV.

"There aren't any crates in there, if that's what you're wondering."

"I wasn't—"

He didn't let her finish. "I went to the police yesterday to give myself up. Turned out the crates were full of *Star Quest* action figures. Can you believe that?" He scratched his head. "So I'm not a smuggler." He shrugged. "Still a cad, though. But you already knew that."

Two beautiful women clad in skimpy outfits and self-confidence passed by, sending long, bold looks at Cary. She waited for him to return their stares, but he kept his eyes locked on her.

"Could I talk to you before you go?" Her throat seized at the thought of him leaving. A boy on a bicycle whizzed by, so close she felt wind in his wake. "Away from the street?"

"Sure," he said. The muscles in his biceps bulged as he slammed the trunk, reminding her that he worked in physical education. Not law enforcement, as she'd previously thought. "The place I'm staying has a courtyard. We should be able to get a table in the shade."

Moments later, they sat catty-corner from each other underneath the canopy of a yellow-and-blue striped umbrella. The pool area was deserted except for a couple of towheaded boys, the larger of whom couldn't have been more than nine or ten.

"Hey, Cary, watch this," the older boy yelled before he jumped into the deep end of the pool. "Cannonball!"

Water shot into the air like a geyser and sprayed out in a fan shape. Cold, fat drops hit the edge of the table and splashed onto Lizabeth and Cary, making her question the wisdom of a table positioned so close to the pool.

"Cool, huh?" the boy asked when he came up for air.

Cary gave him a thumbs-up sign. "Do me a favor, Billy. Keep the water inside the pool and give us a little privacy. We're trying to talk."

"Anything you say, Cary."

"Yeah, anything you say," the younger boy parroted before he and his brother headed for the shallow end with flat, inexpert strokes that emptied the pool of more water.

"They like you," Lizabeth observed.

"They're good kids," Cary said. "I figured out yesterday their parents were leaving them here while they went sightseeing. The boys seemed a little lonely, so I let them talk me into playing Marco Polo."

He lapsed into silence, and the only sounds Lizabeth could hear were the laughs of the two brothers as they splashed each other. She told herself to spit out her apology, but in typical Lizabeth fashion, her tongue froze.

"Go ahead," Cary said, crossing his arms over his chest. "Let me have it."

He looked so miserable that she forgot about being tongue-tied. "Let you have what?"

"The tongue lashing. You didn't get it all out yesterday. I understand that. So go ahead. Call me a snake. A rake. A louse." He turned one side of his face to her. "You can even slap me."

"Would you stop that?" Lizabeth commanded in a strident voice she hardly recognized as her own.

He blinked. "Stop what?"

"Belittling yourself. I'm sick of it."

"But I'm—"

"Just shut up, okay?" She leaned forward, her eyes boring into his. "You are not a bad man. Bad men don't turn themselves into the police. Bad men don't learn the names of strange kids at the pool or teach kids they don't know how to play baseball. I would not have fallen in love with a bad man."

His mouth gaped open. "You're in love with me?"

Lizabeth bit her lower lip and averted her eyes. Her heart had acknowledged that she still loved him long before she said it aloud, but that didn't mean she should have blurted it out. She couldn't possibly be any more gauche.

"Is that what you came here to tell me?" he pressed, and she felt the full impact of his blue gaze. What a fool he must think her.

She shook her head. "I'm cutting my vacation short and leaving this afternoon. I came to say good-bye." She took a deep breath for courage. "And to tell you I've been lying to you."

"You've been lying about being in love with me?"

She ignored the question and stared down at her hands. "I've been lying about who I am. My name isn't Leeza, it's Lizabeth. I'm not a buyer for a department store, I'm a research librarian. I'm not bold and daring, I'm meek and quiet."

"But are you in love with me?"

"Would you forget I said that?"

"I don't want to forget it." He leaned closer to her and tilted her chin up with a forefinger so she had to look at him. She felt the traitorous moisture start to well up in her eyes and blinked it back. "I want to hear you say it again."

"I've been lying to you."

A corner of his mouth lifted. "That wasn't the part I wanted to hear again."

"It's the important part. I lied to you, Cary."

"Don't you think I know that?"

Her eyes narrowed. "How could you know?"

"That you weren't a femme fatale? I'd have to say my first inkling was when we met and you blurted out that a kind of black lemur is the only primate with red eyes."

"Blue eyes," she corrected automatically. "The only animal with red that I can think of is a species of tree frog, but frogs are amphibians, not primates."

He grinned. "I love it when you spout facts like that."

"You're teasing me," she accused, feeling her lower lip start trembling again.

"No, I'm not." He cupped her cheek. "I like that you're a walking reference book but not quite as much as I liked being your first lover."

Everything inside her went still as she thought of the night they'd first made love and the pains she'd taken to make him believe she was sexually experienced. She backed away from his touch as a sense of betrayal stole over her.

"Why didn't you tell me you knew I was lying to you?"

"That would have been a bit like Pinocchio casting stones, don't you think?" Cary put his elbows on the table and began to hope. "Getting back to the part where you said you loved me—"

"I can't believe you keep harping on that." She looked adorably miffed. "A gentleman would forget I said that."

"You're confusing me with my brother Mitch.

He's the gentleman of the family." Cary stopped and swallowed, suddenly nervous. Too much was on the line with his next question. "Speaking of my twin, are you sure he's not the one you're in love with?"

She shot him a look filled with irritation. "Honestly, Cary, how could I be in love with someone I don't know? I had a crush on your brother ten years ago when we were in high school, and I didn't know him then either."

"He's a good man. Better than me," Cary said. "Don't say anything. Just hear me out. I shouldn't even be here in Key West. The only reason I am is that I talked my brother into taking the heat for me."

He took a breath, hardly believing he was going to willingly tell her the story that would kill any love she had for him. Before he could lose his nerve, he launched into the tale, not holding anything back.

When he finished, the only sounds were the splashes the blond brothers were making in the shallow end of the pool. Cary had dropped his eyes to the table. Now he slowly raised them, fearful of what he'd see in hers but knowing he deserved her censure.

"If your brother told you he didn't want you to return to Charleston, why are you going back?"

Cary blinked, because it wasn't the question he anticipated. Hell, he'd been prepared for her to get up and walk away without a backward glance.

"I guess because it's time I started taking responsibility for my actions," he said.

"It's because you're a good man," she said, reaching across the table and taking his hand. He hadn't realized his was cold until her warmth enveloped him. "Right from the beginning, I could see the goodness in you."

"Are you sure it wasn't my imitation of Mitch you were seeing? I'm not a cop, Lizabeth. I work in recreation. I drink. I swear. I don't like wearing plaid. And I hate driving a SUV."

He waited. Even though Lizabeth hadn't budged, he still couldn't quite believe she wasn't about to toss her head, get to her feet, and saunter out of his life.

"You weren't the only one who could see beneath the surface," she told him, her brown eyes fastened on his. "I didn't know you were pretending to be your brother, but I knew you were putting on an act. It was the man underneath the act I fell in love with."

"Ah, Lizabeth, you shouldn't say such things to me." Cary turned his hand over so that their palms were touching and gently squeezed her hand. "I'm probably heading straight for jail, but I'm not above holding you to what you said about loving me."

"If you do go to jail, all you have to do is say the words and I'll wait for you," Lizabeth told him softly.

"Wait for me," Cary said.

"Those are the wrong three words."

Cary smiled as he stood up from the table, took her hand, and drew her into his arms. "I'm starting to suspect that the shy research librarian I'm in love with isn't so shy after all."

"So you do love me?" she asked, her eyes glued to his. "Even though I'm nothing like Leeza?"

"I don't know about that," he said, fingering the ugly octopus brooch he'd given her. "I think there's always been a little bit of Leeza in you. If there wasn't, you wouldn't have asked me if I loved you."

"I wasn't asking as Leeza. I was asking as Lizabeth. Just plain Lizabeth."

"I've been out with plenty of women like Leeza, but I've only been with one Lizabeth," Cary said and traced the bridge of her nose. "Yes, I love you. More than I ever thought it was possible for me to love anybody. More than I love myself."

"I'll teach you to love yourself, but in the meantime I'll love you enough for both of us," she said before she pulled his face down to hers.

The heat of the day mingled with the heat of the kiss until Cary felt as though he were aflame, with love, with desire, and with awe. He was so wrapped up in the unfamiliar feelings that the gleeful shouts coming from the pool hardly registered—until a cascade of water hit them.

"Got ya," a young voice yelled.

He broke the kiss and turned in time to see two laughing culprits swimming as fast as they could to the shallow end. He took an instinctive step toward them, but his foot came out from under him on the slippery surface.

"Watch out," he yelled to Lizabeth, who was still in his arms. He tried to regain his equilibrium, but it was too late. They fell into the pool, one after the other, with a mighty splash.

Cary came up sputtering, his body in shock at the coolness of the pool water after the heat of the kiss. Lizabeth broke the surface an instant later. Remembering her temerity in the water, he wrapped his arms around her and set her down where the water wasn't over her head.

"That was a good one, Cary. Don't you think?" Bobby, the younger brother, called. "That'll teach you for beating us at Marco Polo."

"You little brats," Cary yelled, his eyes sparkling. "I'll make you pay for this."

"Me, too," Lizabeth called, slogging through the water as Cary took a few powerful strokes toward the two boys. Together, they mercilessly splashed the brothers until all four of them were breathless with laughter.

When they were through and the boys had retreated to their room for a snack, Cary turned to Lizabeth, amazed and pleased that she wasn't the least bit upset about the dunking.

She smiled at him, looking more gorgeous wet than she'd ever looked in her full Leeza regalia. Everything about her was beautiful, in fact, except for the brooch pinned to her shirt.

He fingered the iridescent green legs when he got to within touching distance and could no longer hold back the truth. "Sorry to break this to you, but that there's one ugly octopus."

She laughed up at him. "Don't you think I know

that? I only told you I liked it because I was trying to be flashy."

"Then you're going to stop wearing it?"

"Not on your life, buster. Not when the man I love gave it to me." She tapped the Green Monster. "I'm going to wear it to Charleston." She pressed her lips together. "If you want me to come with you, that is."

"There's nothing I want more than to have you with me," Cary said, putting his hands under her arms and lifting her so her body was flush against him, "but we can't go to Charleston in these wet clothes."

"Oh, yeah?" she said, her lips so close that her breath was teasing his mouth. "What do you propose we do then?"

"I think we should take them off and let them dry," he whispered. "Checkout time isn't for a few more hours."

"Y-e-s," she said, and he spun her around before he lifted her into his arms and out of the pool.

Charleston could wait, he thought as he joined her on dry land. But not, his conscience added, for too long.

Chapter Twenty-six

Mitch yanked open the door of Cary's townhouse later the following evening to find Peyton on the doorstep, the soft breeze lifting her short blond hair so that it created a halo effect.

"Hi," she said, a hint of shyness in her Coca-Cola eyes. "I know you said you had to work tonight but I saw the light on and your car in the driveway and I thought you might not mind if—"

"Peyton," Mitch interrupted, grasping her lightly by the shoulders. "Of course I don't mind."

She blinked in that nervous way she had when she was unsure of something. "You don't?"

"I don't," he said and pulled her flush against his body where he tangled his hands in her hair and brought his mouth down on hers.

She smelled of sea salt and strawberry shampoo,

tasted of sweetness and passion. A moment ago, his thoughts had been consumed with G. Gaston Gibbs III, but now all he could think about was Peyton. She responded to him with such unrestrained enthusiasm that his body hardened in readiness for her. It had been that way between them from the first, he thought in awe. In that moment he knew that he would never get enough of her.

"Mitch." She'd turned her mouth away from his and spoke against his cheek. "The door's still open."

"Oh, right," he said, coming to his senses. He drew back, gave a gallant bow and swept a hand in the direction of the house's interior. "Won't you come in?"

"I'd love to," she said and stepped into the front hall. She turned back to him with a siren's smile. "I can even stay a while."

Mitch's spirits sank all the way to the floor when he realized he had to refuse what his heart wanted desperately to accept. "Unfortunately, I have to leave."

"Oh?" Her expressive mouth curved downward. "I thought maybe you weren't going to work tonight after all. It's past nine. Isn't that when you usually start?"

"Yeah," Mitch said and cleared his throat. "But I'm starting a little later tonight."

She nodded, completely accepting his explanation, which made him feel like a heel. He wasn't lying—exactly. He did need to work tonight, but not at Epidermis as Peyton so plainly believed.

Since he'd gotten the idea that Gibbs might be using abandoned properties as a headquarters for illegal activity, Mitch and Vincent Carmichael had conducted around-the-clock surveillance that had thus far proved fruitless. Carmichael was at one of the sites now, with Mitch due to relieve him in less than fifteen minutes, but it was looking more and more like those abandoned buildings truly were abandoned.

"I got finished a little early," Peyton said, then made a face. "Okay, I'm not being entirely honest. I snuck out when Mother's back was turned. I can only take so much Junior Cotillion in one night."

"You still haven't explained what that is," Mitch said.

Peyton held her head at a regal angle and answered him in her most proper voice, "It's only the most important social program a young person can embark upon. Our students receive quality instruction in dance as well as the necessary social graces and customs that will serve them for a lifetime."

She cleared her throat. When she spoke again, she was using her own voice. "That's my mother's stock answer, and I suppose it has some merit. But I'm not any more cut out for Junior Cotillion now than when I was a girl."

"Then why are you helping?"

"Are you kidding? Mother's the director. How can I refuse?"

"By saying no," Mitch suggested.

"Wouldn't work. Mother doesn't take no for an

answer once her mind's set." She sighed and walked a few paces from him. "There's something I should tell you, but it can wait if you have to be at work."

She looked so troubled that he put his arm around her shoulders and guided her to the sofa inside Cary's living room, where he sat down beside her. "Work can wait," he said. "Now what is it?"

Her eyes were worried when they met his. "You know how I told you that my mother wanted me to read Uncle Vincent's report on you but I refused?"

"Yeah?" Mitch asked carefully.

"Well, earlier tonight, she and my father sort of, well, ambushed me." Her eyes dropped and she seemed to be examining the pale pink polish on her nails. "To make a long story short, I had to listen. Oh, not to everything. I did tell them I'd heard enough after about fifteen minutes."

Mitch's gut clenched but he did his best not to betray his anxiety. Even though he loved Cary, a private investigator's report about his brother would be largely negative. Just how negative, he wasn't sure.

"And what did they tell you?" he prompted.

"Lots of things." She was still examining her nails, making it hard to tell what she was thinking. "How you've never held a job for more than six months. How you got fired from your last position for sleeping with your boss's wife. How gambling might be an even bigger weakness for you than womanizing is. How you only have thirty-seven dollars in your bank account."

Mitch was silent as he digested the information. He hadn't known his brother's bank-account balance, but the rest of it sounded fairly accurate. So how could he dispute what was essentially the truth without confessing his lies and putting Peyton in danger from Gibbs?

"If you're waiting for me to defend myself, Peyton, I can't," Mitch said slowly. "But I can promise to try to be a better man."

Finally, at long last, she did raise her eyes. But it wasn't censure he saw in them. It was . . . something softer.

"Oh, Mitch," she said, taking both of his hands. "I had my doubts about you when we first met, but now I know you're a good man. It's not the past that's important. It's the future."

Her belief in him touched him so deeply that his eyes watered. "That kind of reasoning must not have gone over well with your parents."

A dull red stained her cheeks. "I haven't exactly told my parents that yet, but it's the truth." The hands that were holding his suddenly began to shake, and she gave a self-deprecating laugh. "Would you get a load of that? I'm nervous."

"What's there to be nervous about?" Mitch asked softly.

She wet her lips, swallowed, and took a breath. "I guess because it's not every day I tell a man I love him."

Mitch's chest clenched because those were the words he wanted to hear, the words that should bring him joy. But they couldn't, not when she didn't know his real identity. He swallowed. "Peyton, I—"

The piercing sound of the doorbell made them both jump and Peyton released his hands, bringing her own to her quivering mouth. Whatever he'd been about to say was lost, but she'd read enough in his expression to know he hadn't been about to declare his love for her in return.

The doorbell rang again, even more insistently this time, and Peyton nodded toward the front door. "You better answer that."

He looked about to say something else, but then he rose and walked out of the room, leaving Peyton alone. A lump formed in her throat, which seemed to be clogged with pain.

What exactly did it mean when you told a man you loved him and he didn't say it back?

"You were right! I can't believe it but you were right!"

Peyton sat up straighter, recognizing the voice raised in excitement as belonging to her Uncle Vincent. But what would her uncle be doing here? And what had Mitch been right about?

"I was watching the building, just like you suggested, when these men pulled up in a truck and started unloading boxes."

Peyton rose, following the sound of her uncle's voice, stopping shy of the entranceway where he stood talking to Mitch. The overhead light illuminated his face, which was bathed with excitement underneath his fedora.

"So I called the police. I would've called you, too,

Mitch, but the battery in my phone went dead. I didn't want to leave and miss the excitement so I waited until the cops came and made the arrest. Do you want to know what was inside the boxes?"

He paused, probably for dramatic effect, but it was obvious he was bursting with the news. Her curiosity piqued, Peyton took another step toward the two men. Uncle Vincent didn't notice her, but Mitch did. He put a hand on the other man's arm.

"Vincent, maybe you shouldn't—," he began.

"It was drugs. A designer drug called Ecstasy that produces a short high, a *flash.* Get it, Mitch. That's why he's nicknamed Flash Gorman. The guys unloading the boxes gave him up right away. The cops are arresting him now."

"Arresting who now?" Peyton asked, no longer able to keep silent. "Who is Flash Gorman?"

Her uncle's head swiveled in her direction and surprise registered on his face. "Peyton! I didn't know you were here."

Mitch tried to say something, but Peyton interrupted. "Who's Flash Gorman, Uncle Vincent?"

"G. Gaston Gibbs III. The G. stands for Gorman," he answered, almost gleefully. "I did some checking and found out his family disowned him six months ago, about the time they moved to Hilton Head. Probably figured out he owned Epidermis. But who would have guessed that a philanthropist like that would end up being a drug dealer?"

Peyton rubbed her forehead. "Do you mean to

say that Gaston was using those historic properties to warehouse drugs?"

"And laundering the money from the proceeds through his strip club," Uncle Vincent said, then jerked a thumb at Mitch. "But Mitch here had figured that part out already."

"What's Mitch got to do with it?" Peyton asked, staring at him. He was strangely quiet.

"Only everything," Uncle Vincent said. "But then he *is* a cop."

Peyton shook her head, at the same time wondering why Mitch wasn't shaking his. "Mitch isn't a cop, Uncle Vincent. He's a recreation specialist."

"Nah." It was her uncle's turn to shake his head. "He's a cop, all right. All the way from the fine city of Atlanta."

Confusion descended over Peyton, every bit as heavy as the water from the Charleston harbor that had doused them that night she'd asked Mitch to make love to her.

Her eyes sought his blue ones. They were set in a serious, unsmiling face that looked . . . guilty?

"I'm sorry," Mitch said at the same time a couple walked through the door that Uncle Vincent hadn't bothered to close.

The woman was a pretty brunette wearing a hideous green brooch but otherwise simply dressed in shades of cinnamon and chocolate, but it was the tall, handsome man who snagged Peyton's attention.

He had thick, dark hair that grew back from a high forehead, beautiful blue eyes set perhaps a fraction too deep, and a nose that went a bit crooked halfway up the bridge.

With his impressive height and build, which rivaled Mitch's, he would have captivated her even if he'd been a stranger. But how could he be a stranger when he was wearing Mitch's face?

"Hey, Mitch," the man said, his face splitting into a grin as he stuck out a hand to his look-alike. Mitch took it but within seconds turned back to Peyton. The second man also turned.

Peyton looked from one to the other, dimly noting they were mirror images. The only difference she could detect was that the second man's hair swirled to the left while Mitch's curled to the right.

She focused on the latecomer, realizing who he was but hoping she was wrong. "Cary?" she said.

"Hey, Peyton." He smiled at her, then drew the attractive brunette into the circle of his arms. "I'd like everybody here to meet Lizabeth Drinkmiller, the woman I love."

The brunette blushed prettily, but Peyton couldn't focus on her because of the nausea rising in her throat and the question pressing at her brain.

If the man who'd just come in the door was Cary Mitchell, then who was the man she'd told she loved less than ten minutes before?

Chapter Twenty-seven

"Pleased to meet you, Lizabeth," Uncle Vincent said with old-fashioned southern hospitality. Mitch's vocal chords didn't seem to be working any better than Peyton's, but that didn't matter to her uncle, who kept on talking. "I'm Vincent Carmichael, Peyton's uncle. And Mitch's partner, too, but that's a recent development."

"Cary Mitchell," Cary said, sticking out a hand.

"Forgive me for staring," her uncle continued as he took Cary's hand and shook it. "I knew Mitch had an identical twin but darn if it doesn't seem like I've developed a bad case of double vision."

Peyton had known they were identical twins the instant she'd seen them together, of course, but another truth struck her so hard she almost staggered.

At some point, for whatever twisted reason of

their own, the brothers had changed places. And the man she'd come to trust, the man who had let her fall in love with him, wasn't Cary at all. He was a stranger.

"Peyton, I can explain," the stranger said, coming toward her with his right arm outstretched.

She backed up a step. When she spoke, her voice quivered. "Don't you dare touch me."

"Uh oh." The exclamation came from Cary. "Why am I getting the impression that nobody told Peyton about the Bait and Switch?"

"Secrecy is the only way for an undercover operation to work," her uncle piped up, although obviously he hadn't been kept in the dark. "If Mitch had told folks he was a cop, maybe Flash Gorman wouldn't have been arrested."

"I didn't know Flash had been arrested," Cary commented.

Lizabeth clapped her hands. "That's great news. What happened?"

The conversation swirled around them but neither Mitch nor Peyton took any notice of it. He was still advancing toward her, which was the impetus her frozen legs needed to move.

She pivoted and rushed out the open door, wanting only to get away from him and the ugly deception he'd perpetrated.

"Peyton, wait," he called as she dug in her purse for her keys. Damn it all. Didn't automobile manufacturers realize how difficult it was to find those little pieces of metal? Why didn't they make bigger keyholes that used bigger keys? She stopped at the sidewalk and rummaged through her purse, aware he'd caught up to her.

"Peyton, don't cry," he said softly, reaching across the chasm separating them to wipe a tear from her cheek. "It breaks my heart when you cry."

She swiped at his hand. "Maybe I'm not crying over you. Did you think of that? Maybe I'm crying because I can't find my keys. I don't even know who *you* are."

"Grant Mitchell," he said softly, "but everybody calls me Mitch."

"So that's why you were so insistent on the nickname," Peyton muttered, still rummaging for her keys, still refusing to give in to her tears. "It must've made it easier for you. One fewer lie to keep track of. One fewer way for your brother's girlfriend to find out who you really were."

"My brother's girlfriend?" he said, fastening on the remark. "Is that how you think of yourself?"

She could have sworn she heard pain in his voice but she steeled herself against it. She wasn't going to tell him that Cary's introduction of Lizabeth as the woman he loved hadn't bothered her at all.

She wouldn't say that her heart had known the brothers were far different men under the skin even if her brain hadn't consciously realized it. That's why she'd fallen in love with Mitch, while Cary had never been more than a temporary diversion. And that's why his betrayal hurt so very much.

"I don't owe you any explanations," she told him harshly but then gave him one anyway. "But for the record, no, I don't think of myself as your brother's girl. I never did."

"But you thought of yourself as my girl," he said unnecessarily. The night was quiet, the only sound the wind rustling the plants, but he spoke so softly she had to strain to hear his voice. "I never wanted to lie to you, Peyton."

Her hand stilled in her purse and the tears that had been threatening suddenly dried. She felt a hot flash of anger in its stead and shot him an irate look. "Oh, right. That's believable. Especially after you told me one whopper after another. Tell me something else, Mitch. Were you honest about anything?"

"I never lied about how I felt about you," he said. His voice lowered even further. "I'm in love with you, Peyton."

She gave a harsh laugh, aware of how much she'd wanted to hear those words from him mere minutes ago. So much had passed since then, though, that it felt like a lifetime.

"Do you expect me to believe that?" she asked, her voice spiking. "In my world, men introduce themselves before they take a woman to bed."

He ran a hand through his hair, a gesture that should have tipped her off days ago that he wasn't who he was pretending to be. Cary cared too much about his appearance to continually tousle his hair.

"You don't understand," he said. "If I'd told you who I was, I would have had to explain why I was in town. Gibbs was so desperate to keep his secrets hidden that I couldn't risk that. He threatened to hurt you if you found out he was the shadow owner of Epidermis."

Where were those damned keys? Peyton stooped down and dumped the contents of her purse on the sidewalk. He got on his haunches next to her as she refilled her purse item by item.

"Did you hear what I said?" he prompted.

"I'm gullible, not deaf," she answered as she combed through the objects laid out on the cement before her, fruitlessly searching for her keys. "I'm also insulted that you thought I couldn't keep a secret."

"I didn't think that, but I already told you I couldn't risk it." Frustration clouded his every syllable. "I was protecting you."

"You were deciding what was good for me instead of letting me decide for myself." She scooped up the rest of the items, which didn't include keys, and glared at him. "Which is exactly what you say my parents do."

"Your parents dictate to you. I was protecting you," he refuted, a note of anger entering his voice. "Can't you see the difference?"

"You're the one who can't see, Mitch. I already have an overbearing father, not to mention an overbearing mother. I don't need an overbearing lover too, especially one who lies to me."

"So that's it?" Mitch asked when they both stood up. He wasn't touching her and the gulf between them seemed enormous. "You're saying it's over between us?"

"It never should have started in the first place,"

she said sadly. Her hands were trembling so she shoved them in the pocket of her pants. Her fingers met cool metal. Her keys. She pulled them out of her pocket and walked to her car.

Away from the only man she'd ever loved.

"What's the deal?" Cary asked when Mitch hung up the phone later that evening.

Mitch didn't answer until he'd popped the top off a beer can and sank into a chair opposite his brother at the kitchen table. Having refused the beer Mitch had offered him, Cary's hands were empty.

That was quite a switch, Mitch thought as he drank from the can and tried not to think about Peyton. Usually he abstained and Cary partook.

"Gibbs lawyered up but the detective in charge says the case they're building against him is pretty strong." Mitch sighed. Now for the bad news. "He also said Gibbs is making noises about bringing charges against you for theft."

"If he does, I'll pay the consequences," Cary said solemnly. Another surprise. His twin didn't normally do solemn. "I won't run, even if it means I have to go to jail."

"You won't have to go to jail," Mitch said. Not if he could help it.

"It'd probably serve me right," Cary said wryly, "if only because of what I put you through."

"Nobody put a gun to my head and forced me to help you, Cary," Mitch said. "You were in a jam. I wanted to get you out of it."

"Yeah, but I could have told you about bartending at Epidermis. Or collecting debts for Flash. Or cutting out to Key West." Cary paused. "I could have told you about Peyton."

"You should have," Mitch said, sending his brother a dark look as the sound of her name sent fresh pain cascading over him.

"You fell for her, didn't you?" Cary asked, which made Mitch want to thump the table and ask what had happened to his real brother, the one who never noticed anything that didn't directly affect him.

"I'd apologize for that," Mitch said, glaring at his brother, "if recent events hadn't made it clear I didn't have anything to apologize for."

Cary winced. "I shouldn't have let you believe she and I had something good going. Things were never anything other than casual between us. I take it that's not the way it is with you and Peyton?"

"Doesn't matter," Mitch mumbled. "She's never going to forgive me."

A few years ago, after his partner had botched the arrest of a scared kid with a gun, Mitch had taken a bullet in the fleshy part of the leg, and it had burned like red-hot coals. The wounded look on Peyton's face when she discovered his deception had hurt more.

"I could talk to her," Cary offered.

"Thanks, but no thanks," Mitch said. "You weren't the one who lied to her about who you were."

"Why didn't you tell her?"

Mitch took a healthy swig of beer, but the smooth feel of the liquid going down his throat couldn't soothe the rawness inside. "At first it was because you asked me to talk her out of breaking up with you. I thought I was saving your relationship, although you can't imagine how disloyal I felt when it started to work."

"Sorry, bro," Cary said, looking sheepish.

"You should be sorry." Mitch took another swallow of beer. "Eventually I realized I couldn't give her up, not even to you. I made up my mind to tell her who I was, but then Gibbs threatened to hurt her if she found out he owned Epidermis. Because Gibbs was the reason I was in Charleston in the first place, I thought telling her anything was too dangerous."

"Because of your white-knight complex," Cary commented.

"Pardon?"

"You were protecting her, the way you always protect me," Cary said. "The way you think you have to protect everyone. Isn't that why you became a cop?"

"There's nothing wrong with wanting to help people," Mitch said. "And, besides, you never complained about me protecting you before. Somebody's got to look out for you."

Cary straightened his backbone and pulled his shoulders back. "Not anymore," he said with conviction. "It's time I looked out for myself."

Mitch let out a short breath. "Where's this coming from?"

Cary shrugged. "It's the right thing to do. Just like coming back to Charleston was the right thing to do."

"Don't get me wrong, little brother, I'm in favor of accountability," Mitch said, leaning his elbows on the table. "But since when do you recognize what the right thing is?"

"Since I met Lizabeth," Cary said.

Mitch nodded, because he'd thought as much. Pleading tiredness, Lizabeth had gone to sleep thirty minutes ago, leaving the brothers alone. Mitch had seen enough to know she was good for Cary, who had seemed more interested in her needs than his own.

"I like her," Mitch said, then screwed up his forehead. "Did I mention there's something about her that seems familiar? Like I've met her before."

"You have met her before. She was a sophomore at Hatfield High when you were a senior."

"I remember now," Mitch said, snapping his fingers. "I danced with her once in high school, I think."

"I don't want you dancing with her again unless it's at my wedding," Cary said loudly, then lowered his voice. "I love her, bro. I'm praying she'll stick by me if I go to jail."

"You won't go to jail," Mitch said again, as though he could will it so.

"Maybe not, but I can't ask Lizabeth to marry me until I've proved I can turn my life around." He gave his brother a rueful grin. "Lizabeth thinks I'd make a good baseball coach, but first I'm going to try to make a go of it at the rec center." He shrugged. "Unless you've showed me up there, too."

"Are you kidding?" This time Mitch's laughter was genuine. "You're lucky I didn't get you fired. The people over there love you, Cary. And for the record, I don't think you'd make a good baseball coach. I think you'd make a great one."

"You do?" Cary's voice was lacking in confidence and much softer than Mitch had ever heard it.

"I believe in you, Cary," Mitch said, meeting the eyes that were so like his own. "I always have."

He reached across the table and clasped his brother's hand, reestablishing the link they'd always shared. Soon, Mitch would return to Atlanta, away from the city he'd come to love. Loneliness gripped him when he thought about leaving Charleston, because he'd be leaving Cary and Peyton, too.

But, before he left, there was something he could do to make life run more smoothly. For both of them. The two people he loved most in the world.

Chapter Twenty-eight

"It's you again," Mr. McDowell said the next evening when Mitch showed up at the front door of the McDowell's lovely antebellum house.

The stiff breeze from the harbor nearly blew Mitch inside the front foyer, but he held his ground for self-preservation purposes. Neither of Peyton's parents had seen him in more than a week but her father still acted as though that was too often.

"Good evening, sir," Mitch said.

"I thought I just told you to call me Tommy Mac."

Mitch swallowed so he wouldn't let out a disbelieving snort. Was he joking? From the first moment they'd met, Peyton's father had demanded such formality that Mitch had begun to believe the man's first name was Mister.

He was on the verge of asking whether he should call him Mister Tommy Mac or just plain Tommy Mac but stopped himself. What he had to request of the solicitor was too important to risk starting off on a bad note.

"I'll call you anything you want," Mitch said, "as long as you listen to what I have to say."

"Then you have more to say to me?"

"Much more," Mitch said, thinking the solicitor was acting odd. In the past, they'd never said much of anything to each other at all.

Peyton's father swung the door open wide, a far different reception than Mitch had received on his previous visits. But the fact that he was no longer dating the daughter of the house undoubtedly had much to do with that.

Within minutes, Mitch had a glass of port in his hand and the undivided attention of the man who suddenly wanted to be called Tommy Mac.

"Now, what else do you have to say to me, son?" he asked, leaning back in his leather chair.

"I want you to drop the charges against my brother." Mitch met the solicitor's inscrutable eyes. "It might not always seem like it, but he's a good man. Even if he had taken that money from the cash register, which I'm not admitting he did, it was because he was the victim of a loan-shark operation. My brother's not a thief."

"Tommy dear, I was wondering if you'd seen my car keys." Amelia McDowell strolled into the room, stopping when she realized her husband wasn't alone. Incredibly, her face softened when she focused on Mitch. "Oh, hello, dear. How lovely to see you again so soon. Did you forget something?"

"No," Mitch said slowly. He figured it wouldn't hurt to try to find an ally anywhere he could get one. "I stopped by to ask your husband to drop the charges against my brother."

"Someone filed charges against Mitch?" Her eyes went as wide as the Charleston harbor. "What criminal activity is *he* involved in?"

"Mitch isn't involved in any criminal activity," Mitch said, then shook his head. He was so confused he was referring to himself in the first person. "I mean that *I'm* not involved in criminal activity. Except as a cop trying to prevent it. I'm Mitch."

"That's what I gathered when you asked me for the same considerations your brother just got through asking me for," the solicitor said, crossing his leg.

"Cary's already been here?" Mitch asked, but the solicitor's affirmative answer was nearly drowned out by Amelia's gasp of surprise.

"Oh, my goodness. No wonder nobody can tell the two of you apart. Are you the one Peyton's in love with or is that your brother?"

Mitch swallowed painfully. "I'm afraid Peyton would say she isn't in love with either one of us."

"Are you sure, dear? I thought that was why she was so resistant to Gaston, although in retrospect I suppose that was a good thing. Who would have guessed a young man from a respected Charleston family like his could go so wrong?"

"I am sure about Peyton." Mitch turned to Peyton's father, hoping to avoid any additional references to the love Peyton no longer had for him. "When was Cary here?"

"Left about an hour ago," the solicitor said. "He wanted to know if I'd consider dropping the charges against him."

"Will you?" Mitch asked, holding his breath.

"I'll tell you the same thing I told your brother. I'm not about to prosecute a man who was integral in breaking up a major East Coast drug-running operation. Especially when that man had the guts to come here and confess his own crime." He paused. "Your brother wasn't as circumspect as you. He admitted to lifting cash from the register."

"He didn't mean to," Mitch said, leaping to Cary's defense. "He only did it because Gibbs was exerting pressure on him to pay back a loan."

"Relax," Peyton's father said. "I already said I wasn't going to prosecute him."

Mitch let out a relieved breath. "Thank you, sir."

"Tommy Mac," the solicitor corrected.

"Tommy Mac, then," Mitch said. "But you might not want me to call you that after I tell you the other reason I came here tonight."

"You want an apology, don't you?" Amelia said. "I suppose we should give you one, but how were we to know you weren't your brother?"

"My brother's a good man," Mitch said again. "But I don't want an apology. I want to talk about Peyton."

Amelia slanted an unfathomable look at her husband, who seemed to instantly understand her message. He nodded once, as though giving her permission to speak for both of them.

"Tommy and I have decided not to stand in your way," she said. "We still think Peyton would be happier if she married a Charlestonian, but this business with Gaston taught us that even Charlestonians aren't infallible."

"I'm not asking you for permission to marry your daughter," Mitch said, although he would have liked to. But under the circumstances, what would be the point? "I'm asking you to take a good, hard look at Peyton. She loves making Charleston come alive for the tourists who take her carriage tours. She doesn't want to be a socialite. She wants to use her trust fund to buy the business. And I think the both of you should stop standing in her way."

Amelia sighed, a reaction Mitch didn't understand until the solicitor spoke up. "You're a little late on that one too, young fellow."

"I don't understand."

"Peyton told us the same thing last night. She made an offer to buy the business today. It should be hers by the end of next month."

Walking to his SUV a little while later, the irony of the situation struck Mitch as hard as the stiff breeze from the sea.

He'd truly believed he was the only one who could get the charges against Cary dropped, just as he'd thought Peyton's parents would never stop ordering her around unless he instructed them to.

But neither of those beliefs proved to be valid.

Cary and Peyton had solved their own problems,

without the help he thought was so vital. Could it be possible that Peyton was right? Was he so accustomed to protecting the people he loved that he had crossed the line from protective to controlling? Is that why he'd gone to such lengths to get Cary out of his impossible jam? Is that why he hadn't trusted Peyton enough to tell her who he was?

He covered his face with his hands, because he already knew the answers to all of those questions. But there remained one last question, which was more important to him than all the rest, and only one woman could answer it.

Would Peyton ever forgive him?

Peyton breathed in the familiar scent of hay and horse flesh as she finished hitching a sweet-tempered draft horse to a sleek, French-style carriage.

Aside from a stable hand who was mucking out one of the stalls, she was alone inside the large, airy stable that butted up against the Dixieland Carriage Tours office.

She reveled in the peace. Classical music drifted through the air-conditioned building, the better to soothe the horses and make life more pleasant for them until the next work day.

Peyton's day wasn't yet over. In a few minutes she was due to give a private nighttime tour of Charleston, no doubt to a man bent on romancing his lady with the sights, scents, and sounds of a city that retained its old-world charm.

Big Nellie, the draft horse she'd hitched to the

carriage, stamped her feet and nickered. Peyton laughed as she walked over to the horse who came by her name honestly. She weighed a solid two thousand pounds.

"So you want some attention, do you, big girl?" she asked in a soft voice as she stroked the horse's neck. She looked around her at the rows of stalls and assortment of carriages as she did so. "Can you believe this place is going to be all mine?"

Big Nellie nickered again and Peyton laid her face against the soft smoothness of her neck.

"I know, Big Nellie," she said. "It's hard to believe. You're probably wondering where I got the courage to turn away from everything my parents always wanted for me, to go after what I wanted for myself. I wonder that myself."

The horse stamped her foot, causing Peyton to draw back. Big Nellie's large, liquid eye seemed to look into her soul. Peyton sighed.

"Okay, you're right. I know where I got the courage. If Mitch hadn't come into my life, I wouldn't have developed the strength to become my own person."

Not wanting to be on the receiving end of any more of the horse's penetrating looks, Peyton gave Big Nellie a final pat and hoisted herself into the driver's seat of the carriage.

She tried to ignore the hollow feeling that had plagued her since she'd banished Mitch from her life two nights before, but she couldn't any longer. The inside of her body was so empty it would make a perfect echo chamber.

"I'm supposed to be happy," she said aloud, gesturing at the stable. "My dream of owning this place is about to come true."

"But you're not happy, are you?" she asked herself.

Oh, great. Now she was not only having conversations with horses, but with herself. That's what she got for being too pigheaded to allow herself to understand why Mitch had gone to such lengths to protect not only her but his brother as well.

"It's because," she said with sudden insight, "he cares so deeply for the people he loves."

Yes, he was overprotective and overbearing. And yes, he'd carried the charade too far. But he'd done so out of love. He'd done so because he loved *her*. And she'd thrown that love away out of pique.

"Do you know what, Big Nellie?" she asked the horse, having decided talking to one of God's creatures was preferable to chatting with herself. "I'm a fool."

Big Nellie whinnied and shuffled her big body, but this time Peyton didn't think the horse was trying to convey anything besides her agitation to get going.

Peyton picked up the reins, for once not experiencing the thrill she got before giving a tour. The night was cool and lit by the moon, the perfect setting for a carriage ride, but Peyton was anxious to get it over with so she could find Mitch. If he hadn't left the city yet, that is.

She slackened the reins, and Big Nellie clip-clopped out of the stable, out of habit moving to the exact spot where tourists mounted the carriages.

A familiar, dark-haired man waited on the sidewalk, eyes that Peyton knew were blue focused on her.

"Mitch," she whispered to herself as the carriage moved inexorably forward, closer and closer until Peyton could see that MITCH was printed in large red letters on his white T-shirt.

"Hey, Peyton," he said when the carriage slowed to a stop. He didn't wait for her to greet him in return but instead stepped onto one of the footholds and swung himself into the carriage, not into the back where most customers typically sat but next to her. Instantly, the entire left side of her body flooded with heat and the world seemed reduced to the two of them.

She cleared her suddenly clogged throat. "I'm expecting a customer."

"That'd be me," he said as though he reserved private carriages every day of the week. "Shall we go?"

She shot a glance at him but he was looking straight ahead, as though in eager anticipation of the tour. Irritation shot through her. Here she was agonizing over the wrong she'd done him and he wanted a history lesson.

"Well, what are you waiting for?" he asked.

She scowled and set Big Nellie into motion. The carriage company was located a few blocks from the city's market area, so she began her spiel.

"Soon we'll be coming up on the Old City Market, which a wealthy old-town family willed to the town of Charleston in the mid-1800s with the stipulation that it be used as a public market. It features shops, restaurants, and—"

"I'm sure the market has a colorful history, but I don't want to hear about it," Mitch interrupted.

She gave him an unfriendly stare. "Well, then, we're not too far from St. Philip's Episcopal Church over on Church Street. It used to be known as the Lighthouse Church, because from its steeple shone a light to help guide ships into the harbor. In its graveyard is buried John C. Calhoun and—"

He didn't let her finish. "I don't want to hear about guys who died two hundred years ago."

"More like a hundred and fifty," she snapped, then let out a breath. "So what do you want me to tell you about?"

"I don't want you to talk. I want you to listen."

"That's not what a tour guide usually does."

"I thought a tour guide did what the customer wanted," he said and laid his fingers against her lips before she could protest. "And this customer wants to apologize to the woman he loves for not believing in her enough to tell her who he was."

His fingers fell away from her mouth, which dropped open. "He does?"

"Oh, yeah." The moon was bright enough that she could see the regret in his eyes. "I was an overbearing jerk, Peyton, just like you said."

He ran a hand over his forehead. "I probably shouldn't tell you this, but I stopped by your house last night to convince your parents to start treating you like an adult. Funny thing, though. You got there before me and told them yourself.

"It got me to thinking that since I came to town, I never stopped to give you any credit for being able to stand up for yourself."

"Maybe that was because I couldn't stand up for myself until I met you," Peyton said. "Oh, Mitch. I'm the one who should apologize to you. One of the reasons I love you so much is that you care so deeply for the people you love."

"You still love me?" he asked.

She nodded. "I never stopped. Don't get me wrong. I still think you're overbearing and I still want you to lighten up." Her voice dropped to a whisper. "But not too much."

He drew her into his arms and kissed her under the glow of the Charleston moon. They didn't pull apart until they heard applause. A group of foreigners were standing on the sidewalk, smiling and pointing, as though at another tourist attraction.

Peyton laughed and waved. "Come see me tomorrow," she called to them. "Mention the kiss and I'll give you a discount."

"Spoken like a true entrepreneur," Mitch said, smiling at her as Big Nellie trudged determinedly on.

Peyton chewed on her bottom lip as a terrible thought intruded on her happiness, but the decision she made was instantaneous.

"I'd like to stay in Charleston," she said, her voice low. "But you're more important to me than a place. If you can't leave Atlanta, then I'll move there."

"Are you kidding? And leave God's country?" He pulled her against his side. "It's you I can't leave, Peyton. And I won't have to. I already have a job offer from the Charleston police chief. And, believe this or not, the blessing of your parents."

He told her about what else had transpired during his visit to her parents, taking so much time that they were at the Battery before Peyton asked Mitch the question that had been on her mind since she'd spotted him outside the carriage company.

"Are you going to tell me why you're wearing that shirt?"

He grinned and shrugged. "I wanted you to be sure which brother you were dealing with."

"And you thought I needed your name stenciled in six-inch letters for that?"

He cocked his head. "Don't you?"

Peyton laughed, drawing back from him so she could look into his face. "Of course I don't. I fell in love with you, Mitch, not Cary. Now that I know you're an identical twin, it's stunning how easy it is to tell you apart."

It was true. She could see the differences in the set of his shoulders, the slant of his mouth and in the very essence of the man. Mitch had a natural confidence his brother didn't yet possess.

"That's a good thing," Mitch said, grinning. "Cary's not quite ready to ask Lizabeth to marry him, but she is moving to Charleston. If he asks her soon, I was wondering what you'd think about a double wedding."

"Grant Mitchell," she said, tracing the line of his hard jaw. "Are you asking me to marry you?"

"Yes," he said, taking her by the shoulders and gazing deep into her eyes. "But only if you promise not to get the grooms confused when you say, 'I do.' "

"I'll never confuse you for your twin again," Peyton said. "You might have been able to fool my eyes, but my heart knows there's only one man for me."

And then she pressed that heart against his, threw her arms around his neck, and promised him forever with her kiss.

The Last Male Virgin

Katherine Deauxville

Leslie expects a great deal of publicity for Dr. Peter Havistock—heck, the hunk has survived a plane crash, spent nearly fourteen years living with a Stone Age tribe in the wilds of Papua New Guinea, and returned to write a best-selling book about it. But his tour of colleges is too wild. Frankly, Leslie has never seen a doctor of anthropology act the way Havistock does. And while his ceremonial g-string is . . . authentic . . . she doesn't see the need for him to go flaunting his perfect body across the nation. And then he announces on *Harry King Live* that he is a virgin! And that he is looking for a wife! And that he'd like to marry her! Well, she decides, there is a first time for everything. . . .

Marry Me, Maddie

Rita Herron

Maddie Summers is tired of waiting. To force her fiancé into making a decision, she takes him on a talk show and gives him a choice: Marry me, or move on. The line he gives makes her realize it is time to star in her own life. But stealing the show will require a script change worthy of a Tony. Her supporting cast is composed of two loving but overprotective brothers, her blue-blood ex-boyfriend, and her brothers' best friend: sexy bad-boy Chase Holloway–the only one who seems to recognize that a certain knock-kneed kid sister has grown up to be a knockout lady. And Chase doesn't seem to know how to bow out, even when the competition for her hand heats up. Instead, he promises to perform a song and dance, even ad-lib if necessary to demonstrate he is her true leading man.

___52433-3 $5.50 US/$6.50 CAN

Dorchester Publishing Co., Inc.
P.O. Box 6640
Wayne, PA 19087-8640

Please add $2.50 for shipping and handling for the first book and $.75 for each book thereafter. NY, NYC, and PA residents, please add appropriate sales tax. No cash, stamps, or C.O.D.s. All orders shipped within 6 weeks via postal service book rate. Canadian orders require $2.00 extra postage and must be paid in U.S. dollars through a U.S. banking facility.

Name___________________________________
Address_________________________________
City____________________ State______ Zip________
I have enclosed $__________in payment for the checked book(s).
Payment must accompany all orders. ❑ Please send a free catalog.
CHECK OUT OUR WEBSITE! www.dorchesterpub.com